The Interloper

The Interloper

FRANK MILBURN

DOUBLEDAY & COMPANY, INC.
GARDEN CITY, NEW YORK
1983

"Rainbow" by Stanley Plumly, from *Out-of-the-Body Travel* (New York: The Ecco Press, 1977). Copyright © 1976 by Stanley Plumly. Used by permission.

Library of Congress Cataloging in Publication Data

Milburn, Frank, 1945–
   The interloper.

   I. Title.
PS3563.I37157I5   1983   813'.54
ISBN: 0-385-19008-5
Library of Congress Catalog Card Number 82-45837

To my wife, Maria

The Interloper

1

In 1924, the year I was born, my parents purchased six hundred acres of land near Wolcott, Rhode Island. It was my mother's idea: she had been born and raised in Newport and loved the seashore.

Up in Wolcott we had chill mists at dawn. The green crystal lawn opened onto a vista and rolled down to the sea a quarter mile away. The vista was all ours, the sea framed for us. A sailboat on the Atlantic would seem to hang on the water—those mornings after the haze burned off, the foghorns ceased, and the Point Barren lighthouse had been shut off for the day. As a child, the flash of light sought me out in vivid lunges.

Growing up as she did in a sea state, you'd think that Ma—as my brother-in-law, Winston Bingham, called my mother—would have liked lightness and airiness, everything breezy. But the large house in Wolcott, rambling and nicely weathered, was filled with black sofas, lumpy black cushions, and rugs the color of Iowa thunderheads. The dining room table might have been better used to plan military strategy; it seemed to rest not on legs but on implacable shoulders.

I never walked into the Wolcott house—I plunged in from the great light. Our sparingness with electricity made sense to me only once—during World War II when the Army built gun emplacements on the eastern shore of our property. But I was twenty or so at the time, with a war of my own to fight. I didn't care that the house had reached its appropriate level of warmth—the warmth of wartime blackouts.

My father disliked the property in Wolcott. It was too far away from New York City, his Wall Street law firm, and the family's town house on Eighty-seventh Street. He was basically a city person. The ocean frightened him. Sand crackled in his shoes. The foghorn from the Point Barren lighthouse kept him awake at night with blatant mooings. He couldn't stand the damp and humidity, morning ground fog coating him up to his hips when he set off for his daily constitutional.

He didn't like the varied fishes of the sea: crawling ones like lobsters and crabs; stationary ones like mussels, oysters, and clams; deep-water fishes like tuna and swordfish. Any kind of distinct fish taste made him sick. He restricted himself to an occasional filet of flounder, which was examined and separated in the kitchen for possible bones.

The odd thing is that my father never uttered a single word of complaint about anything, on any subject, at any time. His silent protests rode on the air I breathed; they were understood; they were accepted as part of the price, I suppose, for the property.

Dad overdressed for the seashore, and that's putting it mildly. He wore white linen or cream-colored suits from the moment he got up in the morning to the instant he retired to his bedroom at precisely ten o'clock in the evening. He kept an alarm in his head; it rang at 10 P.M. and prodded him to his feet at the appointed hour and set him nimbly off to bed. Gorgeous dreams awaited him, I thought, with places where he could give free rein to a jaunty spirit stifled by a lifetime of devotion to duty.

My father's only concession to Rhode Island and the impact of place, was a Brooks Brothers blazer donned for clambakes. These became a fixture of my childhood, like tennis or fishing. Although Dad disliked the food served, he liked ritual. The clambakes were the only event that could take him away from his musty library and propel him twice a year—on the Fourth of July and Labor Day—down to the tip of our property, where sand and ocean lay in wait for him on muggy evenings to mug him with salty delights.

He spent most of the evening cradling a watery scotch and circling the entire area of the "bake." Sometimes he would come to a full stop, point down at some intricacy of seaweed, subtlety of steam, or Egyptian redness of lobster, and murmur, "Yes, of course," and then continue on his way again. I would watch him through threads of smoke, rich mists of smell. He circled the area in his benign supervisory capacity. Sometimes the only way I knew he was out there was by the glint of moonlight on the buttons of his blazer, spinning out like silver eyes.

Dad was always the last to eat. He stopped circling, filled up a hearty platter, and made a place for himself on a large rock, well away from the ocean. Then he picked away at the neutral foods like brown bread, corn, and chicken. He forced the steaming lobster and inscrutable clams—which he had chosen out of obligation—to one side of the platter until a lopsided mound tipped like dead weight into the garbage at the end of his spare meal. The clambakes were a messy proceeding at best—lots of spilled melted butter, greasy hands, reeks of chowder on your shetland sweater, lapping tides, foghorns, gap-toothed clambake makers; layer after layer stripped away; and my father sitting and circling, circling and sitting through all of it. He needed my protection and love. I understood that from the age of zip.

My mother compared all the clambakes to those of her Newport childhood. They inevitably came up short. The corn wasn't as sweet, the lobsters got smaller every year. Worst of all, an entire generation was growing up without a clue to the lyrics of such grand old standards as: "In the Gloaming," "I Was Seeing Nellie Home," "Tell Me, Pretty Maiden," and a host of other neglected tunes. No voice could follow her into the second stanza of "The Man on the Flying Trapeze," and perhaps no voice wanted to. Quite often these biannual events turned into, or degenerated into, or were uplifted into—depending on your vantage point—a one-woman show, stanza after stanza trilling across the water.

Although my mother sang to an audience perched on rocks or snuggled in cool sand beside the black water, I think the songs were directed toward my father sitting uncomfortably on his rock. The trivial lyrics were really about trust and resentment, seashore and city, town house and country house, grudges, bargains, rugged terrain fought for in the caves of night.

Sometimes during the clambakes I wandered out onto a long, high file of white rocks at the end of our property, a few hundred yards beyond the clambake site. I made my way toward a naturally sculpted rock seat midway in the formation, sat down on it, and dangled my legs over the water. This was my place. In the night and distance I could hear my mother. She called forth the sea and stars and the great clipper ships with keening passion. My father sat; my mother sang; I felt comfortable on my rock seat.

My mother always closed with, "Now the Day Is Over." That was the signal to rejoin them.

As she grew older, the clambakes also meant unpleasant times for my sister Dorothy. She was required to be on display at all times. Her entrance into adulthood—she is eleven years younger than I—coincided with the final glide pattern of my decline. Great things had been expected of me—some golden future and continuation of my athletic youth. Until I developed a problem with alcohol, I had achieved a small renown at amateur tennis.

When it became obvious in my late twenties that my rising star was to be without further burnishment, Dorothy was called on to show the Meriwether family flag. It wasn't a matter of choice. She rose to the occasion as best she could. Her cold comfort was a sense of obligation to my parents' scenario for success. Dorothy's rebellion, when it came—when she married Winston Bingham in 1962—was bound to be commensurate with years of pent-up resentment.

As the Eisenhower decade broke, she was in full dress rehearsal for her role in life. She developed a pert, Southern-belle laugh and steered conversations into avenues of maximum superficiality. She put on a smile that reminded me of a USO girl handing out donuts.

Her coming-out party at the Wolcott house in June 1953 was gala. Two tents, five hundred guests, a ton of flowers. The Atlantic Ocean gleamed like a sheet of strategic metal. My mother was the picture of matriarchal elegance, my father the soul of Old World charm. Dorothy was never more radiant. Yours truly spaced his drinks. Lots of people patted my totemic gut. Lester Lanin or somebody very much like him conducted his heart out amid billows of muted horns. I remember the gracious minuet of Dorothy's politeness. She had come down with laryngitis the night before, which made her sound even more belle-ish.

It was an evening of gorgeous perfection. I reached behind the bar, took a bottle of champagne, and went out to the moonlight-ribboned vista. I plunked myself down on the grass, glass in hand, voices and music behind me. The champagne was nice but what made me happiest was reaching behind the bar and pulling out this whole bottle and walking away. It was the liquid equivalent of a free lunch.

There was a tilt to the dance floor—some engineering miscalculation by the caterers. Several times during the evening, I danced with Dorothy. A certain lack of gaiety surrounded the debutante, perhaps because her eyes were orbs of fear. Whenever I felt things lagging, saw her partners glancing around the tent, I cut in to provide an intermission in her anxiety, sensing her relief as we waltzed around the sloping dance floor.

"How are you holding up?" I asked at three in the morning, taking her for one last turn.

"This is fun," she whispered. Everything in her demeanor indicated she would have preferred to be on Okinawa. "I can't remember when I've had a better time. People are starting to leave now. Do you think they're starting to leave?"

"I guess so." I felt sad that the party was winding down.

"I'll make my exit in exactly half an hour. What do you think?"

"Good idea. It's getting late."

"Who do we hold responsible for this dance floor?" Dorothy's voice had a distinctive rasp. "Old Uncle Billy looks like he's sliding into third base. Did they *grease* the floor? Jesus, Alfred."

"It's not so bad."

"Because you have a natural tilt."

On the morning after her coming-out party, Dorothy woke up and was mute. After a few days it became apparent she suffered from more than a severe case of laryngitis. She began a series of visits to top ear, nose, and throat specialists along the East Coast. One specialist said her vocal cords were bruised; she mustn't speak until they healed. Another nose and throat man suggested she try and talk as much as possible. Another doctor said she should play it by ear. A psychiatrist said my sister suffered from hysterical aphonia. He told her she needed treatment to get at the root of her hysteria.

We didn't like the psychiatrist. A family has its myths. We didn't want him getting at the root of anything. We didn't want him taking a look at my drinking, my father's fast debilitating depression, my mother's manipulativeness. The story went out that Dorothy had swallowed a "large pill"; it had gone down "the wrong way"—whichever way that was—and had somehow ripped into her vocal cords like a strafing thunder jet, putting her out of commission.

My parents hired a therapist to come in and give Dorothy vocal exercises through the summer. He had lots of fancy equipment, a million exercises. By late August Dorothy was talking almost normally. Sometimes, though, she'd be talking away and then lapse into silence while mouthing the words. It was as if her audio portion had gone on the blink. By autumn her voice had returned.

For years after the coming-out party, Dorothy maintained an aura of invalidism. I think she unconsciously cultivated all this lassitude to keep the pressure off. Paradoxically, later in life she found herself happiest at cocktail parties and other social functions. She found an emotional outlet as a hostess. She began to talk more and more in a chitchat style, the stream of consciousness of surfaces.

My sister's semi-invalidism did not help my parents' mood. Now there was no one to keep up the social standards, both in Rhode Island and New York. The family imploded.

In the fall of 1953, Dorothy went off to Vassar. There, I think, she spent her happiest years—not particularly because of Vassar, but because for a while she was out from under the family. If she had boyfriends, she didn't bring them home. After graduation she rented an apartment with a girlfriend on Gramercy Park —a good seventy blocks, three and a half miles, south of her parents and brother. She took a job in an art gallery on East Fifty-seventh Street.

After a period of estrangement from the family, Dorothy took to visiting us again at the house on Eighty-seventh Street. One early June afternoon a pleasant young stockbroker showed up for Sunday lunch, seemingly out of the blue. I wondered how this nice young man had got there with his good manners and background going back to the Framers. I realized that my mother had arranged it.

After lunch Dorothy mimed good-bye to the young man—

whispers of her old voice problem—and gave him a firm hand-shake at the front door.

One week later she was gone, vanished, aboard the British ocean liner *Queen Elizabeth*—outward bound. And that first night aboard ship, Winston Bingham popped out of the shadows and into the moonlight on the First Class deck, and time stood still.

Fresh off the plane from Europe, accompanied by Winston, my sister telephoned me up in Wolcott that late summer morning in August 1962. In a breathless voice she told me she was madly in love. She interspersed a few details about her fiancé. Winston had grown up in a series of orphanages and foster homes around Buffalo, New York. He had been a high school and college basketball star upstate, and now practiced law with a small Buffalo firm called Natoli and Minsky.

"You'll love Winnie," Dorothy said. "We'll be there in time for supper."

2

Winston and Dorothy drove up to Wolcott from New York in a yellow sports car. They walked up the flagstone path to the front door. My parents came out and blinked in the dazzling sunshine. "Mrs. Meriwether," Winston said gravely. "Mr. Meriwether."

"Ah, yes," my father murmured. He looked dapper in a double-breasted white suit. A red silk handkerchief emerged rakishly from his breast pocket.

My mother glared at Dorothy. Then Winston took my mother's hand and leaned down to kiss her on the cheek. She was six feet one inch tall. "Mrs. Meriwether."

"How nice to meet you, Mr. Bingham." There was a hint of red in the hollow of her cheeks, like embers. Then Winston reached out and shook hands with my father. Dorothy's mouth was frozen into a smile. "My parents," she said to no one in particular.

The gravity of the occasion for Winston lightened a bit when he turned to me. "Put her there, Alfred." He dipped for my fingers as his left hand came around to the back of my neck and rested there. "Dot's told me a lot about you." It was the first time anyone had ever called my sister Dot.

My father coughed. His words of welcome were a long time organizing themselves. He was a shy man. Do you know what he said finally? He said, "Mighty fine, mighty fine." Out came the handkerchief and it trailed like blood against his suit. He began to mop his brow in quite ferocious dabs.

"This is a splendid place." Winston opened his arms to bid us welcome. It was a nice reversal.

We hung in space for a moment, like those boats centered in the vista of our property. Then my mother turned toward the front door. The slump in her broad shoulders seemed tactical. She walked through the door and into our front hall. The disembodied echo contrasted with her husky tone. "Dorothy, please show Mr. Bingham to the guest room. The bed's so short I hope he won't have to sleep on the . . ." The word "floor" trailed into the darkness.

"That's okay, Mrs. Meriwether," Winston called after her. "I've slept in foster homes, orphanages, gymnasiums—you name it."

Winston's shadow fell across my father's face. Dorothy came up and kissed Dad on his cheek and the sun beat down on the four of us.

My father waved his red handkerchief. "Dorothy, perhaps you and Mr. Bingham would like to freshen up before cocktails." His gentle words snapped my sister out of a homicidal glance toward the front door.

"Yes, Daddy."

Dorothy squeezed my arm and leaned into my shoulder. "Good boy," she whispered. She always treated me as a younger brother.

My father and Winston moved toward the front door. Winston launched into the virtues of his sports car. "Alfred," he said. "Give me a hand with those bags, will you?" He gave me a wink and a smile, and disappeared into the house with my father.

"Good boy," Dorothy repeated. By this time her eyes had filmed over with the black ice of anxiety. She walked on and disappeared into the house, leaving me standing alone in the sun.

I took the ropes off the luggage rack, the packages out of the trunk. Bingham's suitcase was of battered cardboard, covered with stickers. I couldn't wait to get back inside. I practically ran inside with the luggage. I left Dorothy's suitcase outside her bedroom on the second floor. Then I puffed down the hall with Winston's cardboard suitcase. I knocked on the door and Winston said, "Come right in. "

He was sitting on the bed. His yellow necktie shone, as did the glistening fabric of his green suit. His outsized shoes were made of a material resembling patent leather, but they may have been a petroleum derivative. Winston's general appearance contrasted with the blue china, delicate watercolors, and smallish bed.

He raised his finger at me. "Just put that bag over there, Alfred. Come over and sit beside me. For the first time in my life I've found a home." He patted the bedspread. "Sit beside Thumper."

"Thumper?" I asked.

"That was my nickname when I played basketball at Lake Erie College, for the Golden Eagles. I was Small College All-American in my senior year, but I haven't done much since then. I'm interested in a political career, but can't seem to get started. When I mention I'm a foundling, most people think two words—illicit sex. Sex in the back seats and back streets." He again patted the bedspread, so I went over and sat beside him on the bed.

He placed his hand on my left knee. "Do you know the difference between an orphan and a foundling?"

"An orphan is a child whose father and mother are dead," I said. "A foundling—"

He squeezed my knee. "That's right." Absently, he reached into his pocket and pulled out a wallet bulging with business cards. "Contacts," he muttered. He removed one yellowing paper and then tossed the wallet on the bed. He concentrated on the paper, opening its smudged folds. "I carry this paper everywhere."

"It looks it."

Winston looked grim. "You asked me the definition of a foundling, Alfred."

"No," I said. "You asked *me* the difference between an orphan and a foundling."

His eyes narrowed. The yellowed paper fluttered to the rug. "According to the Oxford English Dictionary," he announced, "a foundling is, quote, 'a deserted infant whose parents are unknown, a child whom there is no one to claim.' Isn't that beautiful, Alfred?"

I nodded. "Very nice."

"Here's a quote from *Barnaby Rudge* by Charles Dickens. 'He roared again until the very foundlings near at hand were startled in their beds.' Or how about this one? 'I myself have seen these

foundlings in their nest displaying a strange ferocity of nature.'
Have you ever been looked at like that?"

I shook my head.

"But my favorite is the line, 'Tho' he a foundling bastard
be . . .' Because it's a line you can hum when you walk down the
street. I've even made up a little rhyme: 'Tho' he a foundling
bastard be, hey, heigh-ho, that's okay by me.'"

I laughed, and for a second he looked bewildered. "I think
you'll fit right in here, Winston, foundling bastard or not."

You see, I thought he was a buffoon. That was the mistake of
my life.

I encountered my mother in the upstairs hall. In black satin,
hands twining a pearl necklace, she teetered on the steep staircase on the second-floor landing. Her eyes focused on me. "How
do we get rid of it?"

"I kind of like him. He's a bit physical."

"You don't just pick someone out of the sewer and bring him
home for dinner." Her long fingers reached out and caressed my
cheek, then squeezed my mouth into a trout expression. She
sighed and I guided her down into the cavernous living room.

A few minutes later Dad entered the living room, reticently. It
was almost as if he were walking backward into the gloom. He
said, "Ah hah," perhaps because the darkness made everything
illicit. He wrung his hands and then proceeded to the bar in one
corner. He assumed an air of confidence and even joviality. "Yes,
yes," he muttered, checking out the *mise-en-scène* and playfully
tapping each bottle in turn. I was already inside a blended
whiskey.

"Edith," he said. "What'll it be?"

My mother sat quietly in her chair nearest the fireplace.
"Sherry," she warned. When Dorothy came into the living room,
looking swank in something blue from Paris, my mother turned
her face to the fireplace.

"Sherry, Dorothy?" my father asked the apple of his eye.
Dorothy nodded. She came over to the deep black couch and sat
down beside me. Her chin dimpled and I felt so sorry for her
that I took her moist hands in mine, lest she threaten to bolt.

Winston reached out and patted Dad on the back as he went by. He sank into the couch beside Dorothy, clasped her free hand and stage-whispered, "How's my baby?"

"Oh, Winnie." She blushed.

"Sherry, Winston old boy?" my father asked.

Saliva bubbles of delight formed between Winston's lips—the word seemed to hold significance for him. "The cask of amontillado," he mused. "They bricked him up."

"La Ina, actually," my father said. "It's the best we can do, I'm afraid."

"I've never taken a drink of liquor in my life, Mr. Meriwether. Never taken so much as an aspirin. Not even when I was playing basketball at Lake Erie College. There were doctors around with amphetamines saying, 'Try just one, Thumper. We need you for the big game.' Believe me, Mr. Meriwether, some days it was a temptation, especially when I hurt those vertebrae in my neck in my senior year. But I've seen too many players—good players, too—go down that road to oblivion."

"Admirable," my father said.

"My philosophy of life can be summed up in six little words," Winston said.

"And what might they be?" my mother asked.

"No booze, no pills, no needles."

"A juice, Daddy," Dorothy said quietly. "Winnie loves juices."

"Winnie," my mother repeated. She watched as Winston's shoe flashed in the air before settling atop his knee. She offered her powdered neck to the gods.

"Tomato, then?"

"Tomato it is," Winston replied. "How does that song go? 'You say tomato, I say tomahto . . .'"

My mother stirred. She looked at Winston for a second, her nose twitching.

After serving the drinks, my father stood before us, holding his glass at chin level, his face dewy with emotion. "Cheers to both of you. Welcome to the Meriwether family, Winston."

"Cheers," I said.

Winston touched Dorothy's glass, then raised his own. "This is the happiest day of my life," he declared.

Moments before the maid rang the bell for dinner, my mother

sensed the reverberations in the air. She rose from her deep chair the way a decked fighter wobbles off the canvas. "Supper's ready," she said with forced brightness. "Come along, everyone. Bring your drinks."

Winston helped Dorothy to her feet with one fluid pull, as if she were a fallen teammate. The bell for supper rang. We followed my mother's elegant prow as it sailed toward the dining room.

The capon was rotten. It arrived on the sideboard juicy and steaming and scrumptious, but an odor of rancidness filled the room when Dad cut into it. The odor permeated the dining room, like sulphur, like an oozing sore. The big carving fork, wielded by my father, quivered in the bird. My mother rose to the crisis over the linen, the silverware, the royal crystal. There were flurries of complaints about the local turkey farm.

We dined on cold cuts and cheese, rye bread and mustard, nutty claret. My eyes glistened. My mother was imprisoned by etiquette into seating Winston Bingham to her right. He had stood beside the table for just a moment, overlooking it and overseeing it and assessing it before he sat down, only to abruptly get back up again to pull out my mother's waiting chair.

The capon crisis briefly enlivened her mood. It was as if this symbol of introduced rottenness was so obvious, so much a portent, so manifestly God-offered, that who could fail to take note?

My mother leaned over to me and whispered, "Do you think it would like some liverwurst?"

And there we were, she and I, the two old veterans of childhood wars, allies against the Goth in his electric green suit and plastic red-hued shoes.

Dorothy was visibly in love with Winston Bingham. She *glowed* beside him, fed him his wurst, drank from his glass of claret, hung on his words like a child on a jungle gym. No longer pale and lank, museum-dead at twenty-seven, she was now taking some first steps toward the world.

My father said, "Natoli and Minsky, Natoli and Minsky. Can't say it rings a bell, Winston. What kind of law do they practice at your firm in Buffalo?"

"Personal injury," Winston replied. "Glorified ambulance chasing, really. It's a cutthroat business."

"Ah, yes." My father smiled gently. Yes, one heard the most appalling stories of distant practices. . . .

"You went to Harvard Law School, I suppose, Mr. Meriwether."

"Yes, I did. The same as Alfred here. Class of 1916."

"Natoli and Minsky was the best I could do, I'm afraid."

My father raised his hand to dismiss any thought of legal inferiority.

"Do you follow basketball, Mr. Meriwether?"

"No, I'm afraid not, Winston. Golf is my game."

"A wonderful game. My problem is that I need an opponent—to watch the roll of his eyes, the dip of his shoulder."

"My big pooh-bear," Dorothy said.

My mother leaned out of her chair. For a moment I thought a slice of American brick had lodged in her windpipe. She was a choker; perhaps it was nerves.

My mother held out her wineglass the way Camille might hold out a hand for a pulse-check. I filled it and she brought the quavering liquid to her exhausted lips. Then she set the glass down again with trembles and poignant exhalations.

Winston pressed his hands against the edge of the dining room table. His thin neck constricted and caused him to nod this way and that. The cords of his neck stood out. Perhaps this was a holdover from his basketball-related injury. The spasm passed. His tongue flickered into the upraised glass of claret. He smacked his lips. It wasn't true that he never took a drink, or was the soul of health and purity. This white lie struck me at the time, but no one else seemed to notice it.

My father looked hunched and small at the head of the dining room table. He wasn't happy in his blazer. Perhaps he felt that something sporty would be required of him—a jovial toast, a string of jokes, a post-supper drive in our J-model Duesenberg. This enormous motor vehicle lurked with pre-Depression gaiety outside in the garage.

Dad would have much preferred to meet the groom-to-be on

some autumn afternoon at the Wall Street law offices of Waterman, Rhodes, Stevenson, and Meriwether—his true home—as the sun withdrew through the window behind his desk. Yes, the new associate paying a call on the firm's patriarch, a half acre of black mahogany between them, the formality and the fumbling, the vest-stretching watch chain, the thumb and forefinger injected with finality into the little wool pocket. Then the snapping open of the filigreed gold watch case, the dry handshake, the "Ah, yes," the pat on the back, the murmured "Welcome to the family, my boy." Formality and decorum—that's where my father's good heart secretly lay. But that evening at supper, the first of many with Winston, only the warmth of my sister's repeated "Daddys" carried him over the burnt valleys of silence and up to the hilltops of benign interjections.

It never occurred to me that Winston might try to set up a winning situation for himself with my father. But it must have been foremost in his mind, from the moment he walked into the house, to get this one nasty detail out of the way—the detail about his future.

Winston shook his head sadly and took Dorothy's hand. "There isn't much golf in Buffalo, New York," he told my father. "I hope Dorothy here doesn't freeze her toes off."

"Don't worry about me," Dorothy said. "I come from hardy Lane and Meriwether stock. Cold weather doesn't bother me."

"I've heard brave words like that before, Dot. I hope you won't be singing another tune when the wind's howling, the mercury has dipped to forty-five degrees below zero—"

Dad stirred himself, coughed, tugged at his blazer button. "*Forty-five* degrees below zero?"

"And a hundred and fifty feet of snow a year, Mr. Meriwether."

Perhaps at this point various career options for Winston were planted in Dad's mind.

"There is one wedding present we could really use," Winston said.

My mother made a faint growling sound. Her eyes snapped open as if a string was attached. "And what might that be, Mr. Bingham?"

"A good wood-burning stove," Winston said promptly and

rather loudly. He might just as well have taken out a gun and shot Dad between the eyes. My old man's shoulders unfurled. Both hands gripped the arms of his chair. His head lolled for just a second. Perhaps he scented the reek—to him, that is—of birch and oak and slow-burning ash, the *buzz-buzz-buzz* of a chain saw. He may have envisioned his beloved Dorothy in something flannel, piling up the cords outside Winston's shack while the young barrister flew over the back roads of upstate New York on the lookout for fender-benders.

My father made no sound—he patted a forefinger across his lips like an ink blot to soak up the sounds, and then used his white napkin. It must have seemed to him like an episode from a silent movie—eviction notices, teetering cabins, shoe-chewings— that had jumped down from the screen to engulf him.

My sister nudged her fiancé. "Go on, Winnie. Tell them."

"I thought it was going to be our secret for a while."

My sister's chin set firmly. "Well, if you won't tell them, *I* will."

Winston sighed. "How do you go public with a private dream?"

"I really wouldn't know," my mother said, and went for her pearls.

"It's something Dorothy and I discussed *ad infinitum* on the boat," Winston said seriously. "The Peace Corps."

My father became alert. "The Peace Corps?"

Dorothy's eyes shone. Winston nodded. "That's right, Mr. Meriwether." He leaned over his plate. "The notion of public service has stirred us both."

"What kind of work would you be doing in the Peace Corps?" I asked.

Winston looked at my father. "Teaching school in Ecuador, digging irrigation ditches in Tanganyika, pitching in at lepro-saria in India. Wherever we can be the most help."

"Lepers?" Something like dignified horror crossed my father's face.

"Hansen's disease, Daddy," Dorothy said.

Winston chimed in: "Hansen's disease is caused by the rod-shaped organism *Mycobacterium leprae*, first described in 1874 by the Norwegian physician G. Armauer Hansen. The mode of transmission is not fully understood. The onset is intermittent and gradual. Symptoms of the disease may not appear until many years after exposure. End quote. I'll skip the mutilations."

Before I could mention that the Peace Corps probably wouldn't be doing much work in leprosaria, I heard a distinctive rustle of satin. My mother stood up. Her hands balled into remarkably large fists. Her powerful white teeth grasped at her lower lip. At least six knuckles rapped on the linen, jouncing the salt, tinkling the silverware. Her chin was thrust so far forward that she reminded me unpleasantly of Douglas MacArthur.

"How old am I, Sloan Wright Meriwether?" my mother demanded of my father. She pointed a bony finger at him. His top gold blazer button sank below the horizon of the mahogany.

"You're sixty-seven years old, Edith," my father said, and added, "There, there. There, there."

"I'm sixty-seven years old," my mother agreed angrily, "and this is the most disgusting dinner-table conversation I've ever heard." She raised the formidable knuckles of her right hand and brought them down like exclamation points. "Leprosy! Mutilations! Darkest Africa! Wood-burning stoves! Car accidents! I ask you!" My mother sat down and stared into the triumphant silence. "I've said my piece. And now I think we're ready for dessert."

Like most displays of family temperament, one is always fingering the dike upstream after the dam has burst downstream, interpreting matters that were misinterpretations in the first place.

Into the silence Winston spoke. "I apologize about the leprosy, Mrs. Meriwether. Sometimes my photographic memory gets me in hot water."

My mother glowed with the tremendous release of pent-up energy, fury, profound and uncontrollable stirrings. Her fulfillment was a more than adequate substitute for the train whistle of sexual desire. She smiled at Winston. "That's quite all right, Mr. Bingham."

"I guess I'm not up on my table etiquette." It didn't seem to bother him in the least. Winston wasn't interested in my mother; she scarcely registered as a person for him. It was Dad he was after.

"Now you must tell me how you two lovebirds met." My mother's head bounced on a little hammock that she had created with her bridged fingers as a listening pose.

She got more than she bargained for. Winston turned away from Dad and focused on her. He looked my mother straight in the eye, riveting her. "Let me tell you the whole story, Mrs. Meriwether." There was a certain sonorousness in his tone, a rumble in the throat indicating he found high drama in his autobiography. "Three months ago I boarded an ocean liner bound for Europe. At the time it seemed my future was all behind me. I was just another aging basketball player with a crick in my neck.

"That first night aboard ship the ocean was covered with moonlight," Winston continued. "Even though I was traveling steerage and practically sleeping with the crew, I climbed over a barrier and found myself on the First Class deck, where the moonlight was even more brilliant. A barrier separates First Class from all the others, but usually it's an invisible barrier."

This fact seemed to annoy him.

"I hugged the shadows and observed a lovely young woman at the railing. Obviously your daughter sensed something, Mrs. Meriwether, because she suddenly turned toward me. And do you know the first words Dorothy Penham Meriwether ever said to Winston Bingham?"

Dramatic pause. We were hanging on Winston's every word. Ours was not a family much given to monologues. My mother preferred the peremptory directive; my father enjoyed the gestures of suggestion—rustling newspapers, drum-rolling fingers, ecstatic coughs.

"Dorothy said, 'Whoever you are, come over here into the light.'

"I stepped out of the shadows. 'I don't belong here,' I blurted. 'I'm traveling steerage.'

"Mrs. Meriwether, your daughter laughed and asked, 'What's your name?'

" 'I'm Winston Bingham,' I said.

" 'I won't give away your secret, Mr. Bingham.' She extended her hand. 'I'm Dorothy Meriwether.'

"Well, that's how we met. In the moonlight at sea. I, a lawyer;

she, the daughter of one of Wall Street's most prominent lawyers." Winston gave a little bow toward my father. "I told Dorothy about my own problems just two years ago, trying to get a job on Wall Street after graduating from the University of Buffalo Law School. Letters unanswered, interviews canceled, phone calls never returned. After six months of feverish activity I'd only managed to hook up with Natoli and Minsky in Buffalo. And Dorothy said, 'How sad.'

"I guess you could say Dorothy and I clicked from the beginning. That first night she leaned out over the railing and asked me what the chances were of the ship ramming an iceberg. We counted the lifeboats in the moonlight, estimated the number of passengers per lifeboat, the temperature of the water.

"Then we talked about the *Titanic*—the lights sliding into the sea, the women and children first into the lifeboats, the band playing 'Nearer My God to Thee,' and all those fine gentlemen singing along. I told Dot that if necessary I would have dressed up in women's clothing and jumped into the nearest lifeboat."

Winston looked angry and his face reddened. "This 'Nearer My God to Thee' business and women and children first and champagne buckets and going down with the ship has always annoyed me. You know, I wonder if everything was so brotherly when the North Atlantic got to the First Class deck, when the water began to lick at the pants legs of the violin section. I think the answer to that question is a resounding No. I think you would have found a lot of your upper-crust Englishmen and Americans, stuffed to the gills with caviar and bombed out of their minds on champagne, experiencing the same emotion as the lower castes—namely, panic."

Winston leaned back to encompass the table. "What the hell," he said, with an enormous shrug. "They always put the cookie jar another shelf higher." He clapped his hands with a sharp sound. He might as well have pounded my parents on the back, for the start it gave them. They had slumped slightly forward and their mouths had fallen open in amazed attention. My mother's blackest satin, Dad's blue blazer, my sister Dorothy's blond hair, my own ruddy round face.

My father cleared his throat, a major gesture on his part. It commanded attention. He mouthed his question before asking it. He looked as if he was undergoing an incantatory trance.

"Winston, of course you've passed the New York State Bar Examination."

"*Passed* it?" Winston said happily. "You bet, Mr. Meriwether."

My father whispered, "Ah, yes." He scurried back into silence. For a moment the only sound in the dining room was the creak of Winston's Queen Anne chair.

I knew there would be no Peace Corps for Dorothy and Winston, no trip upriver, no encounters with the Third World, no heart of darkness. Instead there would be Joy perfume, triplex apartments, delicious pâtés tumbling out of their jellies and splatting on fine china.

My father cleared his throat again and moaned, as if being prodded. "I was thinking that, that, that . . . Young Alfred and I . . . Sit down over brandy and cigars . . . interesting situation now at our shop . . . bright young men . . . always on the lookout. New blood . . . fresh blood . . . Arteries harden . . . Keep things pumping, constant flow . . ."

For some reason Dad climbed onto this metaphor and couldn't get off again. He floundered about in a bloodbath. ". . . transfusions or else a law firm hemorrhages . . . young people . . . the vital plasma . . . anemic. Too much tired blood at the top, ho, ho."

My father tittered and covered his mouth with a napkin. There was a kind of melancholy drapery to his gesture. I had the impression of a piece of furniture covered with a sheet in an abandoned room.

Needless to say, I rushed in to stem the flow, bind the wound, hand out the bandages. Sometimes I acted like an Athenian messenger delivering the tragic news that the Spartans were at it again, knowing all the while it was a subject bound to make everyone skittish. I lived with my parents for almost forty years.

"There are other choices besides Natoli and Minsky or the Peace Corps," I said.

"Other choices. Right you are," my father muttered. "Other choices. Right you are."

Winston's head and words grew pendulous and solemn. "If you don't mind, Mr. Meriwether, I'll pass on the brandy in favor of some apple or grape juice. I wouldn't turn down a good cigar, though."

I noticed my mother. She was slumped against the back of her chair, shoulders sagging, head tilted back. She stirred herself briefly, dropped her hands from the arms of the chair. "Give me strength," she whispered.

Winston smiled at my mother. "I do believe you're playing footsie with me, Mrs. Meriwether."

She blushed. Her feet had evidently been dancing about under the table, searching for the elusive electric buzzer to summon her Irish table-clearing rescuers, Colleen and Mary, from the pantry.

Winston looked at his barely touched blueberry pie. "Mrs. Meriwether, it's good to get back to simple American fare after all that *haute cuisine* Dotsie fed me in the Old World."

My mother smiled at me. "My best baby."

My father stood up. "Is that all?" he asked, swaying a little in place. His hands were restless; he missed his pocket watch.

"Not quite."

My mother's words arrested our movements and scrambles, chair-scrapings and limb-stretchings. Winston was just coming out of a crouch when she said it. I noted that the bottle of claret was still—thanks to the big fellow's abstinence—a quarter full. Perhaps Dorothy was thinking, as she stood up and nervously smoothed her smart dress, that she could get away with bringing home an ambulance-chasing member of the underclass to supper in our sophisticated house with its priceless antiques, priceless history, priceless virtues, priceless *je ne sais quoi*. If so, she had another think coming.

My mother's voice was high and pretty and tinkling and charming. "Why don't *les girls* sneak upstairs and have their own fashion show? We'll let the boys smoke their cigars, drink their brandy, and talk their boy-talk. If you *knew* how I was dying to see all the latest things from Paris."

My mother had absolutely no interest in fashion.

"Yes, Mummy." Dorothy had known what was coming from the moment she'd been smitten with Winston in the moonlight. My heavy heart went out to her. Flee, flee, I wanted to cry.

Grab that big guy by the hand and enjoy your unheated life in Buffalo.

"My cane, Alfred," my mother said. When I handed the knobby oak to her, she flourished it. "I'm an old woman," she asserted, as she frequently did. She leaned on it with her full weight. Of course, she didn't really need the formidable cane, with its ivory handle, thick and scarred staff, dirt-encrusted tip. But with it she became the *grande dame,* the whalebone-spined matriarch. It was as if the call had come from central casting: sensible shoes, tweeds, a 1929 Duesenberg, a no-nonsense mien, property, the lush for a son.

The cane gave her strength. It made her crotchety and peremptory. "Take my arm, Dorothy," she commanded. "We have a lot to talk about." Dorothy obediently came over and latched onto an outthrust elbow. My sister gave me then the weariest look, the quietest sigh.

It could be said that my mother dragged Dorothy out of the dining room then, striding out as if for a trek on the moors. For just a second, before she flew out the door, Dorothy seemed to be trailing at the end of a loose leash. A fragment of my mother's opening salvo drifted back to me. ". . . gutter, young lady?"

Winston wasn't tuned in to any of this. He was watching my father like a condor, hunting the old man's face and gestures for any subtleties or clues that may have eluded him, eating the old boy up with his black eyes.

I did not feel the interior action was with them anymore. I longed to be upstairs, helping out, smoothing the way, being of use to my sister. I felt she was about to be steamrollered. I worried things would get out of hand—something unpleasant would happen. The illusion of rescue is the mini-tragedy of my life.

Whenever I felt myself to be under this particular tension of unwholesome responsibility, distorted priorities, unnatural involvement, I found speedy relief in rectified substances. Indeed, the entire rest of the night began to plan itself out for me. There would be frequent stops to have my frontal lobes caressed at bars and grills, roadhouses and cabarets.

In Wolcott they let me sleep on the cool lapping beach beyond the seawall, curled up in a ball. The beach maintenance crews of sympathetic young men and women knew me. "It's a gorgeous morning, Mr. Meriwether," they would say. "Your spring and your day are wasted in play, and your winter and night in disguise," they would sing. "The dews of night arise," they would laugh.

Winston took my father under his wing, shrouded my dad and bore him out of the dining room.

"Coming, Alfred?" my father pleaded, his voice muffled.

"In a minute, Dad."

While I polished off the wine, pretty maids capered and giggled. They cleared the artifacts of my family's unhappy meal. I found their blue uniforms oddly stirring. Soon my face felt as if it was being expertly dyed a rich blue. "No one knows the troubles I've seen," I said to Mary, the maid, who curtsied. "Tell me about the Emerald Isle," I murmured to Colleen. They clogged the pantry door, tumbling over each other in a clatter of plates and sliding silverware. My mother got her maids fresh off Aer Lingus, practically slave labor, and broke them in. Always after one or two years they married and disappeared into the great city. Even after their experiences in that so-called priest-ridden country, I don't think they could stand the silences.

In the living room my father sat comfortably in his pool of light. He was quite in charge now as the subject was the law. Winston had to read between the lines of the informal contract my father was establishing between them. I'm sure Dad hoped Winston would step into the night air for a breather, and get run over by a Caterpillar thresher, but my father was a gentleman.

There in the distance was the head of Winston, nodding. "That's great, Mr. Meriwether." He held up the thick brown Partagas to the lamp, looked puzzled for a moment, then chomped on the tip. He seemed happy with the jagged remains, wetted and smoothed the tip in his mouth. Then he lighted the thing—gasping, satiated, blowing stacks of smoke, clubman to clubman with my blazered father. He cuddled in the chair and his cigar hand began to conduct Dad, as if the old man was part of his personal Philharmonic's glorious wind section, extracting the pure tones of full employment forever. He patted the couch beside him. "Alfred, come over and sit beside Thumper."

That was the last thing I wanted to do. I carried my golden snifter—perhaps an ounce too heavy in the well—over to a couch near Dad, who welcomed me with rare physicality by also patting a cushion. "I've just been filling Winston in on some of our activities at the shop. More relaxed pace than personal injury, I daresay. Not much excitement for a man of action."

"Pshaw," Winston said.

"Ho, ho," said my father. He seemed to me a man of the utmost fragility. A vein trickled down his temple.

I asked, "Say, Thumper, what happened to all that talk about the Peace Corps?"

The big guy grinned, but there was nothing friendly about it. I don't think he liked me from the start. "Maybe Dot and I will put that option on the back burner for a while, Alfred."

I waved my snifter. "What does Dorothy think?"

It is not enough to say that Winston's black eyes narrowed; they seemed to collide. "Dotsie and I are always on the same wavelength, Alfred. That's part of being in love."

My father grimaced and cast a look of caution my way. He wanted to concentrate on the future now—Winston's past was too much for him. "Winston and I were just discussing the Jensen estate, Alfred."

Winston did away with the bit of business with the cigar. He deposited its mushiness into a copper ashtray. My future brother-in-law leaned forward and the fingers of his huge hands rippled between his knees. Listening for Winston was less a matter of listening than of extracting. He brought to his purpose a fixity of concentration, a profound attention, that seemed almost innocent. He was nobody's fool.

My father meandered around the firm, poking at its history—senile Osgood Waterman, dyspeptic Bruce Rhodes, polo players and camel-coated horse breeders, rolling estates, skeletal dowagers sitting on zillions, great wills drafted like concertos—the whole world of trusts and estates. Winston reminded me more and more of a child listening to a ghost story—open-mouthed, giggly, wide-eyed as megabucks flew around the living room. "Two hundred million," he said. He managed to seem awed and resentful at the same time. He looked at me warily. "Don't you love it, Alfred?"

"I love it too much, old scout," I murmured.

"Well, you can imagine," my father continued. "Olivia Jensen *stormed* into my office."

"Loaded for bear, I'll bet," Winston declared. "In a wrassling mood, I'll just bet."

"Exactly right," my father chuckled. "Loaded for bear, hm, hm, hm."

My face glowed like a sun. "You're sure you won't find Wall Street a mite confining after all those winter sports in Buffalo? Skiing, barrel jumping."

"I don't do any of that because of my neck," Winston said quietly. "I've never done any barrel jumping."

"Maybe we could open an office in Buffalo," I said.

"I don't think . . ." my father said with a gentle smile.

Winston *rat-tat-tatted* his thighs. "Good cigar, good company —not to mention light-hearted conversation with my future brother-in-law." He stared at my waving snifter. "Juices are good for keeping the head clear, I've found."

"Excellent mixers," I exclaimed happily. "Couldn't be more healthy."

"That's for sure," Winston agreed.

At this point I leaned too far forward. I saw myself standing on a Congo riverbank, waving good-bye to Winston. I began to smile inappropriately. I ran along the riverbank until Winston's spangled pirogue disappeared around a bend in the river. "That old man river," I mumbled, and leaned back on the couch. I felt like pulling the pin on my snifter, which I held onto now with both hands.

"My knees aren't what they used to be," Winston said. "The sawbones I saw in Buffalo told me I was an early candidate for arthritis. I guess that'll slow me down, won't it?"

He was on his feet with such remarkable springiness and quickness, had plunked himself down beside me with such speedy agility, that my mind was still waving good-bye to him on the riverbank. There was apple juice on his heavy breath. His thumb found the reflex joint above my knee, and my left leg flew out. A tasseled loafer strutted in midair.

I smelled the whole attic mustiness of his body, the raw forest warmth of it, the closeness of it, the encompassing violence of it.

The strength of it rippled up from his thumb in succeeding waves of concussive force.

"Don't ever do that again," I said.

Obviously, he saw me as some kind of wart on his plans, when nothing could have been further from the truth. He hadn't gotten it through his head that I was given to mild needling, winsome assertiveness when I was under the influence, but no threat to him.

"Sorry, Alfred," Winston declared with a laugh. "I'm a big physical guy."

I took a last gulp of the brandy and showed some agility myself, if I do say so. I more or less clambered to my feet. "I'll just . . ." I murmured.

I ambled over to the well-stocked bar. I looked into the ice bucket. The melting floes reminded me of the *Titanic*. A pocket of dark enshrouded the bar area. It permitted me to linger happily, touching black rums, examining the labels of friendly scotches, hoisting an old favorite like Jack Daniel's, tinkling the mixers and strainers, the tongs and mint julep spoons.

"Let me get the whole structure of the firm clear in my mind, Mr. Meriwether," Winston said from behind me. "You're going to think I'm dense, I guess, not knowing the first thing about how a prestigious law firm works. I'll never forget what my basketball coach at Lake Erie College, Rudy Milchanowski—just a wonderful guy and a wonderful inspiration—I'll never forget what Rudy once told the team after we'd had a mix-up about who was going to set the pick. He said, 'Boys, the only stupid question is the question not asked.'"

My father spoke in a voice of lulling consequence, of maximum civility. Young associates at the firm clambered to work for him. They adopted his hesitant mannerisms and unpredictable aphasia, throat-clearings, bifocals, and eye-rubbings. They developed young paunches and bowed backs; they were concerned about doing the right thing by their clients. They shuffled down the corridors, greeted each other with elaborate politeness. Even saying hello could wind up in a turtle-like minuet, shuffling and snuffling and neck-arching, padded feet moving in place, benevolent and myopic.

I glided out the living room door, up the creaky stairs, and toward my sister Dorothy's bedroom. Everything had been left white and girlish for her return. I was halfway down the corridor when I heard the gloves-off voice of my mother. It was stripped to the essentials of interrogation and information retrieval, a voice that no one, I think, would care to hear more than once in a lifetime.

"So," my mother said. "Are you going to marry that wharf rat?"

Not since the watershed years of the early 1940s had I heard implanted in my brain the imperative to reverse march. It was as if a hidden cortical knot had been carrying around, for all those years, the strangled voice and purple face of an enraged platoon sergeant. And at that moment, in the narrow corridor of my parents' summer home, the big sergeant in his tan puttees and prevent-forest-fires hat finally got out and screamed in my ear. I reversed march so fast that I have the false memory of leaving my snifter hanging in the air—like a cartoon—before grabbing it with a rubber arm from behind me. There was considerable staining and brandy odor on my clothing, dark-marooning of my red blazer.

Dorothy's—Dotsie's—reply caught up with me on the stairs. My sister's voice was really reaching for the octaves, humming the old crystal, and I thought instantly, Well, you have to hand it to Winston. He thinks of everything.

"Of course I'm going to marry him, Mummy," Dorothy said. "After all, you wouldn't want the child I'm carrying to be a foundling like Winston."

It was time to disturb the universe with a couple of Budweisers. My father and Winston murmured in the dim light. I climbed onto my softest tippy-toes and snuck past the entrance to the living room. Even so, I sent out vibrations. Winston's head whipped around. His black eyes nailed me dead to rights.

"Thought I'd pack it in," I said with a shrug. "See you tomorrow."

"You're not sneaking out, Alfred, before I've had a chance to say good-bye." He leapt to his feet and came toward me, grinning. I hoped he wouldn't touch me again, pressure my reflex spots. Winston whirled on my father, riveted and pinned the old man to the back of his chair. "Mr. Meriwether, don't you make a move. I've got a hundred more questions for you."

"Very well, Winston." My father looked rather hero-worshiped and his face was an unusual ego-red color. "Lunch at the Surf Club tomorrow, Alfred?" my father called.

"Sure," I said.

"You smell like a distillery," Winston laughed, prying the empty snifter from my hand.

We walked out into the moist darkness, where crickets chirped and the Point Barren foghorn sounded in the grave distance. My tassels glistened from the ground dew; Winston's shoes shone their brightest plastic in the light from the front door.

"Dorothy tells me you like to hit the hard stuff pretty good," Winston confided. "Glub-glub. It doesn't change my opinion of you. It humanizes you for me."

"Thumper, let's get one thing clear. I don't give a shit what you think."

He had a hand on each of my shoulders. It was dark. He spoke from somewhere far above me. He kneaded my shoulders quite comfortably.

"I'd like you to be my best friend," Winston said.

I shook my head. It was a lonely shake, like a tree falling in the wilderness with no one to witness it.

"'Night, old buddy." Winston released me then—after all, my father awaited him. He walked briskly back through the front door. I hopped into my Buick.

The next morning on the beach, golden retrievers poked their crab-scented snouts into my face. A gentle hand shook me. "Wake up, wake up, Mr. Meriwether," a siren's voice called. "See, even the gulls are pleading."

I rolled over into the sun.

3

In the weeks before the wedding, my father made some discreet inquiries about Winston Bingham. He wanted to know a little more about the background of the man who was marrying his daughter.

With the information Dad passed on to me—and what I picked up from Dorothy and Thumper himself—I got a clearer picture of his life before he met my sister.

Winston was born in January 1934, and within hours of birth had been left on the chapel steps of St. Brigid's of Kildare Church in Buffalo. He spent his childhood in the Sisters of Mercy Orphanage and a series of foster homes.

His prodigious athletic ability showed itself at an early age. When he entered Buffalo Central High School, Winston already stood six feet six inches tall and weighed one hundred and ninety pounds. At Buffalo Central his remarkable basketball career began, and—as I understand it—he first came to be called "Thumper" by the fans. Evidently he earned this sobriquet because of his aggressive "clearing out" under the basket, and a series of expressive facial tics that made him look rabbitlike as he "scented" the action on the court and dominated the play below him. Probably the fans were also making an ironic reference to the playful Thumper in Walt Disney's *Bambi*. Whatever, the nickname stuck.

In September 1952 Winston entered Lake Erie College, a member of the now-defunct Northeast Regional Athletic Conference (NRAC). The college was situated on the outskirts of Buffalo, between Lackawanna and West Seneca, New York, in the heart of the state's steel-making area.

Three years later Winston was named to the center position on the Small College All-American basketball team. He was a third-round draft choice of the Ft. Wayne Pistons, and a second-round choice of the Syracuse Nationals, both of the NBA. But he had suffered a severe neck injury at mid-season and made—as he told me—the "agonizing decision" not to play professional basketball. Instead he decided to enter the University of Buffalo Law School in the fall.

Winston's last game as a Golden Eagle—in which Lake Erie defeated the Albion Redskins 78–40—was christened "Honor Thumper Night." It drew an enthusiastic overflow crowd of six thousand fans to the college's Lakeland Pavilion. Declared Winston in his halftime farewell speech: "I consider myself the luckiest man who ever walked onto a basketball court." His team number—which was "1"—was retired.

In September 1956 Winston entered the University of Buffalo Law School. The institution devoted much of its three-year curriculum to preparing students for the New York State Bar exam. He made law review, became the top student in his class, but after graduation was turned down for employment by several New York law firms. Apparently his background, his obscure college and law school, as well as his overbearing personality, worked against him. In 1959 he reluctantly joined the Buffalo firm of Natoli and Minsky, and for the next three years specialized in personal injury cases.

In June of 1962 he got on a boat to England and immediately made his way to the First Class deck.

Before the wedding I had a talk with my father. I told him that I was extremely concerned about Winston joining Waterman, Rhodes as an associate. It seemed to me, I said, that he had all the classic trademarks of the born hustler. I wondered how Winston was going to fit into our conservative law firm, especially since his legal expertise was based solely on ambulance chasing.

"Isn't he just dreadful?" my father asked agreeably but rhetorically. I detected an unaccountable tone of subdued relish in his voice.

Later, I thought about Dad's bizarre enthusiasm. I suppose it was understandable, considering his personality. I always suspected that my father had spent most of his life in constant fear that nameless barbarian-Philistine invaders would suddenly sweep down upon him. The invaders would destroy all his edifices of routine and civility at one stroke. They would break down the doors of his library and law firm, plunge his careful world into chaos.

They waited out there somewhere in his imagination.

Now the invader had arrived, all six feet nine inches of him. The reality stood on his doorstep. I picture Dad wringing his hands and whispering over and over, "It could have been worse. It could have been worse."

Everything about Dorothy and Winston's marriage was hasty. Meriwether family members were not invited to St. Bart's on Park Avenue: they were corralled, hog-tied, flown in, and dispatched. The marriage ceremony was conducted by the Right Reverend Matthew Madison Gordon, the Episcopal Bishop of New York. He was a formidable figure.

Winston's best man was his ex-basketball coach at Lake Erie College, Rudolph Milchanowski. Rudy was a dapper, boiled, and spiffy little man who bounced around on the balls of his feet, tugging at the confining arms of his blue suit. I don't know why, but Rudy and I hit it off immediately.

Outside the church after the ceremony, everyone settled down into the wedding motorcade. We prepared for the stately processional up Park Avenue, down Eighty-sixth Street, north on East End Avenue, and then a hop, skip, and a jump west across to the Meriwether enclave on robust Eighty-seventh Street.

A photographer leaned in to capture his last candid of the restless couple. I lolled in the third limo with Rudy Milchanowski. He regaled me with stories about the last days of the Northeast Regional Athletic Conference (NRAC), which had suffered financial reversals. Rubber checks, gymnasium floors sold for decorative lumber, over-the-hill semipro ball hawks snuck in as ringers.

Rudy flicked the white ash off his Tiparillo. His voice was permanently hoarse from referee-baiting: "I went up to the guy and I asked him, 'Roosevelt, I ever see you play with the Lenox Avenue Brown Kings?' Well, what could he do, Al, except hang his head? Then I go up to the ref and I tell him, 'Eugene, you eject that goddamn ringer or I'm pullin' my Golden Eagles.' Eugene shrugs and tells me, 'Rudy, I get paid the same.' Al, I'll tell you, that's when I knew the league was on the skids. That fucking Roosevelt. He was throwing forward passes, riding his center piggyback. They won 85–20."

Rudy took a ruminative puff. "It wasn't like that in the Thumper days. We had to put in extra seats at the Lakeland Pavilion those three years. But you know something, Al? It wasn't healthy. Thumper aroused your baser instincts. He'd knock your chin up your nose."

Rudy and I dawdled as the guests milled about on the steps. The sharp sun of mid-September flashed off the black hoods of the limousines. Park Avenue was a gorgeous variety of brown. Each shade represented a fortress-like stability against social accidents. I carried not one but two slim flasks that afternoon.

During the delay in getting the show on the road, Rudy announced through his handsome choppers, with a whistle sounding like a mortar round, as we bumped silver jiggers: "Cheers to you, Al, and here's to the big guy and his little lady." He raised his jigger toward the como-blue ceiling. I did the same, although I was reminded that Winston and Dorothy had decided to forgo a honeymoon. Bright-eyed and bushy-tailed, Winston would present himself to me in my office at Waterman, Rhodes on Monday morning. My flask trembled, and I was filled with great melancholy.

"Here's to the big guy," I said.

At the reception I watched Winston glad-handing everyone in the receiving line. He made sure to get all the names right, mopped his overjoyed brow, dominated the living room. He really put away the champagne, and his face got redder and redder. For the second time, I realized he had lied about his abstemiousness.

After an hour or so I invited Rudy Milchanowski, the diminutive basketball coach, to join me in a sojourn through the city of watering holes.

Rudy was delighted. He looked around the clogged room and wheezed, "I'm with you, Al. This place's not my style." Out on Eighty-seventh Street, I commandeered the same limousine that had borne us to the reception. We were off on the town.

Rudy was an encyclopedia of sports information, a regular

Mister Memory. First, we got into heavy basketball strategy, then moved into football and hockey, and wound up along Third Avenue discussing Sandy Amoros.

"Ask me anything," Rudy said, staring into his Four Roses. "If I don't know it, I'll buy." He had laid down the gauntlet. "Only the major sports," he insisted.

We had a two-bar argument about what constituted a "major" sport. At P. J. Clarke's on Fifty-fifth Street, we finally narrowed the "majors" down to football, baseball, basketball, and horse racing. After a while, working our way uptown, the facts and the figures, the superstars and the bums, the rosters and the lineups blurred in my mind. The afternoon lengthened and I had more and more trouble framing my trivia questions. Frequently, I had the distinct sensation that Rudy was answering them before I had asked them.

The reception was still inexplicably in full swing when we arrived back. Tiparillo jaunty, I draped my arm around my friend's shoulder as we entered the living room. Rudy held me up.

Winston intercepted us in the middle of the living room. From fifty feet above me, he said amiably, "Maybe you should sit down before you fall down, Big Al."

I hated being called Big Al, and made a rubbery motorboat sound with my lips. I wanted to get to the bar. Between the guests I could make out white jackets as we navigated. If I could just make it *there*, I thought, I would regain my steadiness.

I reached the bar and planted my hands on the counter. Then Rudy staggered away—perhaps to find a bathroom. I drank my champagne. Guests came up and greeted me; my words swam in my mouth. I left the bar and made breaststroke motions through the people.

Weaving through the open door of my father's library, I managed to negotiate a red leather chair at the far end of the room, and sat down. I crossed my legs casually, feeling quite propped up and dignified. Then I became sick all over the front of my suit. I couldn't raise my arms, gesture for help, do anything. The sensation in my limbs was fuzzy and tingly and not unpleasant. I've got a big clean-up job, I decided. Golly. I rested my sweating head on the back of the chair.

The corridor was heavily traveled by guests on their way to

the bathrooms on the second floor. They glanced into the library, saw me, popped out again. They said, "Christ," or, "Is that Alfred?" or, "Want to see something?"

Winston filled the doorway. He strode over, picked me up in his arms, and carried me out of the library. He did not say a word. Everything he did was in one fluid motion. Though over two hundred pounds, I was not too heavy for him. He did not mention my state of disarray.

Winston carried me up the stairs, briskly. "Where's Rudy?" I mumbled. "Me and Rudy."

"I put the little fuck in a cab."

"He was very drunk," I muttered.

Winston put me down outside my bedroom door on the third floor. He opened the door, picked me up again, carried me over to my bed and let go of me when I was directly above the mattress—the way a bomb drops out of a B-52. I bounced once and sprawled.

"Alfred," Winston said quietly. "I hope you're not going to be a problem for me."

On Monday morning—his first day at the firm—Winston was raring to go. When I arrived at nine-thirty, he sat in the reception room, leaning forward in his chair and tapping his feet. Before I could apologize for my debauch at his reception, he jumped up and engulfed my body as if it was a long lost friend. "Alfred, what kind of mausoleum is this?"

Winston had put his hand on a sore problem. He had sized things up just by sitting in the reception room, observing our lawyers as they arrived. The problem was tired blood.

We lockstepped down the hushed corridor of Waterman, Rhodes to my office with its gray overlook of Wall Street. His eyes searched my office, checked the walls and windows. He went over and lifted up some papers on my desk, opened a couple of file cabinets, scuffed his feet on the floor. At last he fell into the small chair beside my desk and stretched out his legs. When he finally spoke his tone was almost pleading, very much in the say-it-ain't-so-Joe honest bewilderment of a small child. "Is this where the boss's son works?"

"What's wrong with it?" I asked.

He shook his head. "See what happens when you build things up in your mind? Obviously my dreams outstripped reality." Winston looked around my office again. "I was expecting wood paneling, hunting prints, and leather smells."

"I'm a junior partner."

"You're telling *me* you're junior." He rubbed his eyes tiredly. "Where do they keep the wheelchairs in this place? Nobody except us is ever going to use the stairs."

I laughed.

"The substance part of the business I can handle," Winston said. "Nobody has to give me pointers on how to get to the meat of an issue. That's mother's milk to me. What I was looking forward to were some of the accoutrements, the plush appointments to enhance my new job. Where are they putting *me*, for Christ's sake? Are they going to dangle me down an air shaft?"

"Your office is right down the hall," I said.

"Close to you? So I can just bust in and plop myself down here whenever I have an adjustment problem?"

"That shouldn't be too often. I'll introduce you to our office manager, Mrs. Remsen. She'll be a big help."

Winston brightened considerably. "You like to underplay everything, don't you, Alfred? You don't put much topspin on the old ball, do you?"

It was an unfortunate analogy, but I rallied nicely. "No, I guess I don't."

He wagged his finger at me. "You had me buffaloed for a while, because I'm so dramatic myself. Once you've heard six thousand people stamping their Vibram grips, and scantily clad cheerleaders screaming, 'Gimme a T, gimme an H, gimme a U, gimme an M, gimme a P, gimme an E, gimme an R, What've you got, Thumper,' then there's always a temptation to seize the limelight. I just hope this firm won't be an anchor around my neck and deep-six me."

He looked at me warily for a second and then got to his feet. Still in a basketball mood, he declared, "Let's go, go, go. I want to see everything, conference room to boiler room, the lowest secretary in the typing pool to your dad in his office. I'm looking forward to all of it."

The presence, or the injection, of Winston Bingham into a law firm that defined the word "staid," marked the end of an era, the closing of an epoch, the termination of something. The halls seemed too small to hold more than one little attorney at a time while Winston was in transit. Several of our shyer members, confronted by him, sidestepped into the nearest available office.

"This is more like it," he whispered after we'd climbed the elegant brass-railed spiral staircase to the library. He stood inside the room itself—its teak tables, antique gaslight fixtures on the wall, glass-enclosed cabinets, the whole sense of hush and continuity, the subdued play of the table lamps, the hunched figures of the associates.

Outside my father's office I introduced Winston with great formality to my father's secretary. Obviously he thought the path to Dad's heart would be greased by buttering her up. He aimed compliments at her like light artillery fire, plucked the single rose from the vase on her desk and implanted his nose. "Exquisite, exquisite," he said. "You'll see me cooling my heels out here a lot, Miss Wilson."

She assessed him dispassionately. "I'll let the senior Mr. Meriwether know you're here." She looked at me. "How are you today, Mr. Meriwether?"

"Just fine, Miss Wilson."

"You look a little peaked." She smiled.

"I'm the one who ought to look peaked," Winston said. "I'm the bridegroom."

"You don't look peaked, Mr. Bingham," she said somberly. "You look the picture of health."

"Plenty of exercise, proper diet," Winston said. He put the lightest extra inflection on the word "diet." This was just so the amply endowed Miss Wilson would know where she stood.

My father opened the door a sliver. Perhaps he was stirred by the general disturbance of airwaves, the subtle breakup in a lifelong routine of legal quietude. The firm bore the imprint of his aggressive pursuit of reticence.

Deciding the coast was clear, the mob scalded off the barricades, my father flung open the oaken door and stood exposed— the old thinking reed. His skin was the ashen color of overwork, his head and shoulders were stooped. The whole thrust of his body was floorward. Only his suspenders and gold watch chain kept him propped up to the straight and vertical. I winced with sympathy for him.

"Alfred," he said warmly. "Winston," he said stoically. He extended a bony hand. It trembled amid subtle air drafts, shifting back and forth on its fragile plane.

"Hi, Mr. Meriwether," Winston said. He made a gurgling sound, offered my father a quick five digits, and then roared into the old man's spacious office. He pasted himself like The Human Fly against the large window at the far end of the room beyond my father's long, work-heavy mahogany desk. Dad and I stood inside the doorway and stared at him. Each of us was stunned in place right down to our matching wingtips.

The big fellow had discovered New York Harbor, the Brooklyn Bridge, tugboats and cruise ships, the power plays of light and shadow across the dancing water far below, autumn sun warming the far horizon, oil tankers and coal-carrying barges, a few sleek sailboats tacking smartly. The whole world of bustling commerce spread below him invitingly but almost too far away for comfort. The effect was like a starting gate opening for a spooked racehorse—Winston simply took off and stopped at the furthest obstruction.

He remained attached to the glass for what seemed like several minutes, then turned to face us. He left behind smooch marks, nose breath, and fingerprints at each antipode.

"What a swell view, Mr. Meriwether," Winston said, from behind Dad's desk.

"Like it?" my father asked with real pleasure in his voice. "I'm so glad."

My father—bless him forever—looked for conversational openings in roughly the same way Columbus kept an eye peeled for Hispaniola. Now, with firm tundra underfoot, he perked up and moved toward Winston with what for him was a strut. He assumed the trappings of senior partnership. After long association, I knew pretty well how his mind worked. He would put a fatherly arm around Winston's massive shoulders, lead his son-in-law back over to the window, point out the varied Lower Manhattan sights with courtly nods. Finally, he would gesture Winston to a chair on the client's side of the large desk. The two men would exchange pleasantries for a few minutes.

The accurate prediction of the future as it unfolded must have filled my father with great relief. The certainty of control was very important to him.

My father said, "Allow me to point out the sights, Winston."

I left the two men framed against the glass. Courtesy reigned supreme.

I bid adieu to Miss Wilson and headed back to my office. I did not see Winston again until the late afternoon, and did not miss him. I read through some memoranda prepared by an associate, worked on a brief. At two I shoved off with Kipsy Maginn to the Recess for a long lunch. I was resting at my rolltop when Winston burst through the door. Say one thing for the son of a bitch: he filled a room with energy.

He stood in the door of my office and giggled, snorted, giggled again. "You sly dog, you. You old tiger." He swaggered over and sat down. "I thought you got your kicks from the Traveller's Companion series." He put up a hand, as if anticipating I would ask him what the hell he was talking about. "Don't ask. I have my sources."

"What is it, Winston?"

"Alice Wilson." It was clearly too rich for him. "Does the old-timer know?"

"No," I answered. "I'd appreciate it if you wouldn't tell him."

He put a hand over his heart. The effort to suppress a chortle was tearing him apart. "Wild horses could pull out my tongue."

"You wouldn't say shit if you had a mouthful."

"Exactly," Winston beamed. "Priceless. I thought I detected some body chemistry between you when I was getting on her good side this morning. I hope she's not a sourpuss."

"Winston."

"On the heavy-duty side."

"Winston."

"Built for comfort, not for speed, eh?"

"Shut up, Winston."

It was a mistake. His black eyes opened wide, like thick oil drippings. He whispered, "God, I'm such an asshole sometimes."

"Winston, I didn't mean—"

"I don't belong here, Alfred. You can't drag a boy out of a shithouse and put him on Wall Street. You can't give him beans for breakfast and not expect him to stink up the place."

Abruptly, Winston clambered to his feet. He dusted his knee areas, and then stalked out of my office. I did not see him again that day.

The next morning he greeted me with a light "nuggie." It was as if the scene between us had never happened. I was relieved. I wanted to be polite, and I was still terribly embarrassed about my conduct at his wedding. At lunchtime we got together and subwayed uptown, where he threw a scare into Brooks Brothers. Pinned and chalked, Winston tramped around the store in his new black English-toe shoes.

That evening, the subway squealed under the West Side. The lights in the car flickered. I asked Alice Wilson to marry me. "Yes," she promptly agreed, planting a kiss on my red cheek. No longer would our romance have the back-street prurience that aroused Winston to such swaggers. This did not prevent me from undergoing the hesitations of wariness. I was thirty-eight years old. My emotional development had been arrested somewhere in the late 1940s. Even so, I felt like announcing the glad tidings to the entire subway car.

We walked down Alice's street in the warming fall haze of twilight. It seemed to me as we tossed about gay plans that I had a chance to make a new beginning. All the world loves a lover except my father, mother, sister, and brother-in-law. From casual conversations outside my father's office, supple fondlings against Alice's stationary IBM, romance had blossomed.

We kissed and her quiet street was transformed into an avenue of possibilities. As I rode the crosstown bus later, I prepared and discarded various speeches, finally settling upon a simple declaration to my parents. I would then remove myself from the room.

My father didn't spurt blood from the Brutus-like stabbing I evidently gave him when I announced the news. All things considered, it was a survivable occasion, one must suppose.

"Alice Wilson," he mused. "Have I had the pleasure?" He prepared his warmth beautifully. I hesitated to shatter it. "Clyde Wilson's daughter? First American Corporation?"

"She's your secretary." I thumbed a ride to his office door. "Alice. You know."

"*Miss* Wilson?"

"The same."

My father leaned forward in his chair so quickly that his head nearly bounced off the unforgiving mahogany. It was a two-step movement: he fell back in his chair and loosened the tiny knot of his red-and-blue Games Club necktie. His face went from a beguiling red to its customary ashen.

"We hope we'll be very happy," I added, completing a felicitation he would have made had he recovered in time to make it.

"First Dotsie—" He paused, obviously addled. "First Dorothy, and now you. My God, that orangutan . . ." Tears sprang to his eyes.

"Dad, this is a happy occasion."

"Of course it is." My father hugged himself, as if the office temperature had plummeted. He uncoiled enough to press down the talk button on his intercom. "Miss Wilson," he said. "Would you be kind enough to step into my office for a moment?"

The amplified voice of my beloved came through loud and clear. "Yes, Mr. Meriwether."

When Alice came in my father struggled to his feet, murmured, "My dear, my dear, my dear." He reluctantly bussed a proffered cheek. "Welcome to the Meriwether family."

"Thank you, Mr. Meriwether." I was delighted Alice didn't call him "Pa" or any other sobriquet that would have dropped him to the carpet.

"I'm sure there's a precedent for all this," my father chuckled. He turned away from us toward the window.

"I love your son, Mr. Meriwether, with all my heart."

"Ho, ho, ho," my father said. He turned to me. "How old are we now, Alfred?"

"Thirty-eight."

The window seemed to rivet him. "Ripeness is all."

After it was over, Alice leaned against the wall near her Selectric and said, "Whew." Her delicious body trembled with relief. I felt sexualized—perhaps some connection with the familiar typewriter.

"I don't think your father was suffused with joy," Alice said.

"Give him time." But I don't think Alice believed that.

My mother was a different matter. "This is the happiest day of my life," she said, looking regal. She sat in the living room of the town house on Eighty-seventh Street. Even though the house had been in the family for nearly a century, it still looked as if the movers had just finished carting everything away. My mother's great heart was in Rhode Island.

She smiled at Alice. "I remember your voice on the telephone. It always had a special warmth. Many's the time I longed to meet you, and now of course I have, under the most delightful circumstances. You must call me Edith. Let's be chums."

She took my hand and kissed it and then rubbed it against her frozen cheek. Then she let go of it. "You'll both live with us, of course." She raised a hand to ward off objections. She ignored Alice and focused her undivided attention on me. "It's silly for you to move out, lamb. We never use the top two floors of this house anymore. Why, you'd hardly know your father and I were around. Think of it—your own cozy nest, and for free." My mother looked triumphant. "I call that a pretty convincing argument," she added fiercely.

"I don't know," I said. But I knew it was a bad idea. I said nothing.

"Why not?" Alice asked. "Two floors."

"There," my mother said. She turned to Alice. "I know a wonderful recipe for johnnycakes."

I had not expected my relationship with Alice to take quite this turn. Three or four times a week over the previous year, I had found myself sitting outside my father's office, waiting for him to finish work so we could discuss some firm-related matter.

Alice and I got to talking about this and that. In the beginning I was intrigued by her description of her rural childhood—near the small town of Mapleton, Iowa. Alice told me her family held hands and said grace at the dinner table—all six Wilsons. I wanted to know more; the configurations of the table, which family member held out the first hand, the wording of the grace. It struck me as a slice of Americana. The Wilsons seemed more worried about tornadoes than about those private nitroglycerine moments which preoccupied me. And it had come to pass years before that one of the Wilson girls, after finishing college, had set her heart on the big city.

We went to dinner, the next week we went to dinner again, and then we began to see each other every night. We cavorted at her apartment. My father noticed that I no longer left the firm for my clubs at three in the afternoon. I guess he thought I was putting my nose to the grindstone. But I was just hanging around waiting for Alice, to take her home after the firm emptied.

Alice succeeded in opening up my world a sliver. I hadn't read a book in twenty years, seen a movie since *Hollywood Hotel,* which opened in 1938, the year of the great hurricane. In 1962 I was still humming "Hooray for Hollywood" from that film. I seldom read past the front page of the New York *Times,* rarely saw television unless it was over the bar.

Though worried initially lest my bid for happiness unleash the Furies, I was even more worried that the festooned barque of Life was passing me by.

Alice regarded the city as a kind of permanent state fair. We went on walking tours, did most of the tourist things—Statue of Liberty, Empire State Building, Radio City Music Hall, a Circle Line cruise up to West Point. We attended legitimate theaters and experimental ones, four-hour operas at the Met. We also shared a strong binding passion for food and drink. Drink in my case, food in hers. She had a weakness for pastries. Her Lourdes was the Cafe Stuttgart on Eighty-sixth Street between Second and Third Avenues, which displayed exquisite cakes and pastries at a long counter by the door.

Something interesting happened after my proposal of marriage. Faced with a fear of wedding dress, Alice changed her life-style during the months before our wedding. She got hooked on nutrition and mineral content, vegetables and exercise. She even talked me into playing tennis in Central Park and jogging with her around the reservoir. Every morning she faced the religious rite of the tipped Toledo. In three months she lost twenty-five pounds. Our wonderful times at the Cafe Stuttgart—its display case of mega-calories, its imported beers—became a distant memory. We spent a lot of time in vegetarian restaurants, where they served heaping portions of fresh food. What I did for love.

Alice's self-discipline threw my own lack of it into greater relief. We sat one day at a restaurant in Greenwich Village. She picked at her strawberries. I looked into a glass of yellowish vegetable juice. "Alfred, I'd like to discuss your problem."

"What problem, my little carrot?"

"Your drinking. You seem to drink a lot."

"Oh, hell," I said, as if we might better spend our time discussing Keynesian economics.

"I wondered if it's connected to your family. Your family's really strange, I've noticed."

I wasn't prepared to go quite that far. "Every family has its problems."

"I will not nag."

Usually when people say they will not nag, it means they intend to lay back, mellow-out, and approach the problem from another angle, from the soft underbelly. But Alice meant it.

Even before our wedding, Alice had problems with the Meriwether family. Perhaps her version of us had been idealized—her expectations of old-line elegance, eternal courtliness. My father referred to Alice sometimes as "she" and sometimes as "her," but seldom by her first name. I had not expected him to be so bothered by her lack of social background. My mother clipped fad diets from magazines and left them around the house. My sister Dorothy acted as if the state of Iowa consisted of circled wagons, smoke signals, and prize pigs.

Perhaps I should be grateful to Winston for forcing my hand. I sensed that Alice had got a little impatient over the summer when I didn't go public with our hopes and dreams. Probably she was on the verge of questioning my evasiveness—with Dorothy's wedding bells still ringing in the air—when Bingham snorted his way into my office in late September.

Alice and I were married on a bright spring afternoon at the church of St. David's-By-The-Sea in Wolcott, Rhode Island. I remember so much about the day, but one of the things I remember best is that my father refused to attend the wedding. He stayed upstairs in his bedroom and wouldn't come down. My mother said, "Perhaps you can jolly him out of it, Alfred."

My father sat on the bed, looking frail. I sat down beside him and adjusted the tails of my morning coat. "I'd really like to have you there, Dad."

"I've let you down," my father said.

"Don't say that. I don't feel that way."

"You've been a good son." He seemed to brighten a bit. "I'll come along later, Alfred. Leave me a car. This is inexcusable. My legs are like jelly, I've had diarrhea and splitting headaches since yesterday. See the twitch in my eyelid." Indeed, his left eyelid was half closed and fluttering. He pointed at it with a trembling, near palsied forefinger.

"I'll leave you my car."

"How's Miss Wilson?" he asked.

"Radiant," I answered.

"She was a splendid secretary."

After exchanging marital vows, Alice and I walked up the aisle of the church. I wore a groom-grin. My mother wept; Dorothy smiled; Winston said, "Way to go." I noticed Mr. Wilson, Alice's father. An angular, gray-haired man in a dark pinstriped suit, he was not quite my stereotype of an Iowa farmer. He looked like a prosperous and dignified investment banker with grave financial decisions on his mind. Mrs. Wilson, a tall slim woman, looked supportive but formidable in her own right. Frankly, I had expected them both to be a little more on the rustic side.

Alice and I encountered my father sitting in the last pew of the church. He looked quite small alongside the state trooper. My father's forehead bubbled with sweat, as if it was being deep-fried. There was a dried snake of blood on his left cheek, two more at the edges of his mouth. His color was pale beyond pale—the color of an Antarctic whiteout or Alice's wedding dress.

Alice gasped. I asked, "Dad, what happened?"

"A little accident."

"You the groom?" asked the state trooper.

I nodded, stricken.

"Obviously," said Alice.

"His idea," the state trooper said with a shrug. "Lucky for him, too. This affair's why we're in the neighborhood in the first place." The state trooper nudged my father with his forest-green elbow. He asked grimly, "You ready, champ?"

"Yes, officer," my father answered. He managed a game smile.

"Let's get this guy to an emergency room," the state trooper said. "A medic ought to check him out."

My father was unfamiliar with my Buick Electra and it handled like a boat. I see him poised over the steering wheel, peering down the road like a turtle, sailing through the "Yield" sign outside of Wolcott. He got sideswiped by a surfer-jammed minibus in a hailstorm of shattered glass and crumpling metal. It was a miracle no one was killed.

"My son is being married this very minute," Dad evidently told the state trooper who helped him from the wreck.

Alice and I encountered the remains of the accident on our way back from the church to the reception. The minibus was on its side. Several young people were attempting to right it. One side of my barely recognizable Buick was smashed in, as if it had been caught in a powerful vise. All the glass had popped out of the windows. I counted six state police cars, blue-and-orange lights flashing. A young man sat on the curb, dazedly rubbing his blond beard.

The wedding reception went off as scheduled because "your father would want it that way," my mother said. It was held on the lawn of my parents' summer home in Wolcott, the summer home of my childhood and many grassy memories. It was the perfect afternoon for a party, I suppose—cool and sunny, with a dappled vista down to the sea. There were three hundred guests.

Rumors spread like wildfire. Backslaps and bride-kisses were accompanied by expressions of concern. I accepted congratulations and squelched rumors about my father. Great arcs of perspiration saturated my dress shirt, seeped through my handsome morning coat. I looked malarial and felt scared.

The senior U.S. senator from Rhode Island, Samuel Adams Talbot, grabbed my hand. Eighty-three years old, wispy and hearing-impaired, he yelled, "Alfred!"

"Senator Talbot!" I cried. He was a family friend.

"You rapscallion!" the senator yelled. We were three inches from each other. "How's your pa? Heard he was in an accident."

"That's right."

"What?"

"Right! Hospital now!" This is all I need, I thought.

Senator Talbot grinned at Alice. It hadn't registered. "Born before the motor car!" he shouted. "Me before the motor car!"

Alice nodded vigorously. "You before the motor car."

"Thought you had him!" the senator cried.

"Who had?" I shouted.

"Gonzales! Gonzales!" he said irritably.

(Duty compels me to mention that I qualified for Forest Hills in 1948. In the third round I had the terrible misfortune to draw Pancho Gonzales. He was just coming up in those days—on the brink of stardom, as they say. By some miracle I narrowly took the first two sets. I was full of confidence. The great man—or great boy, as he was then—woke up abruptly in the third set. He made savage work of me for ninety minutes. It is an unpleasant memory, but people still like to remind me of those two sets. The score was 13–15, 5–7, 6–1, 6–0, 6–0. I thought the afternoon would never end.)

The senator clenched his fists, shook them in a prolonged tremor, as if manning an antiaircraft gun. "Almost had him third set!" The senator tapped his temple slyly. I suppose he wanted to let us know that a few withdrawals remained in his memory bank. He was going back fifteen years.

"Ah!" I shouted and nodded. It required too much vocal effort to tell the senator that I never would have "had" him—not if we'd played a thousand matches.

Alice and I walked toward the house. We were intercepted on the too vivid lawn by the flustered maid, Mary. "The hospital, sir." She made a deep curtsy, forever implanted on my brain as the gesture of death. A deep curtsy, a fluttering of wings.

It was a long walk to the telephone, a walk filled with the humblest and most abject apologies. I remembered how my father had watched me play games on a hundred playing fields or hockey rinks or tennis courts. He was always underdressed for winter and overdressed for summer.

Alice and I walked into the dark house. Her wedding dress

shone in flames of white as we strode across isolated pockets of light. I picked up the receiver and it leapt and trembled in my hand. I thought, Why must they live in darkness by the seashore?

"I'm on my way," my father said. "Tell your mother I'm fine."

Dad wore his scattered bandages to the reception as if they were wounds of war. He borrowed one of my mother's flamboyant canes and leaned on it impressively, like a figure from an old hunting print. I heard much talk during the reception about hopped-up young bravos and their surfboards, an insurgence of resort vandalism, all-night parties and drunken driving, the need for beefed-up police protection, sex orgies, and fires on the beach.

In his reticent way, my father basked and glowed. He accepted handshakes with a firm left hand. It was hard to forget his right hand, which hung courageously at his side. He was the bride and groom combined, blushing manfully. In my mind I kept seeing over and over again the upturned spinning wheels of the surfers' minibus, and the dazed expression of the blond young man. Sideswiped. Wet suits had been strewn all over the road like shells of bodies.

My father retired from the law firm of Waterman, Rhodes, Stevenson, and Meriwether. He and my mother moved permanently up to the house in Wolcott. I believe his car accident and near-brush with death—both his death and that of the young people he'd endangered—accelerated a lifelong process of degeneration and withdrawal. For most of his life my father wanted simply to hop into bed and pull the sheets and covers, the fluffy comforter, right up to his chin and wiggle his toes with delight in the snug warmth, and slurp soups, and hear the sounds of the world go by outside his bedroom door.

My brother-in-law didn't help matters any. Winston upset Dad's careful routine at the firm, reminded him of mortality in various subtle ways—the helping hand under the arm, the adjustment of an overcoat lapel, the forgotten hat placed on his head. The phrase "new blood" hovered in the air and became my father's obsession. The firm needed a "transfusion"; it was time for the "deadwood" to make way for the new blood.

My father began to self-fulfill his most secretly desired prophecies. For years he had spoken often and wistfully about his retirement—and the books he would read on the mythical verandah as he welcomed dotage with open arms. And as he spoke the gorgeous skyline of Manhattan, proud and jagged against the sunset, receded. My father thought of his retirement as "golden years." It was almost as if those golden years stretching into the future could obliterate the leaden ones of the past. Like many depressed people, he was an eternal optimist.

My father's retirement was my mother's delight. It brought her into contact with her hearty, clam-chowdering, seafaring roots —Meguntic, Pettasquamsett, Newport. "The sea," she gusted happily. "The sea." You could almost taste the brine in her voice, see the tall-masted spine of her back as we all mounted the poop deck for Dad's death watch.

He took to his bed like a duck to water. For the next two years he puttered around, lost and found and then again lost his memory, snoozed a lot. Instead of sitting out on the old verandah, dosing himself with healthy sea air, reading Lamb and plowing through *Daniel Deronda*, my father had the verandah glassed in. He became like a picture in a frame, so the sound of the sea couldn't get to him. Sometimes he leaned forward in his rocking chair and tapped on the glass enclosing him, and cocked his head, listening. Then he would sigh and gently get back into the rhythm of his rocking. Sometimes Alice or I would adjust the colorful red blanket covering his thin legs—tucked him in, so to speak. His head gradually receded into his shoulders. My mother plopped a jaunty new emerald-colored tam-o'-shanter on his head for his birthday in 1966. She made sure that he got enough southern exposure, and tended to him as if he was a sickly jade tree.

Meanwhile, my mother thrived. She had come home to Rhode Island. This was her place, she was on her own turf, at last the *grande dame*. She prepared for an extensive black velvet widowhood with all the trimmings—sturdier canes, refurbishing and tune-ups of the capacious 1929 Duesenberg with its long hood and downy white canvas roof and plush leather seats and steering wheel big enough to waggle a battleship's rudder. My mother came into her own during the period of my father's decline, became "quite a character" by her own admission.

During the last months of his life, Dad and I underwent a role-reversal, in which he played the role of the passive son. As he retreated more and more from life, I spent as much time with him as I could. I read to him in the afternoons, while he sat bundled on the verandah, surrounded by heavy wicker. From Eliot and Dickens, Trollope and Thackeray, we branched in his last phase toward Robert Louis Stevenson, especially *Kidnapped* and *Treasure Island.* He took special delight in both novels, smiled and nodded, tapped on the glass.

I enjoyed reading to him, but it was disconcerting to find that my father was no longer the remote titan of my childhood. I'd always kept alive a dominant image of him. He stood in his library amid dusty shafts of light. He looked brooding and majestic as he wrestled with what I assumed were legal and ethical questions of great moment.

My father's peaceful slide into death has been overshadowed in my mind by an unpleasant incident that occurred a few months before he died. My mother hired a masseur named Big Red (I never knew his real name) from the nearby Surf Club to give Dad massages on his underused muscles. It was a good idea in theory—getting some of that old blood pumping: new blood; fresh blood. The circulation of revitalized blood was my father's favorite metaphor.

Possibly Big Red was more used to working out on professional football players and muscle-bound weight lifters than on old men.

I encountered my father and Big Red when I returned to Rhode Island on a late Friday afternoon in June 1967. I saw the curls of Big Red's red hair, the portable rubbing table, my father gasping on the verandah. Big Red's hands were placed upward in a dangerous karate position. They descended onto my father's thighs. Then Dad seemed to flip into the air like a large white pancake—caught in Big Red's arms. He looked as if he was learning a delightful new sport called Air Swimming.

"How's that feel now, skipper?" Big Red kept asking. "You starting to loosen up?"

My father lay on his stomach. Big Red's hands were again poised in the air to carve up his back. Dad noticed me then, raised his head as I stood frozen in the doorway of the verandah. He gnawed at the phlegm in his mouth, stretched his jaw to free himself of the molasses for a word of complaint. But what came out was a sticky sound, as though the gears working his mouth hadn't been lubricated.

"That's the ticket," Big Red declared. "We'll get those muskles toned up."

Muskles, he said jauntily.

Big Red's hands spread out. They grasped at the air for a second to gain extra strength before the descent onto my father's back, where all that white flesh needed toning up. Probably my anger to this day exaggerates his movements.

His hands never descended. "Don't touch him," I said.

"And who might you be?" Big Red asked.

"His father," I said.

Big Red looked puzzled.

"I mean his son."

"All right, big shot."

"You're fired."

"Then you get the old man off my table."

I pointed to the screen door of the verandah. "Out." I seemed to occupy a pocket of air between an icy layer and freezing water, where I breathed.

Big Red rubbed his red forearm. "Not without my table."

"Hey," I said.

My father gnashed away.

"Listen, Mac—"

"Out."

"Well, I ain't moving without this goddamn table." He spaced out the last three words. This . . . goddamn . . . table . . . for extra emphasis. "Let's be reasonable."

I took his Surf Club T-shirt in my hands, pulled him over to the screen door of the verandah, kicked it open and pushed him onto the lawn. "What about my table?"

"You'll get your table."

"Tough guy," Big Red said from the grass. "Asshole."

I opened the screen door and went down the steps. Big Red

got up off the grass and walked away, walking backward on the lawn. He gave me the finger. I went after him until he rounded the corner of the house. "That's private property, that table." I turned the corner of the house, saw Big Red hop into his red car. He was yelling—shithead, fuckface. Gravel sprayed and his car fishtailed out of the driveway and onto the paved road running through our property.

I felt light-headed. I don't know if I voluntarily sat down on the lawn or if the lawn came up to meet me. There I sat for a minute or two, outside the front door, making weird facial tics.

I went back to my father on the table. I scooped him up in my arms and carried him from the verandah into his bedroom. I laid him out on the bed. The bedroom had all the kinds of father and cologne smells you associate from a child's age. My father was exhausted and his eyes were closed. He was naked except for his baggy boxer shorts, so I pulled a comforter over him. I kept trying to catch my breath.

That evening I made karate-like descriptions in the gloom of the dining room. My mother seemed shocked about Big Red; he'd had excellent references. I don't think she entirely believed me.

My mother sighed. "I suppose we'll have to send the gardener over with his table. I hope you didn't hurt him, Alfred. I've often wondered what kind of damage you'd do if you ever lost control of yourself."

My father looked at his fish—the white blob of flounder, a pudding of fish. His eyes roved serenely around the dining room. He had the most beautiful eyes in the last month of his life—the eyes of a little boy embarked upon some great adventure, too private to share. Sometimes at supper, toward the last, Dad put his finger to his lips to gently shush us. I'm pretty sure he also did it when no one was around.

My father died in his sleep at the end of that summer, a week before Labor Day. There was medical terminology for the cause of his death—arterio-this, hardening of that—but I think he succumbed from the sheer numbing weight of days.

Although his death had been a long time coming, it still left me with a feeling of abandonment and desolation—like late autumn. If my father had died in old age, then that meant my youth was gone forever. This was particularly hard for me to bear. I was supposed to be an eternal boy.

It bothered me that the funeral was held at St. David's-By-The-Sea in Wolcott. The church was located within sight and sound of the ocean. I felt that Dad would have preferred a funeral in New York City, close to his Wall Street law offices.

The whole service annoyed me, though it moved like clockwork from nave to grave and everyone else was pleased. I wanted the ceremony to last longer. I wanted choirs and testimonials, maybe a reading of Dad's favorite poems—something in there to give a touch of the man. I kept thinking that they probably did this sort of thing better in the South.

My mother bore up formidably. With my help and two canes, she negotiated steps and cars with stately grace, paused for a long moment at the St. David's door to cast a sad look at the ocean. The day was crisp and the water sun-blue. Wolcott was bustling for the Labor Day weekend, but already there were signs that the town was starting to batten down for its isolated autumn and winter.

My mother sighed and I helped her down the steps. The cane in her left hand seemed intrusive and awkward, and I kept getting my footsteps out of sync with it. I was relieved when we arrived at the limousine.

After the funeral the guests gathered at my mother's house. They clustered on the lawn, drinks in hand. Most of what might be called the Old Guard was there. Clients of Dad's; classmates from Harvard and Harvard Law; golfing companions; Games, Union, Century, Down Town friends.

Winston worked the crowd like a pickpocket. He moved among them, somber but energetic, shaking hands, thanking them for coming. Dad's mourners were not Winston's kind of people. They were not used to, and did not appreciate, his brand of physicality, which resembled a Dixie politician's. Dad's friends may not have liked him—in turn, he thought of them as "dinosaurs"—but they found Thumper a hard man to ignore. I think he got around to everybody that afternoon.

While I was standing alone at the bar, Dorothy came up to

me, took my arm, and said quietly but firmly, "Precious, if I can tear you away for just a minute, I think it's time to make some character."

"Making character" was the term Dorothy used when she felt that a person wasn't milling around enough at a party. She had an eye for that sort of thing. Though I didn't just then feel much like mixing, I knew she was right. I wasn't handling the thing properly: I wasn't bearing up; I was mad; I felt like crying.

After the guests had left, our grim little family group inhabited a vast space on the lawn. It was getting chilly in the late afternoon.

"Where's Dad?" I asked suddenly. A sharp pang of loss had given my question too much velocity, and it had somehow gotten loose into the air.

There was a long silence. Dorothy made a clicking sound. Winston shook his head and blew out a long breath. My mother averted her eyes. Alice put her hand in mine, as if to protect me from further humiliation.

"It's okay," Alice whispered. "We're going home in a minute. Hang on."

They thought I was drunk.

As Alice and I were leaving, my mother patted my hand in the fading sunlight and said quietly, "Alfred, you're the man in the family now."

I was forty-three years old. I didn't know how to reply to that one.

4

Even before my father's departure from the law firm in 1965, Winston Bingham had contributed his bit toward its eventual transformation. It only takes one rotten apple to spoil the barrel. He longed for a "fast track," as he called it. More than once he told me that he'd been happier doing personal injury cases in Buffalo. I suggested he might enjoy working for the firm's corporate department.

"Why not?" he asked with a rhetorical sigh in my cozy office. He often came in at day's end to take a load off his feet. "I have to find something commensurate with my abilities." He sucked at his front teeth.

With considerable pleasure I learned inadvertently that Winston was seeking employment with another law firm. I saw him one rainy afternoon in late November 1968, a year after Dad's death. It was shortly after he had been made a partner at Waterman, Rhodes. He was walking along Lispenard Street in Lower Manhattan in the company of two partners from Kearns, Peabody—Brownie Musto and Orrick Hazzard. The three men, Winston huddled in the middle, were locked in deep conversation and didn't notice me. They shook hands, shared a laugh at the corner of Broadway. Winston walked up Broadway and out of sight. The two razor haircuts of the Kearns, Peabody partners bobbed along the other way.

Several months later, I received a phone call from Tom Ruffin, the chairman of First American Corporation, inviting me to lunch at the Golf Club on Lexington Avenue. First American was our firm's most important corporate client.

Because my specialty was large estates, I seldom dealt with the corporate department of the firm, which was handled by

Kipsy Maginn. Naturally, I wondered why Tom wanted to see me. He had recently ascended to the chairmanship of First American at the age of forty-eight, a young age as chairmen go. His dad, Walter Ruffin, had warmed the seat for him.

He was in great shape. He looked as if he could stroke the Harvard crew, which he had. He was about my height, six-three, with close-cropped gray hair and a lean face, covered by a full tan. We shook hands in the Golf Club's oak-paneled bar. For a moment Tom rested his left hand atop our handshake as perhaps an extra gesture of intimacy. He ordered Canada Dry Club Soda with a twist of lemon. I ordered a Coca-Cola, even though I would have preferred a Jack Daniel's.

Tom was one of those people who use your first name a lot in conversation, as if it made you more concrete. "I used to come here with your dad," he said, unbuttoning his coat, spreading a relaxed arm across the top of the warm, banquette-like nook where we'd seated ourselves. A waiter took our lunch order, Tom drum-rolled his fingers and smiled at two older men who passed through the bar on their way to the dining room. He whispered to me, "There go a couple of old-timers." He looked around at the sedate prints of English statesmen lining the walls of the bar. They were interspersed with golfing cartoons and caricatures. "This place brings back a lot of memories," he sighed. "Your dad was a wonderful guy, Alfred. And you're a wonderful guy, too."

"Thank you, Tom. I appreciate that."

He told me that he had recently purchased a helicopter for hunting at his plantation in Georgia. "Extraordinary sensation," he mused. "Shooting down at birds."

"Sounds like fun," I said, which it didn't.

I still didn't know why he had invited me for lunch. We went on to discuss tax write-offs, Vietnam, student unrest, and investment tips.

I loved the Golf Club. What I loved to do most was sit in a big leather chair in the Reading Room and leaf through magazines about English country homes. These magazines were wonderful sedatives and pretty soon, as the countryside kept rolling by, I would find myself romping through a dreamland of English meadows.

The green-jacketed waiter signaled that our table was ready. Tom sighed, rested the palms of his hands, fingers spread, on his lean thighs for a moment. He pursed his thin lips as if at an unpleasant thought, then pushed himself up with all the effort of an older, less athletic and vigorous man.

We adjourned to the pleasant and elegant Golf Club dining room. Hunting prints adorned the walls, sleek horses with elongated necks took fences, hounds closed in for the kill, a pink-coated rider doffed his top hat.

Somewhere between the appetizer of pheasant hash and the entree of venison cutlet we had both decided upon so long ago in the oaken bar, Tom said, "We're taking our business to another firm."

It was so much bullshit after that—streamlining, modernization, pressure from the board of directors, meeting corporate needs, agonizing decision. Tom looked around the dining room, nodded at the tables full of oldsters, the hunting prints, as if somehow the room was representative of our creaking law firm. He folded his hands on the table. He looked like a prep school boy asking to be excused from Lower School dining hall. "Out of deference to your father," Tom added, "I wanted to tell you first. If it is any consolation, Alfred, this is infinitely more unpleasant than I thought it would be."

"I'm sure it is," I said evenly.

"I know you don't handle the corporate department, but I thought it was the right thing to do. Your father was a great man. The legal profession lost a real winner when he passed away."

His voice was tender—the whole thing choked him up. He was choked up, just after he'd fucked my law firm. I watched him with a lack of sympathy bordering on dispassion. "We're not talking about an emergency here," Tom continued. "We're talking about winding up our business with Waterman, Rhodes like gentlemen. There's no fire."

I signaled to a waiter, touched the young man on the arm when he arrived. Waiters are my friends. "I'd like a double Jack Daniel's on the rocks."

"They can muster a wonderful Brie here, Alfred. Or at least they used to."

I looked down at my untouched venison, tried to sound as casual as possible when I asked, "Who's taking your business?"

"Oh—" Tom shrugged. His folded hands became an A-frame. There was a long silence and I watched him. "We've been having some work done by Kearns, Peabody. The feeling down at the plant is they're a better blend for us."

A large bell rang in my head. I remembered the big fellow months before on Lispenard Street, wedged between two Kearns, Peabody partners. "Fast track," I muttered.

"Say, would you like a pear with your Brie?"

"First American has been a client of the firm since the year 1839," I said. "We'll be very sorry to lose you, Tom. I'll certainly relay your decision to the partners."

"Hell, as I said, Alfred. There's no fire."

"Do me a favor, will you?"

"Name it, name it, name it."

"Give me a couple of weeks."

"Sure, sure, sure." Tom nodded. It was hard not to feel a certain degree of sympathy for a man so relieved, who so visibly had had a burden taken off his mind. He spread his fingers across the chest area of his immaculate gray suit in the "Who me?" gesture of a shoplifter. "We're not dialing the Twelfth Precinct about this transfer. Take a month for all I care."

Our luncheon ended, the Brie was runny, the pear underripe. Tom and I shook hands beside the Golf Club's white-bannistered winding staircase. I watched his tonsured head winding down below me. At that moment I wished an ignoble wish, unworthy of a lawyer. I wished I held in my hands a balloon filled with water, so I could drop it on his head.

I repaired to the oak-paneled bar. I ordered another double Jack Daniel's on the rocks. "Christ," I said, and heaved myself off the bar stool. "See you, Bill." I waved to the bartender.

"Leaving, Mr. Meriwether?" Bill seemed almost as surprised as I was. He approached my untouched glass of Jack Daniel's with all the amazement of an archeologist who has dug up an intact artifact. His broad shoulders hovered over the firewater.

I returned to the firm and went to see our chief accountant. We spent the afternoon in his office going over ledger books and billing slips. Yards of figures marched across columned pages.

The only sound in the numeral-charged air was the pleasant *ka-chug, ka-chug* of his adding machine.

There came a time, as the gray February afternoon darkened, when I had to reach down into the morass of numbers and extirpate First American. I spent much time by the window of the accountant's office, looking down at the brown spire of Trinity Church, the old church's gold clock, and the street below. I rubbed my eyes, felt a headache quicken behind the sockets. Electric charges coursed from one temple to the other. I returned to the adding machine and ledger books, and searched for some bright column of figures.

The next day I attended a partners' meeting in the conference room. I noted the absence of Bingham. I stared around me at the white hair of the older men, noticed the vests and glimpses of suspenders, the offbeat noddings, idle finger-taps, crotchety peerings. Portraits of the benign recessional of former partners lined the walls of the conference room. It was a recessional in oils stretching back into the nineteenth century in an unbroken string of benevolent prosperity and poses of satisfaction with the world as it was and the world as it would surely forever be.

Several times during the meeting I opened my mouth—to put the ticking Bingham bomb right out on the olive wood conference table, so to speak. But all that ever came out was an *aaaargh* sound, prompting someone to nudge me and point at a Vicks mentholated cough drop he'd left by my elbow.

The meeting did not so much break up as expire. The partners shuffled out. I asked Kipsy Maginn to remain behind. Surrounded by the firm's ancestors, I retailed my conversation with Tom Ruffin of First American. Kipsy turned purple—the corporate department was his bailiwick.

After Kipsy had left, I asked a secretary to go find Bingham. I didn't have to wait long for Winston to join me. Over the years he had become quite a fashion plate. He wore monogrammed WB silk shirts now, snaffle-bit loafers, tucked-at-the-waist pinstripe suits made for him in London. A hair stylist had quelled the curls around his ears and foliated his bald spot. But the natty outfittings could not conceal his ineffable, rough diamond-like quality, or the brute force of his malevolent appetites.

"Alfred," he said.

"Hello, Winston," I said.

He plopped himself down in Kipsy Maginn's warm chair. He leafed through some scattered papers left over from the meeting, briefly studied one of Kipsy's elaborate doodles. "We don't see enough of each other," he mused. He rapped on the conference table, then rapped lightly on my right shoulder. He smiled at me then, and I got the impression that for the first time I was in focus for him. "So," he said. "How's everything?"

"I'd just like to say what you've done is one of the most unethical, one of the sleaziest things I've ever heard of."

"What's sleazy, what's unethical?" Winston asked. "You should have been able to see the handwriting on the wall. What *I* saw was a client who was very unhappy, a very unhappy bunch of guys at First American."

"They weren't unhappy until you made them unhappy."

He ignored me. "I think it would have been unethical *not* to say at some point, 'Hey, fellas, why the long faces?'"

"Where did my sister dig you up?"

"Fortunately, I have a thick skin," Winston said.

"You've got everything all figured out." It was a minor revelation to me that someone might have it all figured out.

"Yes, I do. Of course, I could step on a high-tension cable when I leave home tomorrow morning. There are chances you take in life, but generally I'm pretty well satisfied with the way things are going. I was sharing a laugh with Tom Ruffin the other day at '21' and I told him, 'Tom, I think you've made the right decisions all the way around.'"

"Thanks, Winston. Jesus. I hope someday I'll have a chance to return the favor."

"Let's cut the crap," Winston said quietly. "Let's talk merger."

"Merger?" I asked. "With Kearns, Peabody?"

Winston nodded. "We want the firm name and some of your livelier geriatric cases. In return, you boys at Waterman, Rhodes get to keep breathing. How does that sound?"

I looked at him for a long moment. "I think it sounds possible," I said. Actually, there weren't too many other options. "I'll have to think about it."

Winston was on his feet and heading for the door of the conference room. "You do that," he said over his shoulder. "You and Kipsy Maginn get in touch with Orrick Hazzard."

He was in a hurry—after all, time was money.

What a shit, I thought.

I salvaged Waterman, Rhodes, calmed down the partners. When I dropped the possibility of a merger with Kearns, Peabody on them, they cooed in their throats like alarmed pigeons, removed and replaced their reading glasses, looked down at their typed agendas. They hummed and murmured, peered over at each other's agendas, muttered about good manners and civility. Why, in Walter Ruffin's day . . .

I gave the partners a long time to hyperventilate before showing them the goat path to salvation. They were not grateful. They caviled mightily, raised problems like emergency semaphores around the conference table. They summoned and grilled the chief accountant, succeeded finally in turning the problem into a position where they could accept it with dignity. One almost had the impression, while sitting around the old conference table, that *they* were racing toward the new age, instead of vice versa.

5

The firm's growth following my father's death—and after its merger with Kearns, Peabody—was spectacular. This was largely the result of Winston's exceptional ability, as he moved into a position of power.

New faces joined Waterman, Rhodes. The atmosphere around the old shop grew more tense. Partners' meetings became hardboiled. Nobody smiled or nodded or made courtly little bows in the corridors anymore. There was more loudness. People pointed their fingers and made points. Associates burned the midnight oil and grafted themselves onto partners and hovered around them and snapped-to. There was a lot of snapping-to, mostly around the figure of my brother-in-law.

Winston moved out into the city. He became a personage, made contacts, brought in business. Evidently many people felt that he had a certain rough charm. The word most often used to describe him was "flamboyant."

From fifteen partners and forty associates in 1967, the firm grew to thirty-five partners, eighty associates. We got involved with tax shelters, international finance, mergers and acquisitions (Thumper's specialty), and, later on, contested tender offers. We hired someone called a design engineer to refurbish our offices. We became color-coordinated and razor-cut, computerized and Selectric.

During the period of expansion, Winston also accelerated his own personal and political growth. As he never failed to tell me. Even before Dad's death, he had taken an interest in New York politics. He wanted it known that he had his sights set eventually on either elective or government office.

By far his most important new association on the national level was with a man named Gerard Charles Ackley. He met Captain Ackley in 1971 at a buffet luncheon at the Naval War College in Newport, Rhode Island. Ackley commanded a nuclear submarine, the two men became friends, and Winston was introduced to several senior officials at the Department of the Navy. Perhaps as a result, he brought the full hammerweight of his concentration and photographic memory to the subject of defense policy. He became something of an expert on the "triad" system of strategic arms deployment, with special emphasis on atomic-powered submarines.

Sometime in 1975 he became a Fellow of the prestigious Washington-based Institute of Foreign Policy. He showed me an article he had written—which I couldn't make head or tail of—for the Institute's quarterly publication, *Global Reach:* "Redundant Second-Strike Advanced Submersion Throwweight—Myth and Reality." He also wrote an article for *Harper's* magazine called, "Steel Hulls, Stern Choices," which crossed my desk. In 1978 he testified before a Senate subcommittee on the need to improve antenna relay systems for hunter-killer submarines on station. He signed on as an adviser on defense matters to the senator from Kansas, who looked as if he might make a long-shot bid for the presidency in 1984.

He took up tennis, kept urging me to play with him. It annoyed him when I refused year after year. He had a tennis pro in New York, a pro in Wolcott. He and Captain Ackley played in the annual doubles championship at the Winding Hollow Country Club near Wolcott. They lost to Carmine Rizzoli, the Governor of Rhode Island, and his partner, Jerome Schnitzler, a local dentist.

Winston placed a scale model of a nuclear submarine on his desk at Waterman, Rhodes. The gray submarine had detachable sections so he could spread out the pieces on his desk and then slowly put them back together again. This seemed to give him a lot of pleasure; he loved subs and other confined areas.

On the domestic side, Winston's life was not so successful. His relationship with my sister Dorothy lapsed increasingly into total indifference, punctuated by occasional outbursts of hostility. After the birth of Winston Bingham, Jr.—who was known as Win —in 1963, the couple more or less went their separate ways. It was as if the two of them had achieved their private goals just by marrying each other. There was no longer any need to keep up a pretense of compatibility, except at the entertainment functions of which they were both so fond. A couple of times Winston even regaled me with details of his larger sexual conquests, steaming up the windowpanes as he spoke, until I told him to knock it off.

Winston's vigorous sexual appetite became well known throughout the firm. For example, he took an unusual interest in the hiring of secretaries, a job normally left to the firm's office manager. There was always one young woman at Waterman, Rhodes with no apparent responsibilities, who was loosely assigned to the typing pool. Winston called her his "tension-easer."

"Have you seen Winston's new one?" was a question heard frequently around the firm.

One night Winston invited me for a drink at his club. When he said club, I expected something like the Racquet or River. I suppose it amused him to think that's what I expected.

"Let's have a drink at my club," Winston said, with some formality.

"Why not?" I said.

The club, located on West Twenty-third Street, was named Bacchanal, though there was no sign over the door. What surprised me, I think, was the extreme tawdriness of the place. There must have been other establishments in the city where a man in Winston's salary bracket could have gotten his needs serviced with more style. But he felt right at home.

There were pornographic films in one room, male and female dancers in another. There was a so-called romper room, where three naked couples cavorted. At the bar we were served by a topless waitress with blue-painted nipples who called Winston Thumper.

I asked Winston how often he came to Bacchanal.

He shrugged. "Once, twice a week. I get around."

I sipped my Jack Daniel's. "It's very interesting," I said.

"The place heats up around midnight. Stick around. Maybe you'll pick up some pointers."

"Do you join in the goings-on when it starts to heat up?"

"I feel very comfortable in this environment." He looked grim for a moment. "I've never hidden my needs."

I wanted to ask him if Dorothy knew—or cared—about this other life of his. But mainly I wanted to leave. I drank up and left Winston at Bacchanal. He had lost interest in me, anyway. I think he was raring to get to the romper room.

Winston's extramarital escapades did not seem to ruffle the surface of his marriage. Whatever substance bound Winston and Dorothy together—whatever glue—proved to be surprisingly strong. I never heard either of them mention divorce, though it would have been the appropriate resolution to their dissatisfactions. I felt sorry for Dorothy, but I thought the real tragedy was young Win.

After the firm's merger with Kearns, Peabody, I entered a dark period in my life. The pressure of the negotiations exhausted me. I felt in some way that I had let my father down. He had passed on to me a happy, prosperous law firm, and I had turned it over to vandals.

I can make out the shape of the next years—coinciding with Winston's rise to power at the firm—but I have trouble with the details. Sometimes I sat at my desk, and sometimes not. I didn't drink all the time, but I drank a lot. Frequently, I failed to return from lunch. Occasionally I forgot to get off the subway at the Lexington Avenue and Eighty-sixth Street stop. I wound up on the open-air platform at Yankee Stadium, bedazzled by the lights of a night game.

I visited my friend Mal Robinson at Columbia Presbyterian Hospital for my annual checkup. I think this was in 1975. Mal had been one of my roommates at Eliot House at Harvard. He was very harsh with me. "You're fucking up. Stop drinking." He detailed the systemic changes my body was undergoing.

Mal took off his glasses and rubbed his eyes. The room seemed very white and I found his white coat comforting. It was all cozy and criblike and warm. I felt wonderful. Mal looked very tired, the fight and scare tactics gone right out of him. But he wanted to say what he wanted to say. "Thirty years ago, if I'd had to pick one person out of our class at Harvard as most likely to succeed, it would have been you."

I nodded and smiled. I was drunk. "Things just didn't work out, Mal." It was difficult, but I managed to get off a rueful chuckle.

There was something else. Alice and I were having our problems. It was clear that my marriage was interfering with my drinking.

Things had been going slowly wrong between us for a long time. Besides my drinking problem, there was also another woman—my mother. When that pull was strong, I found myself looking coldly at Alice, as if she were an unwelcome stranger who had wandered into the wrong house.

My mother and Alice, for all intents and purposes, had not exchanged a word since our marriage. They seemed to agree to miss each other whenever possible, and they largely succeeded. Up in Wolcott they had their separate clubs—my mother, the Surf Club; Alice, the Winding Hollow Country Club—and neither woman ever set foot on the other's turf.

The same situation existed at the house in Manhattan, only in much closer quarters. Despite Alice's repeated entreaties in the early years of our marriage—before my parents moved to Rhode Island—I refused to move out. After all, she was the one who had originally agreed to the arrangement. I made up excuses: my parents were old; they were tired; I was tired; I required peace and quiet to get back on the wagon; the house was free; the real estate market was terrible for selling; it was terrible for buying. Let's wait—I insisted—for the market to "soften"; let's wait for it to "harden."

Harden and soften—the vagaries of the New York real estate market were a good barometer of my boozy sexual life, and therein probably lay the heart of our problem. Alice wanted to have children. We tried for years. We couldn't. We began to drift. She developed her own interests and friends, both in Wolcott and New York. She took courses at Columbia. She had a passion for antiques, and the quest occupied more and more of her time. Increasingly, we became like ships passing in the night —three ships, really: hers, mine, and my mother's ocean liner. Her deep wish for children was fulfilled in a small way by Winston Bingham, Jr., her nephew. From an early age Win's life had long spaces of neglect that were filled in by his Aunt Alice. But it was no compensation for a drunken husband.

If I had to pinpoint the first time I realized that something was terribly wrong, it would be one Sunday lunch up in Wolcott. These lunches with the family were a particular torture for Alice. Since our marriage she had let herself go and put on a great deal of weight, a fact that did not go unnoticed by my mother. At Sunday lunch Alice was forced to undergo the rite of The Second Helping. My mother either instructed the maid to serve everyone a second helping except Alice, or she withheld second helpings entirely so Alice wouldn't be "tempted."

For years Alice said nothing, bore up in silence. But at that lunch up in Wolcott—with Winston, Dorothy, young Win, and myself present—she had finally taken enough.

"Why don't you shut your face?" Alice shouted at my mother, while we waited for dessert. Her exclamation did not seem to have any origin. My mother had said nothing. I had never noticed the problem of The Second Helping.

My mother fell back in her chair as if she had been struck. "Alfred!" she gasped.

I was shocked. Alice had always been so polite. You expected this sort of talk from professional football players at the line of scrimmage.

"You heard what I said," Alice hissed, slapping the table, jouncing the flatware. She was quivering with rage.

"C'mon," Winston said. "Christ."

"I think you better leave this house, young lady," my mother said, her hand clutching her throat. "At least until you learn some manners."

"I'll leave," Alice muttered, struggling to her feet. I wondered why she couldn't lose weight. "But you're the last person to ever talk about manners."

"All right," I said quietly. "That's enough."

"I know why she's upset," Dorothy cooed. "Let's give the poor thing seconds."

"You're just making an ass out of yourself," Winston told Alice. "What say we get into that peach pie?"

"I'm leaving," Alice said, standing beside the table.

"So leave," Winston said amiably. "Who's stopping you?"

"I think you've said quite enough for one meal," my mother said.

"Are you coming?" Alice asked of me.

I looked at my wife, then at my stricken mother at the head of the table. I didn't intend it to be a confrontation, but what Alice had said was incredible. My wife had just told my mother to shut her face.

"I'll be along after lunch," I said.

At which point Alice burst into tears. Emotions scrinched up and mottled her face. A tear dropped symbolically into my wine-glass, which held a decent Petrus.

Alice left the house. My mother reached over and patted my arm. "That was the most outrageous performance I've ever seen." She looked around the table. "So this is the thanks we get."

"No class," Winston agreed.

That was the first inkling I had that something was out of whack. But at supper that night at our house, I got mad. "How *could* you say something like that to my mother?"

Alice was calm then. "I'm not going to argue with you or discuss it. I am sorry I insulted your mother. I want to see a psychiatrist."

"What's the problem?" I asked.

Alice's chin trembled. "The problem is that I'm at the end of my rope."

"Well, maybe if you'd get with the program."

"Get with the program?" We were sitting in the kitchen. She was eating ice cream. Her voice rose. "Get with the program! What does that mean?"

"Well, for starters, why don't you make more of an effort with my mother?"

"Because she's crazy."

"You know what I think," I said. "I think *you're* the problem."

She shoved the carton of ice cream away. "Fine. I want to see a psychiatrist."

I was drinking Schlitz. "That's out of the question."

"Why, may I ask?"

I rested my elbow on the kitchen table, spread out my fingers.

I used the forefinger of my right hand to make my points in an A, B, C fashion by tapping on the first joint of each upraised finger. I felt very lawyerly. "A, I don't think there's any problem. B, I don't believe in psychiatrists." The sound of my finger-blows was oddly loud in the silence of the kitchen. "C . . ."

"I want to see one anyway."

"I will *not* pay for a psychiatrist. I do not believe in psychiatry. We can solve our problems on our own. I will not pay."

Alice took her spoon and stabbed it into the soft ice cream. She stood up and marched off to the bedroom.

When I continued my point-making inside the bedroom—with references to how Dorothy had solved her vocal problems without benefit of psychiatry, with a lot of exercises—Alice said, "Hey, listen. I think you made your point."

"Just as long as we've got this settled," I said, weaving by the bed. The white rocks outside the window stood silver in the moonlight. I could hear the ocean thud.

Alice picked up her remote-control device from the bedside table, aimed it at the television. Then she switched off the lamp on her side of the bed, plunging the room into moonlight. "Know something? This is the closest we've had to a conversation in years. Since the merger when you really began drinking."

"I've always been able to handle it."

"Oh, Jesus. Sure," Alice muttered from her side of the bed. "Good night, Alfred." Her tone was formal and distant. I didn't like this new voice at all.

That was just the beginning. Alice began to see the psychiatrist and without my consent sent the bills to my office. For three months I refused to pay them. I was outraged by the expense. A hundred dollars for forty minutes. I computed the time per minute and ascertained that the man was being paid two dollars and fifty cents a minute. I wondered what kind of racket this was. I spent a considerable time being infuriated by these bills. At one point I told Alice, "You're going to a psychiatrist who charges a hundred dollars a pop. Why don't you go to one who charges fifty dollars? That way you get twice as much help. Anyway, I'm not going to pay."

"Mal Robinson says he's one of the best psychiatrists in New York City."

"How does Mal know?"

"He recommended him."

This made me even madder. "Jesus, Alice. You involved Mal?"

"Yes. How do you expect the man to treat me without Mal's assurances that he'll be paid in the end when you come to your senses."

I felt trapped. "God, this is embarrassing."

"Is this getting us anywhere?" Alice asked.

In fact, she was getting away from me. For the next year we lived in a mild state of siege. She went on a diet. Shamefully, I filled the refrigerator with ice cream, left chocolate treats around the house. In Wolcott I would ask if she wanted to go out and have some fried clams; in New York, if she'd like a pizza or to send out for Chinese food.

"Nope," she said.

One Saturday afternoon in October at our house in Wolcott, I came back from golf in poor shape. That morning we had had an argument about when Alice was going to make peace with my mother. "Never," she snapped. I insisted that she accompany me for Sunday lunch at the big house. "That'll be the day," she said.

When I returned from golf, Alice announced that she was leaving me. "I've had it, Alfred," she said. "I'm sick of your drinking, I'm sick of you, and I'm sick of your mother. I won't let you drag me down with you."

I was stunned. "You're going to end twelve years of marriage just like that?" I snapped my fingers.

"Yes, I am. I'm *not* ending twelve years of marriage just like that. This has been a long time coming."

Alcohol made me feel even more like the injured party. I'd had one mint julep too many at the country club. "Ever since you fell under the thrall of that quack," I declared. "There's the problem. You and that son of a bitch have been spending *my* money to malign me and my family. Now what happens? *I* have to pay for a psychiatrist *and* a divorce lawyer. That's a fine how-do-you-do."

Alice looked away from me. "I can't be married to a drunk," she said. "I'm forty-two years old. I love you, Alfred. Always have. When you used to come into your dad's office to talk to me, I'd get scared. I'd think, This is too good to be true. Well, it certainly was. I'm a middle-aged woman. What is it your mother says under her breath—I'm *dowdy*."

"When did my mother ever say that?"

"All the time. We've been at war for years."

Alice was talking more to herself than to me. We sat beside the bay window in the living room. Alice wore something different from her closet—a blouse and skirt she hadn't been able to get into in years. I saw her dimly through a haze of Bourbon. Her hands were clasped formally on her lap. I had the idea suddenly that she was the client, I the lawyer.

Strictly routine.

Another divorce.

Husband a drunk.

No contest.

I'll have one of my associates draw up the papers, Mrs. Meriwether.

How sad, Mrs. Meriwether.

How sad.

"Let's leave my mother out of this," I said.

"That's what I've been trying to do for twelve years."

That remark got to me. It was completely unnecessary—portraying my mother creeping around insulting people under her breath. "Look, you've made up your mind. You do what you have to do."

"I think it's best for both of us."

"Fine. Great." I made as if to push Alice away with my hands, even though she was several feet from me. Mentally pushing her away before she'd actually gone. I stood up and felt dizzy. "That's that then."

Alice stood up, too. Dowdy, I thought. Who called her dowdy? We drank carrot juice in Greenwich Village, trotted around the reservoir. What was the name of that German restaurant? Cafe Stuttgart—pastries for her, Dortmunder for me. Those were the days. Eighty-sixth Street was never the same after the Stuttgart closed. All the great German places were closing. Then she got worried about her wedding dress and from then on it was carrot juice, fresh fruits. But I could never stay away from the Dortmunder.

"I'm almost finished packing."

"Packing?" I asked. "To go where?"

Alice sighed. "I'm going to New York this afternoon, Alfred. That's what we've been talking about. Sometimes I'm not sure I'm getting through. Are you that drunk?"

I was bewildered. "This afternoon? What about dinner?"

"I'll get something on the road, or wait until New York."

"Oh, yeah," I said, confused. "Right. Well, go ahead then."

"I'm taking the station wagon."

"Sure, right."

"Alfred, do you understand a word I'm saying?"

"Yeah, you're leaving."

"Okay, then. I'm taking the station wagon. Don't wake up tomorrow and think it's been stolen."

That annoyed me.

Alice left me then. She went into the bedroom to finish packing. Still angry, I went into the kitchen, removed a six-pack of Schlitz and headed out to the rocks in front of my house. The haze in my mind contrasted with the clarity of the late afternoon. Everything was sharper—the ocean, the rocks, the white sails of the sailboats.

I made my way out along the left file of rocks. I climbed down with exaggerated carefulness onto my natural rock seat and sat down with the six-pack on my lap. I popped a cold one and leaned back against the slab of rock, which also felt cold.

Sometime in that first hour, as I was gathering forces to examine my marriage, Alice went outside to the station wagon. I heard the familiar house door shut, the familiar car door open and close, the engine start, the sound of the tires on the sand.

Good riddance, I thought. I don't need this.

The sheer injustice of her departure carried me through the late afternoon. The beer ran out and I had to return to the house. In the evening I worked my way through a bottle of Simard and a liverwurst sandwich. Words, sentences, and sentence fragments echoed in my confused brain.

I drained the last of the Simard and glided into the bedroom on updrafts of indignation. I stumbled groggily out of my clothes and was nearly asleep before I hit the bed.

The next morning nearly killed me. I woke up with a splitting headache and no wife. I was fifty-one years old; just yesterday I had been thirty-eight or twenty-four. I felt the silence of the empty house, and grasped for the first time that I would be going into my old age alone.

What made it even worse was the thought of having lunch with my family later. This inexplicably filled me with horror. Going home had been the secret journey of my marriage. A place at the table. My old room on the third floor.

I spent the morning wandering around the house, onto the rocks, inventing little errands. As the prospect of lunch with my family drew closer, I became more agitated. Though Alice wasn't expected, her absence was a disturbing and final reminder that she wouldn't be around at all anymore.

"It's for the best, Alfred," my mother would say. "I never thought she was right for you. Naturally, it wasn't my business to say anything. 'Let him make his own mistakes'—those were my exact words to your father."

I got dressed in my blazer and khaki pants and loafers, left the house, and got into the car. When I arrived at my mother's house, I saw Winston through the bay window. He loomed over the dining-room table with his boardinghouse reach. "No class," he had said about my wife. No class.

I kept on going. Around New Haven I took a couple of aspirins because of my head. I was at the Triborough Bridge in three and a half hours; outside my house fifteen minutes later.

I parked beside the red town house. The street was shady and cool. Carl Schurz Park spread out to my left, verdant; imposing Doctors Hospital stood behind me. Baby carriages, joggers, and strollers moved toward the park. Everyone looked vigorous and happy.

Once inside the front door, I felt more in control. I had had this bizarre fear that I wouldn't be allowed into my own house. I had almost forgotten to shut off the alarm.

Alice wasn't there. For a moment I felt panicky. I searched the house, kept calling for her. It hit me for the first time that she must have hated the house. Everything in it belonged to the Meriwethers—was my mother's, had been my father's, was my own.

I settled down on the terrace, in the bright light. A Sunday *Times* was piled on the garden table, a coffee cup beside it. I began to read the *Times,* kept glancing up at the front door. Obviously, Alice had found numerous ways to entertain herself over the years without me. Maybe she was out right now with some sleek-haired Continental type.

She didn't come home for three hours. I waited on the terrace through the help-wanted and automotive ads and a couple of mint juleps.

When Alice opened the door she stopped dead with the door open. She was not hearing the telltale whine of the alarm. "Who's there?" she asked, the light of Eighty-seventh Street behind her. Evidently, she saw a hulking figure on the terrace.

"It's okay," I called. "It's Alfred."

"Oh, Christ," Alice said. "What are you doing here?"

Winston had once said that Alice was built for comfort, not for speed, a bit on the heavy-duty side. But the woman who came toward me, dressed simply in a red suit, was tall and trim. I saw her having her hand kissed at brunch.

"Where the hell have you been?" I asked.

"That's my business." She sat down in the summer chair across from me. She put her black purse on the table beside the coffee cup, exhaled as if what she was about to undergo would be interminable.

I was in no mood to waste any time. I'd been working on my speech for six and a half hours, since Wolcott. Everything came out in one blurt. "I want you to stay," I said. "I know it sounds silly, but I'm afraid to be alone. I don't want you to leave. We've had some good times."

"I suppose," Alice said neutrally.

"What can we do?"

I wasn't sure if she'd heard the question. She arranged the *Times* on the table. "It's not worth the effort."

"Well, I think it is."

"When do you plan to stop drinking? *Do* you ever plan to stop?"

"I can try," I said.

"*Try?*" she said angrily. "That's not good enough."

"Alice."

"When was the last time we made love—five, six months ago?"

"It's been a while," I admitted.

"I will not—I repeat, *will not*—be married to a drunk. Not for one second more."

"I realize that."

So . . .

It was well into the night before we held anything that resembled a conversation. We did not move from the terrace. It had gotten cold by then. The *Times*'s Monday edition was probably hitting the streets.

At some point my wife agreed to continue living with me for the time being. Nevertheless, the arrangement—its tentativeness, its whole house-of-cards quality—did nothing somehow to ease the sense of foreboding that I had felt since yesterday. We left it at that, with so many things still up in the air.

Obviously, it is one thing to say you're going to stop drinking after a lifetime of putting it away—no matter the shambles you've created—and quite another to stop it.

A couple of days after putting on the brakes, I did not feel my best. Unwell, I went to see Mal Robinson at his office. I described the dizziness, the clamminess, the nausea, the need and the determination.

He gave me a complete physical examination. I spent three days in the hospital. He asked me to see a therapist on the staff, a specialist in alcoholic disorders. With some reluctance, I agreed. This is it, I thought. A nice gentleman in his late sixties. We spent an afternoon meandering through my life. It was not uncomfortable. Rather clubby—this doctor was attentive and courtly.

At the end Mal organized the charts and papers on his desk. He told me I was not suicidal. This information might have filled another man with relief. It had never occurred to me that I might be suicidal. Mal said he was going to prescribe some pills for me. If they didn't work, he and the specialist would consider a different treatment. He went into great detail about these pills—how, used in conjunction with alcohol, they could prove fatal; how a large dose could bring on a heart attack. For a while in there, while he explained all this to me, the cure sounded worse than the disease.

Some days were better than others, but the first week was the absolute worst. I had one disastrous night later, at the one hundred and fiftieth anniversary dinner at the Games Club. One of the members had brought a case of Dom Pérignon pink champagne from his cellar in Cold Spring. This nectar proved irresistible. I had a couple of glasses; a couple of glasses were enough. I tumbled down a flight of stairs. Miraculously, I was uninjured, except for bruises. I did not take a drink after that.

In the first months of our trial period, the barriers remained up between Alice and me. I think it helped when I agreed to let her redecorate the house in Manhattan the way she wanted it. We decided to build separate quarters for my mother on the third and fourth floors—reachable by elevator—should she decide to visit. But she didn't.

Alice continued seeing the psychiatrist. There was no one indicator when things began to improve between us. They did improve, though at times progress seemed awfully slow.

6

Meanwhile, as I was piecing my life together, business was booming down at Waterman, Rhodes. Winston felt secure enough to devote his full time to getting a grip on national affairs. This was one of his great passions. He took to describing himself as "super-Lincolnesque." These were the years when he unchained his ego.

For some reason he liked to impress me. One hot July afternoon in 1982, he took me to "21" to meet the junior senator from Kansas, already familiar to me on television from the evening news. The senator was quiet, almost placid. He deferred to my brother-in-law. Winston waved people over to meet him and kept ordering up telephones as if they were appetizers. There was a lot of commotion at our table. A photographer whirred away with a motor-driven camera and an electronic flash.

While Winston orchestrated the captains, the waiters, the telephones, the senator leaned over to me and asked, "Say, who's running for President here?" His eyes were a rich blue, humorous, interested. His voice had just the trace of a midwestern twang.

The senator was pleasant enough, but I was even more intrigued by his special assistant, a young man named Lawton Randolph. Whenever the conversation turned to weighty matters, Randolph did most of the talking. "What do I think about that, Lawton?" the senator asked at one point during lunch. He sat back in his chair, a broad smile on his face, as if asking us to admire his marvelous toy.

Randolph started in:

"The senator feels . . ."

"We believe . . ."

"As you know, gentlemen . . ."

"It is the senator's opinion that . . ."

"We've prepared a study . . ."

Randolph wore a rumpled blue suit. It made him look harassed, which he wasn't. His pale eyes revealed nothing. Thick glasses only magnified an air of imperviousness. I had the sense of wheels turning behind closed doors.

The senator completed Randolph's recitations by adding humanizing vignettes. These were gleaned from his extensive travels back and forth across the country. A farm family here, a steelworker there, a migrant laborer bending in the sun—something to make the facts come alive. I got the impression that the senator took the high ground and left Randolph to take the low unpaved road, where bargains and trade-offs simmered.

Outside the restaurant after lunch, Winston snapped his fingers for the senator's car. He mopped his brow with a blue silk handkerchief. The senator said to me, "Do you still play tennis, Alfred?"

"Not too often anymore," I answered. "I play a lot of golf."

He seemed a bit disappointed. "Too bad." It occurred to me later that he might have wanted to get up a game the next time he passed through New York. Or he could have just been making idle small talk—the kind of chitchat a man makes when he's waiting for his limousine. But it was nice to be remembered.

We waved good-bye to the senator. This was months before the Secret Service and any entourage. His car drove eastward along Fifty-second Street. Winston turned to me and asked, "What did you think of him?"

"I liked him."

"Alfred, he's going to be the next President of the United States. Too bad he's a lightweight."

We walked east along Fifty-second Street in silence. Winston flung his finger at a Checker and it screeched to a halt beside us on crowded, overheated Fifth Avenue. Winston ripped open the door as if the taxi was a yellow can. He eased himself into the cab in sectional movements—first he ducked his head, then he bent, then he leaned, then he dipped back toward the scarred back seat. Finally, he brought his feet in after him, with a flash of loafer. I closed the door. He tapped on the window and rolled it down. "The die is cast," he intoned. "I've hitched my wagon to his star."

Winston blew me a kiss. He scowled at the Hispanic driver's head, then settled himself into the dark interior of the Checker, and said to the cabbie, "See if you can get me down to Wall Street without killing me." The cab crept away from the curb.

Later, after the election, Winston was on Cloud Nine, orchestrating conference calls with Washington, strutting the corridors, talking somberly about "the difficult task that lies ahead for the President-elect."

His excellent spirits were dampened somewhat when he got word that his appointment in the new Administration would put him pretty low on the totem pole—Under Secretary of the Navy. He had expected a Cabinet post: he felt that he had single-handedly delivered the great state of New York to the junior senator from Kansas. Obviously, the senator thought differently or knew better.

Winston's depression over his appointment lasted twenty minutes. Then he was full of his usual physical brand of camaraderie. "Let someone else be the point man," he growled. "I'll carve out a fiefdom from nothing. I'll burrow from the inside, and"—this was a boffo line that laid his darting-eyed subordinates in the aisles—"I'll make some WAVES down there."

One week before Winston left the firm to make his rendezvous with destiny in Washington with the new and hopeful Administration, Dickie Ramondino, a clerk in the firm's billing department, paid me a visit in my office.

I was in an unusually happy mood that morning. I'd just spent another sober New Year's up in Wolcott with Alice. I felt that I was getting a grip on my life again. The prospect of Winston's departure filled me with pleasure. I was sure the bad times were behind me.

I was always glad to see Dickie. He reminded me a bit of my father—the same hesitancies and advanced courtliness. He always took a long time to get to the point. Probably because I've never been in much of a hurry, never really attacked life, I've never minded people who take a long time getting to the point. This has given me twin reputations, depending on where you come down on the whole Type A Behavior question. I am either a man who thinks things through, or I'm slow on the uptake.

With Dickie I knew we wouldn't be getting down to business for a good fifteen minutes. First of all, there was the matter of finding a place to hang his cane. Then there was the matter of helping him into and making sure he was comfortable in his chair. We exchanged small talk about his retirement, which may have been small talk to me but was big talk to him. He had been with Waterman, Rhodes for fifty years. He was in his late seventies. He was something of an institution around the place, and a repository for much of its history. He remembered me as a nipper, visiting the firm with my father. A lot of people may have had the heart to tell him over the years that it was time to pack up, but I didn't permit anyone to move him out. My only worry was that he might get run over in the corridors. I liked everything about him, from the prewar cut of his suit to the Optimo cigar smoke in his office. I felt strongly that he should have a place in the firm for as long as he wanted one. In the end it had been his decision to retire.

Dickie was a tall, almost gaunt man with brown eyes of immense sadness. Seeing him over the years, I was reminded of a character in a Eugene O'Neill play facing another Sunday night with the family. Grave emotions pulled on his face, dragging it into melancholia. The sandy hair of my first powerful childhood impressions of him had long since turned white. Its waviness and lustrousness gave him a hint of rakishness, of a great matinee-idol youth that had used up his face with exotic experiences. I also had the impression of a man who had experienced fear or shock. Perhaps some dream or life-plan had been handed to him on a silver platter and then been whisked away before he had had a chance to get a taste. Perhaps it was the Depression.

Dickie arranged himself in his chair, as if he wanted everything to be just so. His beautiful tapered fingers took up a rather portrait-like positioning on his lap. For a few minutes we reminisced about the Kearns, Peabody merger, discussed his retirement plans, some matters of billing, my golf game, the latest design engineer who had been roving the corridors, subway crime, graffiti, straw boaters.

We could have gone on like this: I was just getting comfortable. But while we were shooting the breeze, Dickie got nervous. His laugh came out in a mini-gasp; he seemed preoccupied with lint on his suit. He said, "Is that so?" in the middle of my detailed description of my duck hook. He ran his hand through his wavy hair, coughed delicately and then coughed again. I thought it was too bad Dickie had succumbed to the drum-tight tension of the firm, that two old duffers couldn't get it together at the start of the work day.

He cleared his throat again, reached into the inside pocket of his immaculate and old-fashioned black suit. He removed several sheets of yellow legal paper and a dozen or so Xeroxed copies of what looked like billing slips. He unfolded the documents, smoothed them down. "There is something," Dickie mumbled to the papers. ". . . here . . . that bears . . . looking into." His mellifluous voice—which went superbly with his luxurious hair; almost microphonic—chopped at each word with tsks and whistles and lip-lickings. A lot of seconds passed before the whole sentence stumbled across the desk to my ears. Whereupon I reassembled it.

"What's that?" I asked.

"Oh, Alfred," he said softly.

Dickie leaned forward in his chair. For a moment I thought he wasn't going to stop leaning, that he was on his way down to my rug. I almost said, "Whoa, Dickie," nearly leaned across my desk to catch him by his shoulder. I was transfixed by the prolonged swoop of his right hand. The hand came toward me on the momentum of its dramatic and uncontrollable tremor. It approached me like a form of scribbled skywriting or a signature in the air. The papers clenched in his hand rustled above my desk.

Dickie planted the papers in front of me. He pressed them down with his dancing right hand. Then he pushed himself off from my desk and began a long backward glide. It was less alarming than his forward motion had been, but amazing nonetheless, almost thrombotic in the deadness behind his eyes, the painful bob of his head when his thin white neck reached the back of the chair and his backward motion stopped. He groaned the way an invalid might groan who is being repositioned in his sickbed. He turned his face to the wall, or in this case my window. I had a full view of quite a noble profile pointed toward the Brooklyn Bridge—meldings of nobility.

I may be slow on the uptake, but I know when a man's got a problem. It was probably my imagination, but it seemed to me that Dickie's suit had gotten blacker. His body had shrunk a bit within it, and his clothes were about to literally make the man, creep up his neck in tickles of material until his face was shrouded in wool.

I pounced on the reading glasses beside me. I picked up the papers, read them through once. After I'd finished, I took off my reading glasses. With dignified formality, I folded them beside the papers. Then I repeated the same procedure: I put on my reading glasses, picked up the papers, and read them again. I was so agitated that I probably could have performed this repetition compulsion until the cows came home. Some people rise to the occasion; others are destined to repeat it.

"What a mess," I said. "What a goddamn mess."

Dickie's face was drawn down again in that familiar expression of infinite sadness. "I wanted to be sure before I came to you with it."

"Who else knows?" I asked.

"I know, and now you know," Dickie said, almost apologetically.

"I appreciate that."

"I would not have done otherwise."

I read the papers a third time. Dickie activated himself, looked away from the window and directly at me. There was a fierce dignity in his look. "I want to make it clear that whatever you do is all right with me. I wouldn't do anything to hurt the firm."

We exchanged a glance of complete understanding, but even so it was now my problem. "Thank you."

"This firm has been a home to me."

"I know, Dickie. What a note to retire on."

"Yes, yes. I've known it was bad for six months. It was just a matter of pulling the evidence together."

"I want to think this through before I decide on anything."

"Whatever you say. I'm with you on this."

"Thank you, Dickie. I'll keep you informed of whatever I decide."

"My God," Dickie exclaimed, just as if he had seen a ghost over my shoulder.

American Steel and Pipe Systems, Inc. was one of Winston's pet clients. He was close friends with the chairman of the board. In this case, the company paid Bingham directly for his services and Bingham in turn reimbursed the firm—or at least that was the way it was supposed to work. But Dickie Ramondino had noticed something. During the past few years Bingham occasionally paid the firm with a bank draft, instead of with the endorsed check from American Steel or with his personal check made out to the firm and stipulating it was for services rendered to American Steel. Bingham didn't pay the firm with a bank draft all the time—just sometimes.

Dickie had become suspicious. He made a note of the times Bingham paid the firm with bank drafts. Then in December he had called the accounting department at American Steel and Pipe Systems. He explained there was a problem with the computer at Waterman, Rhodes, and requested an itemized list of dates and payments made to Winston Bingham for services rendered to Waterman, Rhodes over a period of five years. Dickie soon discovered a discrepancy between what had been paid to Bingham by American Steel, and what Bingham had paid to Waterman, Rhodes. That discrepancy—or theft—amounted to one hundred and twenty-five thousand dollars, and change.

Once I had it clear in my mind that morning how to proceed, I asked my secretary, Ms. Cook, to tell Bingham I wanted to see him as soon as possible. I sat back and waited, twiddling my thumbs or drumming my fingers on the mahogany of my late father's desk. I couldn't help but wonder how Dad would have proceeded. Probably he would have gone ahead with a tasteful ritual suicide.

Winston arrived in a burst of impatience. He flung open the door without knocking, just like in the first stage of a drug bust, and strode toward my desk. "What is it, Alfred?"

"Have a seat, Winston. I'd like to talk to you."

He looked at his watch. "Alfred, you've caught me—"

"Have a seat. This won't take long."

"Yeah, yeah, yeah," he muttered. "Yeah, yeah, yeah," exhaling himself into the chair vacated by Dickie Ramondino earlier that morning. He again gave himself a time-check to indicate precious seconds were ticking away.

I whipped around my desk like the roadrunner in the cartoons and closed the door to my office on the startled Ms. Cook. I leaned against the door for just a moment with my hand over my heart, and took a deep breath. Winston's was the voice of calm. He spoke to my chair just as if I was still in it. I don't think Winston focused on people until they had something he wanted. Then he was all ears and all body. He knew how to love you to pieces.

"Alfred," he said, without turning around to look at me, speaking to my chair and making little thrusts of his right hand for emphasis. "It's always great to talk to you, but I'm having lunch with the Governor of the State of New York in fifteen minutes."

"This is more important, Winston."

"I'm sure it is," he said reasonably. "I think the pension plan is great. Let's go ahead with it. Great. Why don't your boy wonders get together with my boy wonders? Why do we have to involve the movers and shakers in this?"

Winston was in the habit of referring to the associates as "boy wonders," though some of them were female.

"It isn't the pension plan, I'm afraid."

"Yeah, okay," Winston said. "So?" He shrugged. *Get on with it*, he meant.

I took my seat. At a moment when bluntness was called for, I chose to break the ice with him. Somewhere in my psyche I had the belief that events could be shaped, that the only thing preventing life from being a joyous experience was better rehearsal. "When are you off to Washington?"

"I'm off to Washington next Thursday." He winked at me. "Why, you need a couple of ducats to the Inaugural Ball?"

"Ducats," I repeated under my breath. "No. Thanks anyway."

"I'll miss you," he said absently. "I'll never forget what you've done for me."

There was a moment of silence. Winston looked around my office knowingly, as if this was just the kind of office you'd expect of Alfred—the coziest den for sleeping it off.

"I won't miss you."

He was craning his neck with impatience, getting the cricks out for his confrontation with the governor. He stopped abruptly in mid-crane. His head was cast in a dauntless leadership mode for just a second, exposing his jugular.

"What?" His head whipped around to face me. He was instantly alert. There was something ominous in his black eyes. Pleasure and the embers of anger combined to contort his face.

That would have been the appropriate moment to get down to cases. It would have gotten him out of my office faster. But instead I became circumspect. Perhaps I expected him to grasp the point without me ever having to quite get to the point. I also wished this whole thing could have taken place at another location more suited to the occasion—like the second level of a parking garage.

"Winston," I began, looking directly at my desk, embedding my words in the wood, "I wish you well in Washington, but I don't think you should ever come back to this law firm."

"*What?*" he asked. I wasn't sure about his body, but I could certainly feel his mind poising. Since I didn't look at him, I did not observe the transformation of his mood, the pints of blood pumping into his face and darkening it, creating squall lines across his cheeks.

"I think you're a very unhealthy influence here," I said to the mahogany, polishing it with my dulcet tones.

"Whuh," he said. "Whuh," he repeated, which is just the sound people make when they've had the wind knocked out. Only Winston was in the process of topping off his lungs with a little extra air.

"And I think it would be best for all concerned if you resigned," I concluded. It didn't occur to me that he had no idea what I was talking about.

That doesn't excuse his disgraceful conduct. I might have badmintoned and worried the whole thing around for another fifteen minutes or so if his conduct hadn't brought me to my senses and forced me to raise my eyes. The very wood of my late father's desk made me realize that once again I had failed to see the forest for the trees.

Winston flew off the handle. He began by shouting, "Go fuck

yourself." Obviously my request for his resignation was just the trigger pulled on years of accumulated hostility. Perhaps he broke down over class lines—my silver spoon versus his entrepreneurial spirit that made this country great. But I tend to think it was much more *ad hominem*. Also, it shouldn't be underestimated that Winston powerfully believed his crowning achievements exposed his flanks to sudden onslaughts. This personality characteristic made him suspicious by nature.

It was like being in the same office with a menacing, constipated Brahman bull. At one point Winston was so overcome with rage he developed a nosebleed. He yelled at me with his head thrown back and a silk handkerchief stuck into his nostrils. His protuberant Adam's apple ripped up and down along the length of his spasming throat. He suggested it was I who should resign, since over the past few years it was obvious I preferred to conduct the firm's legal business in bars and grills all over the city.

"Glub, glub, glub," he declared. "Glub, glub, glub," presumably doing an imitation of me hurrying to down a fifth. It had never registered on him that I'd stopped drinking. "Don't ever talk to me about being an unhealthy influence."

"This isn't getting us anywhere," I said quietly.

"I built this goddamn law firm from nothing." He pointed theatrically at his chest. "You and your sainted father ran it right into the ground. I dragged you people bodily into the twentieth century, and all I got was ingratitude and knives in the back. Let me tell you something else. Your family owns six hundred acres of prime Rhode Island real estate. You sit on that gold mine like you're trying to hatch it." The property was a continuing source of annoyance to him. "You don't even take a tax break. I could put *cattle* on that property. What's wrong with calling it a farm, for Christ's sake?"

"You've told me about the cows," I said. "It's not a farm."

"You're an asshole," Winston said.

"Winston . . ."

"If you like undergrowth so much, why don't you and your goddamn family move to Thailand?"

"Winston—"

"You came to my wedding and puked all over yourself. Remember that?"

"Yes."

"That's when I knew you were a fuck-up."

His monogrammed WB pale yellow silk shirt was spattered with blood. He wiped his nose with his claret-soaked handkerchief. He looked at his designer handkerchief with amazement, as if he couldn't believe he had been so grievously wounded.

"You're a shit," I said.

He heaved himself to an upright position and snarled. For a moment I thought he was off and roiling again, but this time he restricted himself to a vigorous point-of-order jab at my Games Club necktie. "Listen, buster . . ." Probably because I rarely declared my opinions with such frankness, he realized something was up. I should have let him know something was up fifteen minutes ago. He might have spared himself a nosebleed; I might have spared myself a tirade.

Winston listened calmly to my restrained recitation of the pertinent facts. His composure was remarkable. The case against him was pretty cut-and-dried. It was just a matter of laying out the evidence, which I did without any particular inflection. It was time to get it over with and get him out of there.

"I can explain," he said with an air of indifference, folding the handkerchief on his tweed knee. "I deny everything, naturally. Someone has it in for me. Someone's trying to set me up. Who is he? I promise the name will never leave this office, Alfred. I want you to know I'm shocked and surprised by these allegations. Obviously I've stepped on a few toes at the firm—sometimes I forgot the niceties. Was it Orrick Hazzard?"

"No, Winston."

"Let me tell you something. Orrick Hazzard is a pederast."

"No one has it in for you," I said. "As I told you, I don't think it's a good idea for you to return to this law firm. I don't care what reasons you give—ill health, new career in government."

"Now, listen here," Winston protested, but his voice was unusually quiet.

"I want your resignation in writing. I want it before the partners this afternoon."

"Would you like to hear my side of the story?"

"You don't have a side." For the first time my voice began to quaver.

"Is this justice?" Winston asked. "Am I not to be allowed to clear my good name?"

"If you like, I can draft your resignation statement, and you can sign it."

"I'm not going to sign shit. I think it's *you* who has it in for me."

"I don't have it in for you. I just can't believe you've done this. Last year you drew six hundred thousand dollars from the firm. You don't need the money. Why did you do it?"

He shrugged—so much for motivation. "I don't have to listen to trumped-up charges and wild accusations from a drunk."

"Okay." I reached for my telephone. "I'll call a partners' meeting for three this afternoon. You can explain to them what you did with the hundred and twenty-five thousand."

Winston leapt out of the chair and pounced on my hand with the receiver halfway to my ear. He was sprawled over my desk. We grappled for the receiver. Rather, he grappled. I was impressed with his viselike grip, wondered what cologne he used. He laughed in brisk little snorts. For a second he grappled with his own hand for control. Then he had the receiver and replaced it with a dainty pat onto its cradle.

"Let's not be hasty, heh-heh-heh," he said. His eyes were wide open from this near-brush with the long arm of the law—glistening orbs of relief. He sank back into his chair. "Whew," he said. I wrung my tender hand.

Winston shrugged. "You're so hepped on having my scalp. Okay. Here's my scalp. We can settle this like gentlemen. We don't need the other partners. Winston Bingham resigns."

"I *know* you're going to resign," I said. "You don't have to act as if you're doing me a special favor. You should be counting your fucking blessings."

Winston dug his elbows into his thighs, placed his head in his hands, and began to rock back and forth. He did this for an uncomfortably long time. Just that morning he had rolled down the corridors of the firm at the center—his old basketball position—of a legal juggernaut.

I would have gotten up and left, except it was my office. Once or twice I cleared my throat, tapped out the opening chords of Beethoven's Fifth Symphony a couple of times on the mahogany. I said briskly, "Well, okay," and, "That's that," and I even said, "All right," the way athletes do, drawing out the "right." But I didn't get any response from him. He continued rocking back and forth, leaning on one swaying thigh and then the other. They reminded me of the shaky footbridges in jungle films.

His eyes brimmed and dispensed identical bulging globules that rolled down his nose creases, until they reached his thick ruby lips, where his tongue licked them.

"I've let everyone down," he said. His shoulders rose and fell as though receiving electrical jolts. "I've let you down, my wife, my son, the firm. God almighty." His head fell into his hands again.

"You should have thought about that before you stole the money."

"I'm sorry, I'm sorry, I'm sorry," he said. At least that's what I think he said, since his voice was muffled by his hands.

"Enough is enough. I suggest you go back to your office and prepare your resignation. Good luck in Washington."

He nodded. He stood up. He sighed. He brought his hand toward me on a wide arc, and we shook hands. I couldn't escape the idea that he regarded this whole thievery as an athletic event. If it hadn't been for the refs, it might have gone the other way.

He held my hand for an extra moment, brought his other one around and plopped it on top of our handshake. Then, taking a few steps backward, he gave me a somber wave and removed his blood-flecked presence by tiptoeing out the door.

In the afternoon I went to see Dickie Ramondino and told him what I had done. I thought he was going to cry, too. Eagerly he pressed the documents related to American Steel into my hands —six manila envelopes. "This is all I have, and I hope this ends it."

"So do I, Dickie," I said.

But that didn't end it. Only the location changed. In fact, Winston Bingham had only begun to cause trouble for me.

7

It was a Saturday morning in June. The early summer weekend in Wolcott coincided with Winston's first vacation in Wolcott since he had taken Washington by storm, eighteen months previously. My brother-in-law had proved to be more than equal to the job of Under Secretary of the Navy. Indeed, as promised, he had carved out a Pentagon fiefdom from nothing.

That morning I sat in the warm sand of the Surf Club, nursing a soft drink. Above me was the wooden porch of the Meriwether cabana, laden and stuffed with wicker furniture. An oval mirror decorated with tiny seashells reflected the sun and tinges of blue. My mother had owned a cabana at the club since 1925.

From my position in the sand I could look across to our property in the distance. It was separated from the three-mile-long Wolcott beach—which included the Surf Club frontage—by the Piscotaug River. The white rocks beside my house formed a blistering funnel for the headwaters of the river.

At noon I heard the long siren from the Wolcott Fire Department. I wiggled the metal poles of my beach chair and sat unexpectantly. I wore a knee-length surfer bathing suit covered by spangles of yellow and red. My Dominican straw hat's cloth rim of como-blue and black acted out in several tableaux the joyous gigs of a *merengue* orchestra.

The previous day I had received, in a white Department of the Navy envelope, a long newsmagazine article from, and about, you-know-who. It was entitled, "Rough-and-Ready Ramrod of the New-Look Navy."

Significant passages in the article had been underscored in red Magic Marker by the Under Secretary himself. Also enclosed was a photograph of my brother-in-law. He sat at an oblong con-

ference table. Easels stood deployed to the right of him and
charts and graphs were affixed to the walls behind him and a
scale-model of a nuclear submarine was positioned in front of
him. The conference table was top-heavy with the arms and hats
of Navy brass—gold and filigree and egg salad and inches of
starched white cuffs. At least to the eyes of this former second
lieutenant, the table threatened to collapse from the sheer
weight of rank.

In the photograph Winston's big hands were outthrust across
the table to catch a pass; but he was obviously making a point.
The article focused on Thumper's eagle eye in the awarding of
lucrative Navy contracts; his concern about cost overruns; safety
standards; improved and streamlined administrative procedures.
He was bullish on women in the new-look Navy: "They're pulling their weight," he declared proudly. Confided an admiring
aide: "The old man's tough but he's fair."

As for the Bingham life-style: he jogged at five in the morning, chuckled about having to go easy on his favorite food—
lobster thermidor. Invitations to his house in Arlington, Virginia
were "coveted."

" 'It was love at first sight,' declared the elegant Dorothy
Bingham, member of an old-line New York family who met her
man, appropriately, on a cruise to Europe in 1962." But, sighed
Washington's latest hostess-with-the-mostest: "Winston is full of
surprises. One night he'll bring home the Chinese ambassador
for pizza and chat about diesel submarines. The next night it
could be candlelight for six or a formal dinner for twenty. I'd be
lost without my Filipino houseboys."

The Secretary of the Navy, Ray Perry, was regarded in Navy
circles as a "nice guy but ineffective." Confided one topsider:
"Bingham's the guy who makes the decisions when the going
gets tough." Added Thumper: "I like to think I'm a soft touch
who can play hardball."

In the margin alongside his picture, with a red arrow running
into his assertive mouth, Winston had scribbled, "See you Saturday!"

From my secure position in the sand, I had an unobstructed
view—under the raised cabanas, between thick tar-treated stilts—

of the Surf Club parking lot a hundred yards away. A space had been reserved for my blue Caprice Classic.

I watched the Bingham party arrive in the parking lot. They piled out of a silver Cadillac Eldorado. I heard Winston's finger-snaps in the still air—a finger-snap for each door of the Eldorado and one for the trunk area. A cabana boy attempted to carry off a green duffel bag holding the big fellow's collection of graphite tennis racquets. Winston pointed at the young man and said, "Hold it right there, son." He took the bag out of the fellow's hand.

My sister Dorothy, dressed in a pink-and-green Lilly, followed the three basket-bearers up the steps. She looked at the steps before she mounted them and announced, "Heavenly," as if in thanks for all the massive doses of sea air.

Winston was accompanied by a wiry, slightly bowlegged man in his late forties. The man wore khaki pants, a pale yellow linen sports shirt, and tennis sneakers. His salt-and-pepper hair was close-cropped in the military style. He stood a shade under six feet. In his right hand he carried a blue flight bag with a shoulder strap. As he approached the cabana steps, deep in conversation with Winston, he nodded crisply once or twice, as if digesting a fresh bit of information.

I waved to my sister and called, "Hi," to her as she followed the cabana boys down the boardwalk. She came toward me, smiling, while the cabana boys lugged the picnic baskets onto the porch. I screwed my soft drink into the sand and clambered to my feet to intercept her for a brotherly kiss before she ascended to the cabana.

"Precious," Dorothy said. As I approached her cheek I heard the hum in her throat signaling kissy-kissy. Her left hand swept around and made a series of affectionate thumps on my upper back. "Heavenly," she murmured. After giving me an extra thump, she released me into the waft of her Jean Patou. "Winston practically *commandeered* a Navy transport to fly us into Quonset. It was too convenient."

"I read you're the toast of Washington." We hadn't seen each other in eighteen months, but talked frequently on the telephone.

Her ivories vanished abruptly. Dorothy said, "*I* didn't make the regulations. As far as I'm concerned, the Navy can take all their Filipinos and put them on aircraft carriers doing the boys' laundry. Maybe that would stop newsmagazines from barging in and humiliating a decent wife and mother."

Blue tinges of anger surfaced on Dorothy's cheeks. She said in babyish tones, "'I'd be lost without my Filipino houseboys.' Jesus Christ." Straightening her shoulders, she smiled at the whole sandy acreage of the seashore—the pounding curlers of waves in the distance and northward to her house, which stood just beyond the Piscotaug River, a quarter mile from my own.

Dorothy stood on tiptoes and peered into the cabana. "Oh, hell. I thought Mummy would have arrived by now." She turned back to me. "Have you met her new companion yet?"

"What new companion?" I asked.

"Alfred, I don't know how we got so lucky," she said. "The most I'd hoped for was some little Wolcott High School senior with a driver's license. I didn't expect a mature, accomplished college student from the Rhode Island Art Institute, no less." Dorothy gripped my biceps. "Now be nice to her. Mummy is very keen on her, and we're going to be keen on her, too. I think we both know how *not*-keen Mummy can sometimes be."

My mother, who hit ninety in April, had run through a series of nurses and companions over the years. There always seemed to be personality conflicts.

"This time I didn't ram anyone down her throat," Dorothy said. "I left the decision completely up to her. I just made sure the girl wasn't a drug addict. Her name is Kate Latham, and we're going to see she has the best time, aren't we?"

"We certainly are," I said.

"Good boy."

Actually, I was glad I wouldn't have to spend a weekend interviewing prospects for this difficult job.

"She moved right into the big house, brought down all her art things from Providence. She's going to be as happy as a clam. She's got the beach, room, and board. Her afternoons are free for painting, when Mummy goes beddy-bye. I call that a pretty good deal," Dorothy sighed. "Let's just try and get through the whole summer with her." She blew me a little kiss and headed up the cabana steps to supervise the unfolding of the picnic.

The handles of Winston's graphite tennis racquets pointed out of the duffel bag like tiny antiaircraft guns. "Alfred!" he said. He and his companion approached me along the boardwalk.

Winston dropped his racquet-choked bag and spread out his arms. He sank into the hot sand and walked a few feet toward me. "Alfred," he whispered, pulling me into the general chest area of his blue sports shirt. He released me for a second as if to get a good look at me.

Our reunion.

"Winston." I stared into the white alligator of his La Coste. I'd forgotten how much I hadn't missed him.

"Alfred," he repeated for the third time, as if we'd shared a lifetime of trial and hope.

"Winston."

His eyes were slicked over with inexplicable emotion. "Eighteen months," he said.

"You call," I said evenly.

"Hell, that isn't the same. I need to *see* you. I've shared every triumph and every tragedy with you."

"The tragedy part doesn't seem to have affected you," I said.

I was willing to let bygones be bygones, but didn't have to be happy about it.

"Look, I've learned my lesson. The same way I've learned everything else. The hard way."

"Thanks for the clipping. From that magazine."

"Got it?" Winston beamed. He looked relieved to be off the subject of our last meeting, which took place in my office at Waterman, Rhodes, Stevenson, and Meriwether. The subject of that meeting had been theft. "I'll tell you, Alfred, it's a world of Lilliputians down there. If memoranda were excrement, there'd be a worldwide shitstorm. That newsmagazine got it right— tough new ramrod of the new-look Navy."

"Say, how long are you staying?" I asked.

"A few days this trip," he said. "I don't need to tell you about the recent buildups in the arsenal of democracy. I haven't had a day off in a year, but I'm looking for some time in the fall. Speaking of which"—here Winston's voice took on a special resonance and he cut loose my aching arms—"Alfred, I'd like you to meet a crackerjack guy." He turned to his companion. "Gerard

Charles Ackley, meet my brother-in-law and ethical compass, Alfred Meriwether."

Ackley stepped forward, leaned down from the boardwalk, gave me a vise of a handshake. "How do you do, sir," he said in a soft Southern voice.

"Pleased to meet you, Gerard."

"You can call him Jerry," Winston said. "'Course, I call him X."

Jerry stared at the ocean—wincing at one of the little in jokes that the chain of command demanded. Regrettably, I contributed to his discomfort. Obviously my left hemisphere was tuckered out. This left me open to the missed guffaw, the head-'em-off-at-the-pass chuckle. "X?" I asked.

"X. Ackley," Winston said. He sucked away in silence until the good news arrived from his belly and he broke himself up. "Get it?"

I got it. My cheeks spoke for me with twin dimples of exasperation.

"Jerry here is part of the new-look Navy we're building. He's captain of the Neptune nuclear submarine, the *Avenger*."

I expected more of a run-silent-run-deep gruffness from my sub skippers.

Winston patted Ackley on the arm. "The two of us thought we'd get in some tennis while his boat's laid up in Groton for modifications. We're shooting for the seniors tournament next month. I handle the net area."

"Is Jerry a senior?" I asked.

"He is now," Winston declared. He licked his lips. "Even if we have to dye his hair white."

"Well, good luck," I said. It pissed me off. I nodded to the Atlantic, longed for my beach chair.

"Jerry was champion of Annapolis in his day," Winston said.

"How's Win?" I asked, referring to his difficult son and only child, Winston Bingham, Jr., who was my godson. A recent graduate of Yale, he was still uncertain about a career. His literary inclinations annoyed his father. I had meant to ask my sister about him, but the question had been mislaid during the welcoming ceremony. "Is he up from New Haven yet?"

It was a sore subject. "The poet?" Winston asked. Disgust

thickened his basso. "The poet is in residence. Do you know what he's doing this summer, Uncle Alfred?"

I assumed from Winston's tone that whatever my godson was doing, it was not career-oriented.

"He's mowing lawns in New Haven, Connecticut and taking poetry courses. Don't get me wrong." Winston put up his hands in that pass-catching way of his. "I'm not going to song-and-dance you about the Protestant Ethic. But when I was the boy's age, I was Small College All-American. I held down *two* jobs. I sent the boy to Exeter, I sent him to Yale University, but I didn't expect the return on investment to be skill at mowing lawns." Winston paused and cocked his head quizzically. "But I'm an insensitive clod from Lake Erie College by way of the School of Hard Knocks. What do I know?"

"Well, Winston . . ."

"You know, you should have a tête-à-tête with him and define some career areas. Then I could get on the phone and make some appointments for him."

"Are you asking me to be your intermediary?" I asked.

"You have a way with the boy. I've got a communications problem with him."

"Maybe you'd help things by not calling him 'the boy.'"

"I think I'm too gruff," Winston said. "When I ask him a question at the breakfast table, his hands tremble. The boy's twenty-three years old and he's got this uncontrollable tremor in his hands. A simple request like, 'Would you please pass the Tabasco, Win?' Jesus, you'd think I was telling him to land on Omaha Beach."

Winston made a *click-click* sound with his tongue on the roof of his mouth. "And I think the reason is that I've always been too gruff. Sometimes he starts gasping for breath. So," Winston asked crisply, "what's your secret?"

"I don't have any secret."

"You and Junior must have many intimate conversations together when he's up here. What kinds of things do you talk about?"

"Winston—"

"Baseball? The owner of the New York Yankees is one of my closest friends."

"We talk about a lot of things. Just casual stuff."

"Sometimes I think my son comes from another planet."

"That's nonsense."

"You don't have any children," Winston said irritably. "What do you know?" He turned to Ackley. "You ready, Jerry?"

"Yes, sir," Ackley replied softly.

"Then let's do it to it."

He took the steps two at a time, bussed his wife, and disappeared into the men's dressing room. Captain Ackley followed him up the steps at a more stately pace.

I dug my toes into the sand and settled under my sombrero for the afternoon. Winston and Ackley headed down to the ocean for a swim.

My mother and her companion arrived in the Duesenberg. The canvas top was down. Bright tan leather poured over the seats in an infinitude of spaciousness. One did not drive the gleaming Duesenberg; one piloted it and looked for block-long parking spaces. It was an anachronism but so was my mother. The yards of hood took Proustian seconds to pass into view before the driver herself—Kate Latham—actually appeared. She was intensely concentrated in the sun as she swung the green snout into my mother's parking space across from the cabana steps.

My mother wore a white pleated cotton dress and a large white sun hat. She waved at the cabana boys and cried, "Hi, hi, boys." She waited for one of them to open the car's glinting door. The door might have taken up a parking space all its own. It always reminded me of a biplane's wing.

Before my mother could sink into her favorite wicker chair, a substantial Meriwether effusion of greetings took place. Kate Latham's expressive hazel eyes looked wide with astonishment.

Dorothy adjusted her Lilly, threw back her shoulders and advanced upon my mother. On the boardwalk beside the cabana, they fell upon each other. They pierced the air with cries of delight.

Of Kate Latham, Dorothy exclaimed, "Isn't she the most beautiful creature you've ever seen?"

"She's saved my life," my mother declared, going "one on one" with her daughter in the hyperbole department.

Although there was the usual ummm-ummm undertone of heavy cheek-kissing and back-patting, I could tell that my mother's eyes were after bigger game. They darted around the cabana circle with a pinpoint accuracy belying the siege of years. This was so Winston wouldn't take her from behind, possibly hood her eyes with his huge hands and whisper, "Guess who?"

Winston was distracted by larger thoughts, perhaps nuclear thoughts. He was remarkably restrained when he appeared from the cool darkness. "Mrs. Meriwether," he said, giving my mother a dainty peck.

"Winston?" she asked, holding onto her bonnet with her left hand.

With a humble but riveting little bow, Winston said gravely, "Mrs. Meriwether, I'd like you to meet Gerard Ackley. Captain Ackley commands the Neptune nuclear-powered missile submarine, the *USS Avenger*. Jerry, this is my wonderful mother-in-law."

"I can't stand it," my mother exclaimed. She removed her hand from her bonnet, enveloped the captain's hand with both of hers, and gave it a vigorous pump.

"Pleased to meet you, ma'am."

My mother's eyes clouded over, her color heightened, she fumbled with her pearls. "You boys"—she shook her head—"you boys." She recovered and raised her chin proudly. "I pray there'll be no more wars."

"I'll second that," Winston said, letting his somberness seep into the already humid air.

"We all do, ma'am," Jerry said.

My mother looked down at me. I stirred in the sand nervously, tugged at the brim of my straw hat. I knew what was coming. There was no escape. "My son," she declared, "served in the Second World War."

"Really, ma'am," Jerry said.

It looked as if my mother's sensible shoes had sprung elevator heels. My eyes rolled upward. "I suppose Winston told you that my son won the Distinguished Service Cross in Italy," my mother said. "*And* the Purple Heart."

"Actually, Mrs. Meriwether," Winston began. "Jerry and I have been so involved with this nation's nuclear resolve—"

"Alfred received the medal from Vice President Truman, isn't that right, Alfred?"

"Christ, not again," Winston muttered. "Who would've thunk it?"

"Obviously, Franklin would have awarded the medal himself had he not been so pressed with war matters," my mother sniffed. "*We* always thought it was because Waterman, Rhodes turned him down for a job after Columbia Law School, so he went to another firm. I daresay we'll never know the real story."

"No kidding." Jerry looked down at me on the sand. I wished he could have seen me twenty pounds and forty years ago in my brand-new steel pot.

My mother gave an irritated little wave in my direction. "*He'd* never tell you about it, Captain Ackley. My son has always hidden his light under a bushel. If I hadn't pirated the medals away for safekeeping, he would have thrown them out a long time ago."

"Heroes don't grow on trees," Winston said. He was annoyed. I had taken away his nuclear moment.

My mother made a kissing sound. She blew the kiss toward me on a chute of love that she had created by placing her outstretched palm under her lower lip.

"Best brother," Dorothy said.

"I hope individual heroics aren't a thing of the past," Winston said. "Now everything's missiles, first strike, payload, telemetry encryption, throwweight. Compared to this new generation of weapons, World War II was kindergarten. Jerry's the expert on that. He's a walking computer."

"I'm so proud of all of you," my mother said.

There was a gathering then—chicken and chablis waited. I was left beached on the sand with my GI memories and shell-shock dreams.

In the early afternoon, when the gorgeous Kate Latham settled down on the sand and undid the strand of her bikini halter, Winston appeared from the depths of the cabana. He stood on the porch, staring down at her, holding a half-munched fried chicken leg in one hand and a fluted glass of chablis in the other.

"You're invited for supper," he said to me. "Eight o'clock. You and Alice." Then he disappeared again. His glance alone might have given Kate a permanent tan.

A little later, Winston plucked at a chicken breast. He balanced a paper plate atop his thighs. His scarred knees were welded together demurely. "Know the first thing I did when I got here this morning, Mrs. Meriwether?" he asked from his wicker cantonment. "After I checked in with the Chief of Naval Operations to get my daily fix on the global picture?"

The accumulated ounces of chablis had made my mother merry. She doffed her snappy bonnet, removed a few pins from her white hair. "Oh, Winston. You've been calling me Ma for twenty years."

"Ma," Winston said. The word dipped sheepishly around the cabana and onto the sand where Kate Latham and I lay at prostrate rest.

"I took a walk around the Meriwether property, from the entrance gate all the way to that last point of the white rocks out there." He jabbed his finger toward the rocks in the distance—beyond me, beyond the tops of the cabanas, beyond the Piscotaug heaving and shimmering in the afternoon downpour of heat and light. "All six hundred acres of it."

"Sometimes I think I've died and entered heaven," my mother sighed from the wine-dark cabana, following Winston's left jab.

"You must have had many offers," Winston said quietly.

"Dozens. I've told Alfred not to bother me with them anymore. I hope after I'm dead and buried that some nature conservancy or land trust will want to take it over."

Somber shock waves of disgust registered in Winston's voice. "Nature conservancy." He yanked on the chicken breast.

"We can only hope. Sometimes I dream at night about my beautiful herons."

The marshland on our side of the river is a fine nesting spot for blue and white herons. They clobber small fish in the Piscotaug rivulets with brisk smacks of their serrated bills, then strut off into the marshes to their secret heronry of weeds. They have delighted me for five decades; they should be non-profit.

I listened to Winston—idle conversation for a summer afternoon. But he didn't see it that way.

"The natural state," Winston mused. "All that undergrowth."

"It's a treasure," she said. "Alfred and I think of the Meriwether property as a trust."

"That makes three of us, Ma. Those were the exact words I found myself using during my little tour this morning. Treasure, trust, virgin state, protection, family."

Winston toasted me with his fluted glass, ablaze with golden facets. "I don't think Alfred has ever gotten enough credit for what he's done."

"He takes after his father," my mother said wistfully.

Their conversation continued inside the cabana. Winston went on and on about his high-level treks to the White House; the naval maneuvers evidently staged for his personal edification; how he bestrode the Pentagon like a Colossus. I turned to Kate Latham, tanning below me on the sand, and asked her how she enjoyed driving the Duesenberg.

"It was a little scary at first," she said, "especially getting through the gates of the club. You don't drive it—you sort of aim and hope for the best. It's sure a change from my Honda."

"How are you getting along with my mother so far?" I asked.

"She needs someone to talk to." Kate paused. "Actually, I think she needs someone she can teach." She looked up at me quickly, as if she might have said the wrong thing.

"I know what you mean," I said.

"It's a beautiful piece of property, Mr. Meriwether," Kate said. "I didn't know places like that existed. It's a wild place."

A wild place. "My sister says you paint."

"Mostly abstract. Originally I went to the Institute to study fashion design, but then I took painting courses and that was it for me. Now I'm getting a little worried about what the Institute calls my career path."

"You should have a lot to paint this summer."

I thought to myself that it would be nice having Kate Latham around through the summer, doing landscapes and seascapes. It sure beat talking to Winston. I looked at the stunning young woman below me, tanned legs in the sun, and hoped that at some point she might ask me to oil her exquisite back.

"My nephew should be getting here pretty soon," I said to Kate. "He's a poet."

"Mrs. Meriwether told me. I gather Mr. and Mrs. Bingham aren't too thrilled."

"I think they're a little worried about *his* career path," I said.

Kate and my mother left the beach club at around three o'clock. When talk shifted away from her immediate concerns, my mother grew sleepy and once or twice patted her lips with a fist. Her sun hat began to shift over her eyes.

"It's nap time," she said finally. She was on her feet in a twinkling, heading for the stairs, trailed by her solicitous companion. She raised her hand and wiggled her fingers at me in silent good-bye.

Kate Latham eased the green Duesenberg out of its parking space. My mother sat hunched beside her in the silver chrome of sun, against the swirl of the younger woman's blond hair. Home to her dark house, silent memories, and a long nap through the shank of the afternoon. The matriarch.

Winston came out to the dappled porch of the cabana holding one of his graphite tennis racquets. He acted out for my benefit an awkward little ballet, or mime, of tennis stances. He stroked forehands through the air and leaned into powerful backhands. He climbed onto his tippy-toes for his crunching first serve. He scraped the angled boards of the porch roof with each on-point thrust of his racquet. He jogged in place for a few seconds to indicate he was raring to go.

"How's my form?" he asked.

"Okay."

"Governor Rizzoli and that dentist have beaten me for the last time. That's why I went to graphite."

"Maybe bend your knees a bit more," I said.

"I've had lessons. The game's changed a lot since 1948."

I shrugged. "Maybe so."

"I've got a pro in New York, I've got a pro in Arlington, I've got a pro up here. I spend about five grand a year on lessons."

"A suggestion, Winston. Just a suggestion."

"Want to play?" He rolled a topspin backhand in my direction.

"Nope."

"C'mon, a little *rally*. Don't you ever long to hit a few?"

"Not very often."

"Canadian doubles—you and Ackley against me. That little nuclear engineer will run until he drops. All you'll have to do is stand there and I'll drop some grounders at your feet. Where are those competitive juices?"

"You've been asking me to hit a few for twenty years."

"I have a dream. My brother-in-law and I win the senior doubles championship of the Winding Hollow Country Club."

"Fifteen years ago we were going to win the doubles," I said. "Now it's the senior doubles."

The dream didn't seem to amuse him. "You know, it's sure easy for noted retired amateurs like yourself to say, 'Bend your knees,' as if it was the simplest thing in the world. They forget that a basketball court is hard. It's a nightmare world under the boards with jabbing elbows and falling bodies. Thumper lived as a superstar in that world for three years."

"So you have trouble bending your knees?" I asked.

"I didn't say that. I just don't feel comfortable." He tossed up an invisible ball. "What do you say?"

"I'm playing golf with Alice at five-thirty."

"Golf," Winston muttered. "I'm not going to stand out here and beg you every summer."

Winston bounced the "sweet spot" of his racquet off his knee for a few seconds, then stalked back inside the cabana.

My family left the Surf Club to pursue their varied afternoon activities. Dorothy came down the cabana steps in her Lilly dress. She flapped her hand at me from the wrist in a gesture of good-bye. "If you *knew* how I was dying to see Alice," she exclaimed. "There's so much news, I hardly know where to begin."

Captain Ackley looked spiffy in his immaculate tennis whites. Even his Izod socks seemed alert and not droopy. He wore an elastic knee brace over his right knee, but it didn't hamper the general springiness of his movements. He gave a couple of tiptoe jogs in place to get the kinks out. Then he did a nice thing by coming down to the sand to shake hands and say good-bye to me. I suppose it was partly in appreciation for my war effort.

Winston's terry cloth hat resembled a small white animal that had pounced on his head. He pointed his racquet barrels at my red nose. "Drop on over after golf if you want to see the pros go at it." Meaning, presumably, Ackley and himself.

The silver Eldorado left the Surf Club amid a covey of cabana boys. The young men stood at loose attention and Winston told them, in his element, "You're doing a great job," and "thanks a million," and "wonderful, terrific." He tipped each of them from a gold money clip shaped with his initials, WB. The Eldorado took off in an immense thrust and scatter of sand.

The cabana circle was nearly deserted, cool and pleasant amid serrated shadows. I sifted sand and waited for my nephew, Winston Bingham, Jr., to arrive. At the far end of the circle two cabana boys removed furniture from the porches, slid chairs and chaise longues across the wooden slats.

My nephew liked to come over and swim when the beach club and the beach itself were empty. I wanted to say hello to him before I met Alice at the Winding Hollow Country Club.

Win parked his red BMW next to my car. The parking lot and cabana circle were empty. It was five o'clock and a breeze still carried gusts of heat. I sat up in my beach chair, kicked at the sand, and smiled.

Somewhere Winston Bingham, Senior, must have sprung a good gene in the wintry steppes of his recombinant DNA. My nephew had the build of a rugged lacrosse player. He was six-four, blond, and blue-eyed, as far removed from garret paleness as a poet could be. His habit of running long distances at a brisk pace—marathons and mini-marathons—had given him a healthy glow, as had his intense vegetarianism, which included the easy-to-find kelp.

I waved my sombrero and called to him as he got out of the car. Win searched for my voice as if he was afraid to find it underfoot. He tossed me a tight little wave and said, "Hi, Uncle Alfred," over the hood of his car. Barefoot, wearing faded jeans and a blue T-shirt advertising a multi-kilometer run, he tiptoed over the rough tarmac to the stairs. He disappeared from view for a moment, then reappeared at the steps leading down to the cabana circle. "How's the water?" he asked.

"Haven't been in," I answered. The ocean holds limited appeal for me.

He sat down on the boardwalk across from me. The physical similarity between Win and his father was in the large hands.

"Your mother and father were here a couple of hours ago."

"Uh-huh," Win said. His blue eyes kept fixed on a point slightly above my head. "How's Aunt Alice?"

"We're playing golf in about fifteen minutes. Want to come?"

"Nah." He looked away, pressed his arms against his chest. "You coming for supper tonight?" he asked.

"Eight o'clock."

"Terrific. That Ackley guy seems okay. The submarine commander."

"He and your father are in training for the senior doubles."

"I was wondering—how old do you think Ackley is?" he asked.

"Hard to tell," I said. "Late forties, maybe."

"I wondered."

"He's not a senior," I said.

There was real tiredness in Win's eyes. "Jesus, the guy's fit. He looks like he runs."

I said, "Why don't you take a quick swim and come over to the club with me? My game hasn't improved since the last time we played."

"Could you beat my father?" he asked abruptly.

"He doesn't play golf."

"At tennis."

"I doubt it."

"He's not that good," Win said with a shrug. "That's why he's got this Ackley guy. You'd think, to hear him talk, if it wasn't for his neck problems . . . I'm not taking anything away from him."

"He runs every morning. Why don't you two—"

"Yeah, we've tried that together." I noticed the slight tremor in Win's hands. "Uncle Alfred, I've won *races*. I was afraid Dad was going to have a heart attack. And then he began to *limp,* so he was dragging himself along, holding his leg and shaking his fist at me."

Win looked out to the sea for a moment. He sighed, and stood up. His sharp profile was framed against the sloping wood of the cabana porch—a tall young man, but not with intimidating height, unlike his father. His shoulders sloped gently like the cabana roof. It was odd that both Winston and his son, in their different ways, saw themselves as targets.

I held out my hand to him. Sometimes I became planted in my beach chair through a day's relaxation. I dusted sand from my vintage body. Win went inside to change. I policed my area, gathering up my *Daniel Deronda*—"Oh, Gwendolyn," I murmured—my Paba, my sand-wedged glasses case, and then folded my metal beach chair.

Win emerged from the men's dressing room. He wore a red bathing suit and had a Surf Club towel draped over his shoulder. I lugged my stuff up the steps. "Drop over to the house tomorrow," I said. "We could go fishing, play chess, or"—and here I made a Churchillian thrust with my reading glasses toward the white rocks in the distance, beyond the last cabana, a mile and more away, white in the perfect clarity of the late afternoon— "declaim some poetry from those rocks."

I think my blond nephew smiled from the shadows. "I'd like that."

I watched him walk down the boardwalk in the sun, slog over the sunny, grass-tipped dunes. Soon I could see only his blond hair, bobbing against the sheet of ocean. Then he seemed to plummet into a background of whitecaps—a roiling commensurate with his conflicts and tremors.

At a time when Win should have been opening up to life, he was closing himself down in the way a floundering ship seals off its compartments to keep afloat. It was the saddest thing to see.

8

From the deep verandah of the Winding Hollow clubhouse, I observed Winston and Captain Ackley, playing. We were separated by the club's wide front lawn and nine-hole practice green.

There were groans from their court, lots of animation and scurrying back to the service line. The two men were taking the senior's tournament seriously, hitting the stuffing out of the old ball. Especially the one who wasn't a senior.

I was relieved we'd decided to play the back nine. The tenth tee was located on the other side of the tennis courts. The first hole was right beside Winston's court. The proximity would have necessitated banter with him. I was content to let him remain a shape in the late afternoon light, across a green distance.

I set off for the tennis courts and the tenth tee beyond. Trees lined the left-hand side of the tenth fairway. It was not a good hole for a man with a natural hook, impervious to grip-changes and foot-replantings. The problem with my hook lay in the mystery of the backswing and some primal tension induced in the clubhead. I've noticed that most ex-tennis players have the same over-steerage.

I felt an extra spring to my Footjoys when I saw Alice. She stood with her back toward me, wearing a dark blue sports shirt and white golf skirt. She was deep in conversation with her friend, Jessie Robinson, who was all wiry intensity and point-making and crisis situations—honest and great-hearted—electric and gray on the tee in pale yellow shorts and matching blouse. Two close friends in conversation.

I came up to them and slipped my hand around Alice's waist. Jessie said in her husky voice, "I love that shirt, Alfred," referring to my filigreed *guayabera*.

"How are you, Jess? Where's Mal?"

"Working on his long irons," she said, with a nod toward the practice tees.

Mal and Jessie owned a summer house in Meguntic. He walked toward us from the practice tees, which were obsolete polo fields across the club's driveway, concealed by a high hedge-row. He was a balding man of medium height with a barrel chest and an easy smile. When he reached me, he stopped dead and planted his feet. He assumed a golfing stance with a two-iron, and said, "It's not in the hands, Alfred."

"Where is it?"

"It's in the wrists," he muttered. "Out on the practice tee, a voice said, 'Mal, it's in the wrists.'"

On the tenth tee Alice leaned into her drive and socked it about a hundred and fifty yards down the center of the fairway. Jessie hit a short fly to right field. She was the best golfer in our foursome, and would settle down as the course deepened. But she always hit the pop fly on the first hole. Mal sliced—it wasn't in the wrists. I hit my usual skyhook, prayed for the woodsy ricochet, and watched my ball land in the far left rough.

Our carts gave off a soothing electric whirr on the hilly back nine. I approached my putts warily, eyes slits of studiousness. I did my "homework" on other putts, sank a twenty-footer on the fifteenth and found myself making piston-like motions with my right arm, just like the pros do on television. "All right!" I cried, bouncing on my spikes, strutting into the sunset.

I loved golf because there were pockets of time between strokes where it was possible to insert the details of real life. There were always threads to be picked up again, details to sort out and time to say what you meant to say, and say it again, deep in a landscape of green and white.

Mal shuffled along beside me as we approached the sixteenth green—head down, thick neck tucked into his shoulders. He rubbed the bridge of his nose, looking something like an aging middleweight about to break into a trot for his morning road-work.

"I saw your brother-in-law out on the tennis court," Mal said. "Is he back for the summer?"

"He tells me he'll be commuting between here and Washington."

Mal didn't say anything for a moment, as we walked. "How are you feeling these days?" he asked finally, putting his hand lightly on my shoulder.

"Pretty good. I take it one day at a time."

"How long has it been? I forget."

"Not since that incident at the Games Club," I said. "When I fell down the stairs. I guess that was four or five years ago."

"Miss it? The sauce."

"Oh, yeah. Much as I like soft drinks."

Mal squeezed my shoulder. "Never thought you could stop." That was nice—for some reason he thought I needed support. Perhaps it had to do with the presence of Winston. Mal knew that my relationship with my brother-in-law was not the best.

We walked up a slope to the green. I could see the black roof of the clubhouse in the distance, the high mesh fence surrounding the tennis courts. We were on the homeward leg of the course. The clubhouse and the fence were visible through a mist of light.

On the seventeenth, directly facing the clubhouse now, I went to my mental golf manuals. I came up with a grip variation—a bit of an overlap. A rising line drive flew off my Toney Penna driver with a satisfactory hum of power—enough to provoke "ooohs" and "aaahs" from the gallery in my head. But the ball neglected to hook back and sailed onto the adjacent eleventh fairway.

On the eighteenth—a five hundred and seventy-five yard par five—I felt the serene whippiness of my driver, the extension of my left arm. I laced into the ball and sent it humming down the fairway. It gave a kick and rolled to a stop one hundred and seventy-five—oh, say two hundred—yards away. The ball "sat up" ripely on a hillock. I wasn't above going—with a flush of unorthodoxy—to the big driver again.

I charged down the fairway, dimly heard the carts behind me. I pulled out my scorecard, with its drawing of the Point Barren lighthouse on the cover. Barring complete collapse, I'd come in after nine holes at forty-six or forty-seven. On a spring morning in 1952—during the Truman presidency—I broke eighty on the course, despite a double-bogie on the eighteenth hole after my legs turned to jelly on the green. The year 1952 was the last time I saw eighty. In the next decade I kissed off eighty-five. Ninety disappeared like a jackrabbit, even after years of lessons with laconic young men from Texas and Oklahoma. I putted in my office, watched every tournament on television—Pebble Beach, the Tournament of Champions, the Masters, Jackie Gleason's Inverrary Classic, the Hawaiian Open. I had my heroes—Arnie, the Golden Bear, Don January, Gene Littler, Julie Boros. Ken Venturi had a great swing. Tom Weiskopf never realized his potential, as we know.

I hitched up my khakis and stalked up to the ball. I tramped in place for several seconds and let the club face of my two-wood get a long look at the Titleist. I descended into a mental grotto—there was me, there was the red flag in the distance.

My hands lingered behind the swivel of my body as though mired in gravy. I hit an acceptable two-wood, but not a shot up to my expectations. Everything had been in order—my frame of mind, backswing, and downstroke. The clubhead had connected with a marvelous *tick* sound indicating raw power. The ball headed straight for the flagstick, but then sagged. It rolled to a stop a hundred and fifty yards from the green, at a point where the fairway narrowed between two sand traps.

I trudged over to the cream-colored cart and climbed in beside Alice. "Not bad," she said, as we drove up the fairway. It was no consolation. I sank back into the seat. Air exhaled from the cushion.

"Have you seen Win?" Alice asked.

"He was at the club," I said. "He likes to come when no one else is around."

"I'm worried about him, Alfred. He's gotten so withdrawn lately. I know he's always been quiet, but it would be nice to see a smile once in a while."

"I was going to talk to him, but he didn't seem very receptive. Maybe you'll have better luck."

"When I think of that child. Does Winston still go on about him?"

"He was in rare form this afternoon. Kept calling him 'the boy.'

Said he didn't expect his return on investment to be skill at mowing lawns in New Haven."

"Return on investment?" she asked. "What did he mean by that?"

"I guess all that money he spent on Win's education."

"My nephew is not a stock."

"I know, Alice."

"For God's sake, he's only twenty-three years old. Already he's had four poems published in good literary magazines."

"Winston associates poetry with something he thinks women do, like baking. He told me this afternoon he thought his son came from another planet."

"Another planet," Alice muttered.

"He meant it."

Before we reached my ball, there was a wide dip in the fairway where Alice had deposited her long drive from the ladies' tee. As the cart moved into the dip, I had a clear view of Winston and Captain Ackley going at it in the far court beside the first tee. I watched them from my depression in the fairway, while Alice made her club selection and went through her practice swings.

Winston's basic serve-and-volley game counted for its effectiveness on looming intimidations at the net. He had a vicious overhand putaway. Sometimes the yellow Dunlop lodged midway up the mesh backstop behind Captain Ackley. He had good anticipation and a certain grace around the net. He had an excellent first serve—flat, with good speed—but a poor second serve. Half the power in his second serve was generated by his aggressive forward movement—all legs and clump of hat and waving racquet and big knees.

Captain Ackley was a different matter. I could see why Winston had selected the younger man as a doubles partner. Ackley ran down everything Winston fired at him, and was a textbook picture of form. His shots were not powerful, though they gave that impression off the racquet.

To mock my assessment of his power, he hit a stupendous backhand from deep in the backcourt. It was a tribute to the Navy's fitness program that he didn't rip muscles sequentially down his back. He responded to one of Winston's overhand smashes by leaping after it like a terrier after a bouncing ball, all instinct and reflex. He leapt ahead of the high bounce, whipped his upper body around. With both feet off the ground, he sent the ball toward Winston's backhand side. The shot forced Winston down and then down some more, racquet fully extended. The ball lashed by untouched, with enough topspin to send it hurtling into the backstop on one bounce.

"Great shot, great shot," I exclaimed to myself and patty-caked my hands in silent applause, because Alice was about to hit her second shot. My lips twitched and I felt competitive prickles along my bald spot.

Winston wound up like Princess Aurora in *Sleeping Beauty*. Hands and neck bowed to the grass in an elastic supplication of white. The terry cloth hat rested upon his extended left thigh and his right sneaker poked the net. Captain Ackley had fallen onto his trim right side and the racquet had cakewalked away. He rolled over on his back, briefly shaded his eyes, and then seemed to lift himself off the grass by the sheer strength of his thighs. He did a series of stretching exercises and arm windmills, trots in place. He retrieved the racquet and headed briskly for the ad court.

Winston used his racquet as a crutch and the net as a handhold to get into a kneeling position. He located his crushed hat, limped across the half court while massaging his serving arm. He pawed at the service line, creating puffs of chalk. He took a hesitant practice serve, winced, and clutched at his armpit. He said something, Ackley agreed to it by shrugging, and Winston retrieved several balls from the backstop. He indulged himself with a few pitter-pat practice serves into the net and a wild floater into the deuce court. Then he was ready for a lethal ace "for real" right down Ackley's periscope—a flat chalk-kicker. The serve caught the captain glued politely in place.

I told Alice that it looked like Ackley and Bingham were really going at it. We left the dip of fairway and headed for the eighteenth green. Occasionally I peered out over the steering wheel toward the tennis courts, but the two players were obscured by the canvas partitions used for wind protection.

Jessie and Mal and Alice and I parked our carts and putted out on the eighteenth hole. Most of the empty back nine was spread out before us. Alice and Jessie folded their arms against the gathering chill. Looking out over the green world we had passed through, I felt that I had just put on glasses too powerful for my eyes. There was the faint sound of the sea. Soon the shaft of the Point Barren light would dart across the sky.

"This could be the start of a beautiful summer," Mal said, as he and Jessie climbed into their cart. "Maybe it's in the hips." He looked out at the ribbons of fairways.

I turned to Alice. "I'm going over to watch Ackley and Winston for a while. Want to come?"

"No," she said. "You go if you want to."

"Ackley's good," I said. "I almost forgot. Barbecue tonight at the Binghams'."

"Okay," Alice said. "I guess we have to go. It's been eighteen months." The prospect did not thrill either of us.

I kissed Alice, waved good-bye to Jessie and Mal, and watched them drive away toward the clubhouse and the attached golf shop beyond. Sprinklers sizzled across the tennis courts. Mists of water rolled along the greens on the back nine, mottling sand traps, sending waves of spray in my direction across the fairways on the breeze.

I walked across the empty courts toward Winston and Captain Ackley. Their skins glistened, their white shirts were soaked at the shoulders and stomach. Winston's hat sat well back on his head with a deceptive casualness. Before serving, he seemed to present the ball to Ackley and then dipped down and tossed it up. He compensated for the dip by arching his back in jerky motions. Much of his considerable first-serve power was derived by the gathering of his whippy right arm, which rose from the direction of the grass—dragging a reluctant racquet behind it—to crush the ball. It was an effective serve but Winston was too admiring of it. He hung back for an extra second, as if to get a damage estimate. He had the fatal vanity of the hacker.

I took a seat, unnoticed, on a low wooden bench beside the court. Winston went into his first-serve routine—the presentation of the ball, the mighty heave, the herky-jerky spinal dislocation. Just as he was about to bring his racquet up to strike, Captain Ackley said, "Foot fault."

Winston's graphite racquet quivered. He staggered backward

a step and his knees buckled—quite a buckle. The ball bounced off his noggin. This made him mad. He whacked at the stationary ball, took a few lumberman strokes at the grass. Words seemed to blubber in his mouth, suck at the gums, and die away.

For the only time in our lives, Winston Bingham and I achieved a communion of thought, a harmony. We stared at Ackley. You expect this kind of behavior from gunsels at the junior level.

Captain Ackley strode over to the opposite side of the court and took his position. Winston paced in a circle. Ackley trotted in place on the other side of the net.

"Fuck you," Winston declared.

"Winsun," Ackley said. "Your left sneaker—"

Winston gestured with his racquet toward Ackley's nicely arranged face. "How would you like to command a midget submarine?"

"You upset yourself, Winsun. Love–15." I liked the way Ackley honeyed up the word "love." It came across the net riding on blossoms.

"What we're playing out here is not Wimbledon. It's just a friendly game. Can't you get that through your goddamn head?"

Ackley smiled. "Winsun, I feel *compelled* to call these things. That's love–one first set, love–three in this set, and the score in the game is love–15."

"We're not playing for money, Jerry. We're trying to hone our games. That's why I've been running around on my fucking backhand for an hour and a half. I'm not carrying a calculator in my pocket."

"Winsun, this is just to keep track."

"If you want to play for seventy-five thousand dollars a point, hell, let's play for seventy-five thousand dollars a point."

"I'm going to be seizing up here in a minute, if we don't get this game underway," Ackley said.

"We peak during the tournament. We don't peak in spring training. I'm not going to leave my game in the middle of nowhere."

Ackley jogged in place. He wanted to see the ball; he wanted to hit and run. A vein in his temple throbbed.

Winston registered my presence. "Alfred!" I think he saw me as a breather.

"Don't mind me."

"Just fooling around, old buddy. Let me polish off young Jerry here, and I'll be right along."

"Take your time. Looks like a good match."

"Mr. Meriwether," Ackley said, with a curt nod. I think he was annoyed by the added interruption.

"We ready to play, we ready to do it to it?" Winston asked. He presented the yellow ball to Captain Ackley. Over his shoulder he announced, "Alfred, you be the umpire. We've had a lot of questionable calls today, so don't hesitate to sing out. This set belongs to me."

My brother-in-law raised his game to its topmost level. Any resemblance to spring training or a rally in the sun vanished. Winston was delighted. After harsh volleys he would strut back from the net. "How'm I doing?" I would nod to indicate he was doing well. "See the way I'm bending my knees? I'm big enough to heed good advice. Did that rolled backhand remind you of Don Budge? Did Pancho have a faster serve?" He whispered, "That son of a bitch will run all day. You have to admire him."

In the fifth game I murmured my allegiance. "Lob, for Christ's sake."

"Thumper doesn't lob," Winston panted. "Wasn't that last shot in?"

I shook my head.

"Whose side are you on?"

"I call them as I see them."

"I couldn't beat this guy with a bazooka."

"Come in on your first serve."

"Tell me about it. I'd like to see your heroes after they've had a whiff of graphite."

The more the match heated up, the more Ackley smiled. It was not a smile of certain victory or of any particular warmth—it was a nervous habit of the mouth. He tossed the ball up smiling at it, hit backhands and forehands with a smile. From a distance, from the verandah of the club, say, it would have looked as if Ackley was having a wonderful time out there.

Several times during the remainder of the match, Winston

pranced by me and promised, "I got him now." Hope sprang eternal, but he lacked the shots. He didn't have a lob or a second serve, and no one would mention his forehand in dispatches. But he'd play you with what he had.

In the ninth game of the third set, Ackley went down. The score was five to three in his favor. Winston had staged a gritty mini-comeback, but the match was on Ackley's racquet. At 30–love, after Winston had netted two returns, Ackley's smile vanished. Perhaps this was a sign that things were going well. I guess he wanted to go out in a blaze of speed and hit a couple of crusher volleys. At the net he leapt for Winston's floating passing shot, his right sneaker rolled on its edge, his ankle followed and for an instant his leg strained outward. There was a faint popping sound at the kneecap. Ackley fell onto the grass, shoulder first.

"Whoa!" Winston yelled.

Ackley did not utter a sound. He wore the benign grass marks of his previous fall on his shoulder. His nose was buried in the grass, his body raised a little at the buttocks, as if he was snuggling into pillows for an extra minute's snooze. His legs sawed at the grass, twitching in that first clarity of seriousness when time expands.

As I came up to him, Ackley tried to get away. Both hands gripped his right knee, and he kept trying to push off with his left sneaker. His shoulder dug into the grass. He breathed in stuffy gasps through his nose, sniffing the dangerous air. "I'm all right," he murmured. "I'm all right."

Winston crossed the net. Ackley's left sneaker continued digging into the grass. With a sigh he rolled over onto his back and held up the damaged right leg. It was probably the illusion given off by someone else's pain, but it did seem as if the ill-fated limb had swollen to twice its normal size.

Ackley lowered his right leg onto the grass and rolled down the elastic pharmaceutical knee brace. His knee looked surprisingly healthy and tanned. Ackley smiled and rubbed it. He seemed to find the injury acceptable, familiar even. He shook his head. "Sorry, Winsun."

"Hell," Winston said.

"Let me give you a hand," I said.

"I think I've got it now, sir." Ackley looked up at me with liquid blue-gray eyes—the way he once must have looked up at a stern father. He used the net as a crutch to stand up, then hobbled around the near court. Occasionally he reached down and rubbed the knee. The backs of his white shirt and shorts were grass-stained. His close-cropped hair was matted on one side where he had nestled into the turf.

Winston folded his arms and watched his partner's knee. Ackley tried to put a little weight on it, and his smile nearly broadened into a scream.

Winston said, "Ah, shit."

I escorted Ackley to the bench beside the court. He hopped a bit to get comfortable before sitting down. "I've got two choices. Have an operation or get one of those hospital knee braces. That's if Winston and I are going to continue to play tennis going at it the way we do."

"I don't want you to move," Winston declared. He used his large hands the way a third base coach makes a "slide" sign, the way a politician reluctantly silences overwhelming applause. "You gather your forces, you take it one step at a time. Take my neck, Jerry. I came back too fast. The coaches pushed me. They said, 'We can't win the N-Rack Conference without you, Thumper.' Now I've got a neck like Howdy Doody's."

"I'm all right," Ackley said. "'Course, I may need a cane for a couple of weeks."

"There's no sense rushing things. Are we in a hurry, Alfred?"

"Of course not."

"Supper doesn't start until the king arrives. Right now the king is standing watch over his fallen friend."

Ackley began to flex his leg. "Feels better."

"Don't put any weight on it," Winston said. "I advise against it, Jerry. We've got all the time in the world."

Winston looked over at his canvas bag beside the bench, choked with graphite racquet handles.

He looked over at me and smiled.

"There's still plenty of vigor left in this old afternoon," he said. "Right, Alfred?"

I don't know what made me agree to play him. I played only a few times a year. Perhaps I agreed because this was the first time I'd seen Winston's game up close. I'd imagined him as being good. Of course, it was always different once you got out there on the court.

"How about it?" he asked. "Come on. One set. What the hell, Alfred. I need the work."

Something in his smile, some challenging quality, annoyed me. I wanted to wipe that smile off his face.

"I won't run you around too much," Winston said jovially. "I'll go easy."

I stood up. "Let's see who runs who around."

"Ooh, tough guy," Winston said, taking a quick step backward as though I'd alarmed him.

"One set," I said.

Ackley loaned me his sneakers. He seemed to forget his own pain and shifted on the bench eagerly. If his sneakers had not fit, Winston would have gone over to the pro shop and bought me a pair that did. He wanted to play me. Perhaps something about my early tennis career had gotten puffed up in his mind. Generally, he regarded me with contempt.

While lacing up Ackley's sneakers, the air went out of my competitiveness. I knew that it was going to be awful. He would work me over and I would lunge and waddle. Worse, I would never hear the end of it.

Winston made a big deal out of the racquet selection. He proffered me his duffel bag as if it contained dueling pistols of the most exquisite craftsmanship. I saw no reason to give him his moment. I just picked a racquet and headed out to the court.

We began to rally. There was an indescribable thrill in not embarrassing myself. After about five minutes, it dawned on me that Winston wasn't going to be a problem.

I moved in slow motion and had to think through every shot. I had to plan where to arrange Winston. I was forced to cut down the court on him in order to minimize my own exertions. It was more like a chess game than a tennis match.

He began in triumph—strutting around, playing up to the wounded Ackley, saying, "Watch this, Jerry," making rhumba movements at the baseline, trying a few blooper lobs.

"I can't see one fucking thing out here," he said after I took the first three games. It reminded me of the line about the athlete who never beat a well man.

In the fourth game I started to loosen up and enjoy myself. It would be too much to say that I toyed with Winston, but the effect on him was the same. I got into the net and forced him into a series of erratic crosscourt backhands.

"Goddamn," he yelled, after hitting his second straight line drive into the backstop.

At 40–love and again at 40–15, he swung out with the full power of his modest backhand, aiming at my throat. My returns bounced back to him in puffy yellow cotton balls and died at his sneakers.

He approached the net, motioning to me with his racquet. "Look, Alfred," he said with a controlled homicidal rage that mottled his face. "Let's play the game the way it's laid out."

I bounced around on Ackley's sneakers. I felt terrific, but didn't want to get too close to his menacing racquet. He was extremely upset.

I shrugged and said quietly, "Winston, I'll play it any way you want to play it."

"No more pussy shots," he snapped.

He turned on his heel and stalked away. At that moment I felt no sympathy for him. In 1948 I played Pancho Gonzales and he beat me as badly as you can beat an opponent, but I didn't stomp around and ask him to go easy on his second serve or beg him to give me a chance around the net. I didn't think that what Winston did was right.

In the fifth game, I felt comfortable enough to air out a couple of forehands. I hit three forehands in a row down the line, playing the game the way it was laid out. Those shots took something out of Winston; they hurt him. His lips trembled and I thought he was going to cry at the service line.

On the fourth point of the fifth game, I wrong-footed him on a crosscourt backhand of my own—the best shot that I hit in the set. Winston swatted at the ball like a deranged lepidopterist and sagged into the net. I looked at my racquet in amazement.

He had misjudged me—I wanted him to know that. I had not

spent a thousand afternoons on tennis courts like this one to be beaten by a man who refused to lob and had no second serve.

Winston leaned against the net for a long time. His terry cloth hat was askew; it had slid down over his ear, making him look rakish.

Well, that was enough for me. I gave him the sixth game on my serve. I should have known that such leniency would only revive his hopes. He began to swagger again. He looked over at Ackley a couple of times to indicate that maybe he had at last got my number.

I didn't want the set to slip away from me. I thought that maybe the magic wouldn't last. There was still plenty of dusk left in which Winston could run me around. I decided it was better to win than to face the prospect of his gloating. I'd always had this firm belief that magic accounted for my tennis ability. The gods gave and the gods took away. I think that this neurotic conviction was one reason why I quit playing in tournaments before I was twenty-five.

In the seventh game, I mustered all my concentration and went to work on Winston's forehand. I was tiring, my shoulder hurt, and I didn't want to wait around for an eighth game. I had adjusted to his first serve pretty well. It had speed but no variety, so I knew where to encamp for my return.

At love–40—on the final point of the set—I indulged myself with an irresistible towering sunset lob from the deep backcourt. Winston, who had been poised at the net, went back and back and circled under the ball like a parched man with heat exhaustion. When the ball did bounce finally, Winston struck at it with a quizzical stroke and hit a forlorn blooper into the net.

The match was over. Winston was breathing through his mouth only, like a tired fighter. I had wanted to beat him; I hadn't intended to humiliate him. Guilt set in immediately. While we were milling around the bench, I admired his first serve, replayed for his benefit a few of his better volleys. I mentioned how often I'd seen this same goddamn thing in golf. You get a guy who hasn't picked up a club in years and he goes out and burns up the course, but the next day shoots a hundred and forty and couldn't find the pin with a seeing-eye dog.

"Why don't you shut up?" Winston said. In truth, I *was* getting a bit smarmy. "How's that knee, Jerry?"

Ackley had been taking little practice walks around the bench. "Mostly numb, Winsun."

"We got a big day tomorrow."

"I know that. First thing when I get back to the base tonight, I'll see what the doc can do to strap me up."

"There are all kinds of painkillers. No sense biting the bullet."

"Mr. Meriwether, you must have been good," Ackley said, as I handed him back his sneakers.

"Thank you." I glowed.

It was nearly dark when we crossed the lawn to the parking lot. My aches were just setting in, but I still felt exhilarated. The golf course had a mysterious softness; deer had been spotted in some twilights.

We kept to Ackley's slow pace. Winston carried the duffel bag and brooded. I still held in my blistered hand the graphite tennis racquet. I didn't want to let it go, such a splendid example of advanced workmanship. I couldn't stop twirling and examining it, taking zippy little strokes with it. If I'd had this in 1947, I kept thinking. . . .

Winston sidled closer to me as we padded across the dewy lawn before the club. He put his arm around my shoulders and I really felt the weight. "This just goes to show my swelled head. I've been looking forward to playing you for twenty years. So what happens? You kick my ass. A man can't hang around this club very long before some old fart starts blabbing away about Ellsworth Vines and Big Bill Tilden or the old club championship you won in nineteen forty whatever." My shoulder bounced against his rib cage as we trundled. "I'm a very competitive guy, Alfred. Sometimes my competitiveness blows up in my face. The fact is, you beat me and I congratulate you."

"Thank you, Winston. I played well."

"I'm sorry I didn't shake hands with you after your great victory."

"That's all right. I've felt the same way."

"I remember when the Golden Eagles lost to the Salamanca Spartans in '54. Everybody was shaking hands and patting each other on the back. It was the last game for a lot of seniors. Some of the guys were in tears. But I kept shouting, 'We'll get you next year, you bastards. We'll get you next year.' And all our guys were telling me, 'Cool it, big fella. Stay loose, Daddy Eagle.' They used to call me Daddy Eagle—after all, I *was* that fucking conference for three years."

"Sure."

"I shook hands with Governor Rizzoli and that dentist two years ago. You'd think I'd be able to shake hands with my own brother-in-law."

"Yeah, you would."

Later that evening Winston looked down the length of the supper table. "I don't know what you've been feeding him, Alice. You must have put something in his Wheaties this morning."

"What was the score?" asked my nephew. It was one of the few times he raised his head that evening.

Winston leaned on the rough-hewn cookout table and pointed his finger at me. "Your uncle beat me six games to one."

"Wow."

"Don't annoy me," Winston told his son. He was into his third martini, which did not bode well for dinner.

"The important thing is now you're home," said my sister Dorothy.

"I'm home," Winston agreed. "What is this crap?"

"Billi Bi soup."

"What are all those black things?"

"Mussels, baby."

"Great," Winston said without enthusiasm.

"Did you have a nice day?" Dorothy asked, less to Winston than to the whole table—Alice and me and Win and also Winston. I thought of Captain Ackley driving back to Groton, using his left foot on the brake.

"It sounds like they played a lot of tennis, Mom," my nephew said, coming to her aid. She was out of it. He never looked at his mother—he heard her in the candlelight.

Dorothy patted my hand. "Every Saturday and Sunday Daddy and Mummy and I would take the Duesenberg over to the country club to watch you play. At least it *seemed* like every Saturday and Sunday. I hope that women's liberation won't force women to play games they're not good at."

"Not bad," Winston said of the soup.

Dorothy refilled her glass from a bottle of white wine that she kept on the ground beside her chair. She did not touch her soup —mussels squeezed out of the ruffled congealment. She leaned back in her chair, sighed. "I was almost raped by a dog today."

"Jesus, Mom." Young Win fingered the glinting flatware.

Winston looked down the table. "How do you mean—raped?"

My sister looked around—at every movement arrested—and her cheeks reddened. "Maybe that isn't the word, but I don't know how else you'd describe it. It was that yellow Lab of Evan Tyler's. He tried to climb up my back. I've told Evan to keep it chained, but then he takes it down to swim in the river, and the first thing it does is trot right up here, covered with muck and slime. It should be banned from this property. I've told Evan it ought to be neutered. The dog has a congenital hip displacement, and should have been put to sleep a long time ago. They keep that poor dumb animal in pain. I said to Evan, 'The least you can do is make sure it doesn't breed and cause more suffering.' Guess what its name is?"

There was a silence.

"Ergo." She took a delicate sip of wine. "What kind of name is that for a dog? Such a macho dog."

"Macho?" Winston asked.

Dorothy's left hand reached down for the half-full bottle. "I don't know of any other word to describe Ergo."

Winston stood up. He looked distracted, as if something was out of place in a pattern that he enjoyed. "Is all in preparation?"

"Of course it is, precious."

Winston moved over to the stove and peered down at the coals. On a table beside the stove were the various implements of his cookout. They had been laid out from left to right with a step-by-step precision worthy of intricate surgery, starting with his apron and a puffy French chef's hat.

Winston put on the chef's hat and gave it a jaunty tilt. He hoisted a couple of tongs and arched a spatula. He lifted a dripping steak. "Let's hear from the well-done people first."

Moments later there were the sounds of sizzle, the smells of fry brought to us on a tolerable haze of smoke. While Winston cooked, I listened to Alice and Dorothy. The only thing they had in common was an interest in antiques—small shops and attics and bargains up and down Rhode Island and Connecticut. It was a world of Econoline vans and deals closed in overstuffed rooms. Dorothy and Alice had enough Shaker furniture to start a community.

The conversation and the note-comparings rolled along as Winston commandeered the meal from his wheelhouse at the stove. Alice filled Dorothy in on some new finds in nearby Meguntic, as they related to an ongoing search for a highboy.

As they talked, I nursed aches and pains with little flexes and light rubbings. There was a raw gouge in my palm and the pillow of my thumb lacked feeling. My eyes were rheumy from peering into the dusk at Winston's thrashing service motion.

While Winston stood at the stove, my nephew recited to me softly:

"Taking its time
   through each of the seven vertebrae of light
   the sun comes down. It is nineteen forty-nine.
   You stand in the doorway drying your hands.
   It is still summer, still raining.
   The evening is everywhere gold: windows, grass,
   the sun side of the trees. As if to speak
   to someone you look back into the dark
   of the house, call my name, go in. I know
   I am dreaming again. Still, it is raining
   and the sun shining . . . You come back out
   into the doorway, shading your eyes. It looks
   as if the whole sky is going down on one wing.
   By now I have my hands above my eyes, listening."

Winston stood over the table, clutching a spatula. "You write that?"

"Not me," Win said and his hands flew to his chest. "Another poet—Stanley Plumly."

"That's great stuff." Winston tapped the spatula against his palm. "'It looks as if the whole sky is going down on one wing.' That's the way I felt this evening, playing Uncle Alfred here."

I said, "That first serve of yours—"

"Yeah?" Winston asked, ignoring me. "How's your Shakespeare?"

"Okay." Win looked down at his plate.

"Remember this?" Winston tapped the spatula on the rough wood for attention, and all the glasses tinkled.

> "What infinite heart's ease
> Must kings neglect that private men enjoy!
> And what have kings, that privates have not too,
> Save ceremony, save general ceremony?
> And what art thou, thou idol Ceremony?
> What kind of God art thou, that suffer'st more
> Of mortal griefs than do thy worshippers?
> What are thy rents? what are thy comings-in?
> O Ceremony, show me but thy worth."

"Why, lamb," Dorothy said.

Win had the answer at "kings neglect." He could barely conceal his delight. *Henry the Fifth,*" he snapped.

"You got it," his father said. "I have all the tapes. I have Olivier. I have Sir John Gielgud. I fill my bathroom in the morning with mellifluous voices. Same with my limo."

There was an extra burst of sizzle behind him. Winston brandished the spatula. He hurried back into the night and stood framed against the blue haze of the distant shoreline.

I have no explanation for what happened next. Perhaps Winston's tennis loss had been barbecuing in his mind for some time. I kept waiting for my steak, which I had ordered rare. I waited for an uncomfortably long time. Suddenly I heard a crash sound in front of me. Embers sprayed across the lawn near the kicked over stove.

Winston approached me. His whole face seemed to be twitching from eyebrows to chin. He held up my smoking steak, which made hissing noises. The steak was burnt to a crisp and curled back onto the tines of the large serving fork. He loomed spectrally over the table and the steak fumed. "Sorry, champ. Got a little overcooked."

Alice put a hand to her forehead. Dorothy reached for her bottle of wine. "Such a nice butcher," she sighed. From the corner of my eye, I could see my nephew's hands suffering leaps and tremors in the candlelight, like amber wings. I decided that discretion would be the better part of valor.

"Maybe we can give the steak to Ergo," I said. "Next time he comes around."

The meat smoked on the plate. Staggering a little, Winston walked across the lawn toward his house. He returned a few moments later holding a bottle of red wine. "A '52 Petrus."

Winston sat down at the head of the table. He beamed. I looked at the bottle he had placed in front of me. The label certainly went back in time.

"Three hundred dollars," Winston said.

"I wish I could," I said.

"Can we change the subject?" Alice asked. She glared at Winston.

Winston had that look of menacing friendliness mean drunks sometimes get. "Thought you'd want to celebrate your victory." He slurred his words. "Special occasion." He was leaning back in his chair.

I sensed that the moment was very dangerous. "That's a beautiful wine. I wish I could."

Winston lunged across the table at me, grabbing onto the lapels of my blazer and pulling me up out of my chair. Everything clattered—silverware, glasses, plates. "You don't like my hospitality?" he shouted. A glass broke. He was tremendously strong. The lapels were right around my ears.

"Take your hands off me." I smelled the liquor on his breath, saw his frizzy hair and red eyes. I knew that if he released one of his hands from my lapel, I'd have to take a swing at him.

Win grabbed at his father's hands, prying them off me. He looked scared. "Come on, Dad. Whoa. Calm down."

Winston seemed to be in some kind of shock. He was sprawled across the table and Win lifted him off the table and back into his chair, the way you might gently lift a man who has suffered a seizure. Winston sat in his chair, gasping.

"Let's go," I told Alice, adjusting my blazer. My hands were trembling. "Goddamn it," I said in a high voice.

Dorothy took that moment to pounce. "How could Alfred beat you?" she asked, speaking from her own time zone. "He practically doesn't play anymore."

Alice and I got out of there in a hurry. We moved off into the darkness toward our house. Behind us the grass glowed.

I heard Winston say, very distinctly and soberly, "There are reasons why husbands kill wives."

9

I did not see Winston again for nearly a month. Presumably, he was occupied by naval matters. Then he woke me up at seven o'clock one Sunday morning. At first I thought it was a burglar or a raccoon, or Evan Tyler's excitable yellow Labrador, Ergo. But it was Winston Bingham throwing pebbles at my bedroom window, then scratching on the glass.

"Don't shoot," I heard him call. "It's Thumper."

Alice stirred and groaned. Her right hand landed gently on my side of the bed.

"Come out, come out, wherever you are," Winston crooned from the great outdoors.

The only thing handy to my nakedness was a red velour siren suit that I sometimes wore for casual padding around my house in the evening. I noted the time—7:02—on my digital clock-radio.

"Where are you, Alfred?" Winston asked from the region of my back door. He was circling the house.

I shook a leg through my Shaker living room, turning on every light I could find, illuminating rusticity in isolated glows of spare wood.

Insects whirled around the light over the back door. "Winston?"

"Alfred." He stood beside my heavy-duty garbage cans. "Did I wake you up?"

This struck me as an amazing question. "Yes, you did."

"Sorry."

He wore a blue Windbreaker with a Navy insignia, a blue sports shirt and new-looking pressed blue jeans, as well as white Ked basketball sneakers. He had his hands in his pockets and a broad grin on his face. Tucked under his arm he carried two rolls of paper resembling blueprints. He was clean-shaven and his curly gray-black hair had been given extra fluffing.

"I thought we might drive into Wolcott this morning," he said. "There's something I want to show you."

"Can't it wait?"

He tapped the blueprints. "I just got these last night. I have to share it with someone."

"Share what?"

"You'll see."

"How about sharing it with Dorothy?"

"She's out like the proverbial light. Anyway, I thought of you first. I'm really sorry about that little incident at dinner. I don't know what came over me, must have been drunk. I'm prepared to get down on my knees and beg forgiveness right here beside your garbage cans."

"Don't do that," I said. He was capable.

"Come on, Alfred. I'd like you to come with me. One, two hours of your time. I've got a ten o'clock appointment in Groton, so this is the only time we can get together. I guarantee this will interest you."

"What you did at the cookout was pretty bad," I said.

He shrugged. "I'm the world's biggest asshole. Let's face it."

The rolled papers under his arm had piqued my curiosity a sliver. I rubbed my eyes and thought for a few moments. "What do I have to do?"

"Nothing." He smiled. "I'll get the station wagon and see you back here in fifteen minutes. You'll probably want to change out of that cute bunny suit."

"Want coffee?"

"No, you go ahead. There's a sense of adventure in the air. Do you feel it, too?"

"No," I said.

"It reminds me of the early days of our friendship." What friendship? I wondered. "Back when we were pulling together at the firm." Winston scuffed Hucklike at the pavement. "I really enjoyed those days. It was a more innocent time."

I heard the throb of innocence in his voice, and stepped back inside my kitchen. In the bedroom I sat down on Alice's side of the bed. Though still half asleep, she slipped her arm around my neck.

"Alice," I whispered.

"What's happening?" she asked in a clogged voice. Alice was not a morning person.

"Winston and I are taking a little trip into Wolcott."

It had sunk in, finally. The prospect of him. "Oh, no," I said. Heavy and blue, I rolled over onto my side of the bed, tucking in my shoulder. "What have I done?" I cursed my stupidity.

"Why a trip?" Alice asked groggily.

"It's Winston's surprise. Something he wants to show me. We'll be back in a couple of hours."

"Ciao." She grabbed a flower-pattern pillow from behind her head, hugged it to her body, and pitched away from me. She settled into the softness in a no-nonsense way. I turned on a lonely lamp. Everything felt like a night in the Army.

After showering and shaving, I dressed in a less snazzy approximation of Winston's attire. No insignia on my yellow Windbreaker or creamy-clean look to my sneakers. I heard a car pull into my driveway.

"Hey, Alfred," Winston called.

I kissed Alice, left my house, and got into the station wagon beside Winston. "Here we are," he said and patted my knee.

I felt enclosed. His cologne was very sweet; his Windbreaker rustled. "Sorry to get you up so early, but I've got this goddamn meeting in Groton. We're having all kinds of problems with Ackley's submarine, the *Avenger*. She's why I'm up here and not down in Washington. Just to keep everyone honest. Christ. It's Sunday morning—they want to have a meeting."

"How do you mean—keep everyone honest?" I asked, settling into the seat. Honesty was not my brother-in-law's strong suit.

"If it isn't the joystick, it's the pipes. If it isn't the pipes, it's the precision depth recorder, the antennae, the satellite navigation receivers, the shower stalls, outlets for the hair dryers. It's mostly bullshit stuff for the electronics people to fool around with, but there's still lots of deadline pressure. So I come up, put in an appearance, walk around the poop deck, and then go home."

Winston shrugged. "They've got all these mathematical equations, and I tell them, 'Boys, I just sign the requisition forms. You build the boats. I'm here for the salt air.' I love it when they start explaining things to me as if I'm a moron. As if Winston Bingham hasn't been involved with the nuclear capability of the United States for fifteen years."

"Do you ever have any major problems?" I asked.

"Nah." Winston smiled. "The usual stuff you associate with a nuclear submarine that has enough firepower to destroy every Soviet city with a population of over 135,000."

He lowered my electric window from the master control at his side, then raised it again. The station wagon left our property and eased onto Route 3, heading toward Wolcott.

"You ever get tired, Winston?" I asked. I was suddenly tired.

His left sneaker was tapping to a private rhythm. "Sometimes I droop a bit after lunch if I've gone heavy on the starches like potatoes and dumplings. Then I'll put my head on my desk for fifteen, twenty minutes. As one of the perks of office, they offered to move in a couch. But I had them leave it in the Secretary of the Navy's office with my compliments. He's got nothing to do, anyway. Don't get me wrong—I like Ray, but he's a bantamweight."

We sat in silence for a few minutes. I looked out at shuttered roadside vegetable stands, the rough curves of stone walls. The car dipped down toward a deserted traffic circle.

"I've never ordered soup in a restaurant, and generally I don't like having soup at home," Winston mused. He massaged his troublesome neck with a pincer movement of the thumb and fingers of his right hand. "I always suspected that the cooks took turns pissing in it. That was the rumor at the Sisters of Mercy in Buffalo—round-robin pissing contests and then four hundred pounds of saltpeter dropped into the giant soup tureens to prevent the constant buggery."

He wiggled farther down into the driver's seat, glanced at me briefly—Windbreaker crinkling, aglow with companionship. "Alfred, want to know Thumper's First Law?"

"Sure," I said.

"A big fish in a small pond is better off than a medium-sized fish in a big pond."

He laughed.

"Does Thumper's First Law have a practical application?" I asked.

"Naturally—I even have a timetable," he said. "A lot depends on the incumbent President of the United States. His spineless attitude toward every major issue facing this country could work in my favor."

I considered for a moment and asked, "So you think you could make a political career?"

"The top media people tell me I come on too strong. They want to know what I'll do when a little tyke pulls at my pants leg and asks, 'How's the weather up there?' Will it be the first media strangulation? They push restraint like it was a new breakfast cereal." He sounded disgusted. "But my credits far outweigh my debits. I'm of the people. Blacks play basketball. I'm a lawyer, a family man, a success, and so forth. Of course, my greatest strength almost goes without saying."

"What's that?" I asked.

I guess the answer should have been obvious to someone who knew more about politics.

"I've been to the nuclear arsenal and I know what's what."

He nuggied my Windbreaker.

"Maybe that should be your campaign slogan," I said.

He nodded. "Who knows? Politics is a strange business. Look at Jimmy Carter. A man who came from nowhere. But then look at John Connally. In the 1980 primary campaign he spent eleven million dollars and picked up one delegate, who later defected to George Bush. I only use the Connally example because he was once Secretary of the Navy."

"And Governor of Texas, as I recall."

"Senator, governor—I'm not particular. The important thing is that a politician has to put down deep roots in a state. Like Rhode Island, for example."

"Is that the way it works?"

"I'm counting on it," he said.

The sky was clear as we entered Wolcott. Mists lingered in the dips of the road. My thoughts turned petulant. I longed to be home in my warm bed and in the arms of my wife.

What am I doing here? I asked myself.

I need a drink, I grumbled.

Something with orange juice, I ordered.

A mimosa! I exclaimed.

Just the thing! I cried.

Scrumptious, I sighed.

The gigi bubbles tickled my nose. I extended my tongue into the expensive fizz and the gay caress feathered the lobes behind my eyebrows.

We drove down deserted Main Street. Winston turned left at the Georgian solidity of the Wolcott Post Office, and pulled to a stop at the seawall. The whole curve of the beach was before us then—the public beaches, the gold cupola atop the Surf Club roof, the white rocks in the distance at the tip of our property. The ocean was a sheet of light.

"Don't go to sleep on me," Winston said. "Here's what I want to show you."

Grumpily, I shifted position and rubbed my eyes. Winston picked up a blueprint from beside him on the seat. He unrolled it and spread it out. Without a word he shoved the blueprint onto my lap, then rested his head against my shoulder.

"What is it?" I asked.

"You're looking at the new Wolcott, Rhode Island. As a matter of fact, we just might call it New Wolcott."

I looked at him and then back down at the undemonstrative blueprint. I popped the question softly. "Where's Main Street?"

For all the delight illuminating Winston's face—really like an instant face-lift—you might have thought this nation had just elected him President by acclamation. "There *is* no Main Street."

I repeated, "There is no Main Street," staring once again at the incomprehensible blueprint. My forefinger traced along row after row of little squares. They took up half the paper. "What are these things?"

"Condominiums."

"What's this?"

"That's the Atlantic Ocean," Winston said. "The condominiums face the ocean. We envision a barn-wood design, rustic and weather-beaten. A nice balcony, sliding glass doors, one or two bedrooms, central air conditioning, a total electric-living concept. There'll be a supermarket, drug store, gift shoppeys, recreation center, tennis courts, free parking."

I couldn't tear my eyes away from the blueprint. "How much will these condominiums sell for?"

"Two hundred and fifty to three hundred thousand dollars."

"What happens to Main Street?" I asked.

"We're going to raze it. We're going to bring in bulldozers and a battalion of cranes wielding spiked wrecking balls. We can do the job in ten days—level the town and gut it. Six weeks after that—after they've hauled the shit away—we can bring in the construction people."

"Is we a rhetorical we?"

"We is"—and he sounded a bit like The Kingfish on "Amos 'n' Andy"—"Mr. Charles Garozzo of Meguntic, Rhode Island, and myself. Mr. Garozzo's construction firm is responsible for this blueprint. He's a very close and very dear friend of mine."

"How much does Mr. Garozzo—"

"Charlie Tuna," Winston said.

"Charlie Tuna?"

I gave a little bounce in my seat.

"Now don't get upset. That's his nickname." Winston anticipated my question. "It derives from his chunky build. He's on the heavy side."

I studied the blueprint, angled it this way and that, imprinted the new town over the old one. I tried to remain calm. "You don't think these condominiums are a little overpriced at three hundred thousand?"

"Charlie Tuna and I have big plans for the northern section of the town. Right there along Ocean Drive, next to this seawall."

"What sort of plans?" I asked.

"Something along the lines of Atlantic City, New Jersey."

"What do you mean?"

Winston shrugged. "Yeah, like what they did in Atlantic City."

"Gambling casinos?"

"You got it, Alfred."

I was stunned. Winston went into a detailed explanation of the enormous difficulties that would be involved with passing gambling legislation in Rhode Island—the people who had to be "got to" and convinced that legalized gambling was in their financial interest. He assured me that he didn't envision anything as tacky as Las Vegas.

"What gave you this idea?" I asked.

"From the moment I first saw Wolcott, Rhode Island in 1962 I thought it was an eyesore. It still is. Some of Alfred Meriwether's favorite watering holes are lit up like Caesar's Palace. Roving bands of surfers tie up traffic day and night. Sheriff Jim Sprague informs me there are drug parties on the beach. He tells me he's come upon young couples having unnatural sex in the dunes near the Surf Club."

"What's his idea of unnatural sex?" I asked.

"I'm not defending Jim Sprague's prurient interests. As far as I'm concerned, those kids can go fuck a duck just like I did in Buffalo."

"You fucked a duck?"

"Listen," Winston said. "There was enough sexual activity, natural and unnatural, at the Sisters of Mercy to keep me aroused for life. I didn't need a duck."

I traced my finger through the rows of condominiums. "So what's the next step?"

"At the moment there is no next step. New Wolcott is just an idea in someone's head. Charlie Tuna and I enjoy thrashing it out, adding extra stores, another row of condominiums."

"I see."

I felt deeply relieved that there was no next step.

"I've been calling people since last year," Winston continued. "You'd be surprised at the feedback I get, especially among the Old Guard. 'What happened to the pretty little resort town of our youth?' they ask. 'What happened to the pretty little town that once rivaled Newport?' And I tell them, 'Mrs. Winterbottom, Mr. Knapsack, there's another way.' And then I describe Charlie Tuna's planned community, the substantial burghers who would be attracted to it, the elimination of drug addiction, pornography, and loitering."

"Do you mention gambling casinos?" I asked.

"It would only confuse the issue at this time."

"How does the Old Guard respond to your pitch?"

"In many ways the rich see themselves as powerless, threatened by forces beyond their control. I take pains—even though all this is limited to casual telephone conversations—to explain

they are *not* powerless. It isn't necessary for them to hide behind
the wrought-iron gates of their elegant mansions, making a dash
once a day for the Surf Club or the Winding Hollow Country
Club. There's another way, I tell them."

"What's that?"

"Activism," Winston said. "Wolcott has a town council, a Zon-
ing Board. Some members of the Old Guard think you can com-
promise with sleaze. I tell them, 'Mrs. Winterbottom, Mr. Knapsack, sleaze is like a cancer. Every cell must be extirpated. You
can't eliminate Vinny's Grocery and still keep Abdul's Cards and
Gifts. You can't keep Jan and Dean's Surf City and eliminate
Bobby Twinkle's Roller Skateland.'"

"What do you get out of all this?" I asked.

"A staggering amount of money." Winston smiled. "Do you
begrudge me it?"

"No, of course not."

"I wonder," he said. "Maybe if you'd had to walk a mile in my
moccasins . . ."

"Winston, I don't want to rehash your early career."

"Of course you don't." He leaned forward in his seat, peered
over my shoulder at the blueprint. "So?" he asked.

"So."

"Well?"

"Well what?"

"What do you think of New Wolcott?"

"I hate it."

"What do you mean, you hate it?"

"I hate it."

His mouth stayed half open for a long moment. He glared
down at the blueprint. "I thought you'd love it. Why the hell do
you think I showed it to you? I thought of all the people in the
world, you'd love it the most."

"You can't come in with bulldozers and spiked wrecking balls
and uproot people. I'm not going to lecture you. As for gambling
casinos—"

"You haven't even heard the figures. Do you have any idea
what we plan to pay these people to leave?"

"I'm sure it's very substantial."

"Substantial is not the fucking word," he snapped.

"The drug charges and accusations about unnatural sex, pornography, and—what's the other one?—loitering—are wild and unsubstantiated. I would also remind you that my mother and I hold seats on the same town council through which you seek to implement your dastardly plans." I felt connected to my surging blood pressure. "You and what's-his-name—Charlie Tuna—would be better off looking for another town."

Winston leaned into me and ran his finger along a wide, crowded area where my beloved Main Street had once stood. "But Alfred," he said in a tone that was almost pleading. "I thought you'd be glad to get rid of the old Wolcott. This is the scene of your perdition."

"*What* perdition, for Christ's sake?"

"You've gotten very aggressive lately. That's what I don't like. The old Alfred was more laid back."

"Especially after a few drinks."

"I've always been sympathetic to human frailty. You have to say that about me."

"If I don't say it about you, you'll say it about yourself."

He looked hurt. "I thought you'd like my plan. I feel pretty foolish now."

I didn't think Winston felt foolish, but kept my own counsel.

"I've been looking forward to discussing New Wolcott with you for almost six months. Let's put it on the back burner for now. Keep the blueprint. If you have any further questions, I'd be happy to discuss them."

"There's nothing to discuss," I said. "*You* keep the blueprint. Your plan stinks."

The odd thing was that he was perfectly happy and perfectly calm—peaceful almost. Not for the first time did I think that Winston was like one of those submarines that obsessed him—vulnerable on the surface, dangerous when submerged.

"What the hell," he said, whisking the blueprint off my lap. A forest of condominiums clustered at the corner of my eye. "Another time, another place."

I shrugged and looked up into the new day, relieved of the New Wolcott.

Alice and I sat in front of our house that evening in a cool breeze. The only sound for a long time was the splash of the waves. The two files of rocks rose before us and scrub vegetation waved against the sky. A finger of black water stirred between the rocks. I wondered idly if that natural berth was wide enough to hold a submarine. I pictured Captain Ackley's *Avenger* tethered in the night, held to the rocks by clean white ropes.

Alice and I listened to fishermen passing along the road beside our house. After running a gauntlet of PRIVATE PROPERTY signs, they moved down a narrow path through the scrub and then leapt onto the first plateau of rocks. They climbed up to the dragon's back, negotiated narrow footholds in the dark and then disappeared down the other side of the hump and moved toward the outer rocks. They'd fish for bass through the tides and before dawn move back across toward their cars.

Winston and New Wolcott and Charlie Tuna seemed a long way off, in another time and place. I thought about how far Alice and I had come since the years of my hard drinking, stumblings, absences, indifference. Which was not to say there weren't still unresolved problems. She had resigned herself to my afternoons at the Surf Club and Sunday lunches at the big house with my mother, though she never accompanied me. I straddled two worlds uneasily.

But Alice and I had a marriage. It was not as good as some or as bad as others, but the absence of alcohol had made an incalculable difference. There was a hum between us that I'd never expected or even knew existed. I was more used to long silences, sudden outbursts, gestures that had to be interpreted on the spot for hidden meanings.

There was the lapping of the sea, the cool breeze, a fisherman's silhouette in the distance. She wore a yellow cotton sundress and held a coffee mug with her initials on it. I had bought it for her twenty years ago on Second Avenue.

There was the sea and the fragrance of her freshly washed hair.

10

In the morning I was full of beans. On the lawn facing the rocks, I choked down some coffee and ballparked the coming day.

I would read the Providence *Herald;* cut some weeds; climb on the rocks to survey the fishermen's catches; mutter with them about the Bosox; have lunch with my mother at the big house; play eighteen holes with Mal Robinson in the afternoon by fringed cart; take a swim at the Surf Club; have supper with Alice at Cap'n Andy's in Wolcott.

My mother was ninety. She was in splendid, almost fiercely good shape, shape good enough to be remarked upon. She still wielded her cane, but didn't need it. Her carriage was erect, her hair a mellow white, and her skin glowed with health. She was the brightest thing in that house. The immaculate grounds, flower garden, towering elms, never prepared me for the gloom. The sun escaped at the front door and the coolness of the interior seeped upward from the flagstones.

Before lunch we cleared away some business involving the property. I explained tax and insurance matters to her, detailed easement rights for the fishermen who used our road to get down to the rocks. I gave my mother an update on the town's proposed water treatment plant, which might involve running pipe under a small section of our land. Since the plant had been on the drawing board for fifteen years, it was just a matter of keeping up with the latest proposals and counter-proposals. Nothing much about the business side of the property ever changed, which was the way I liked it. All in all, it was a routine meeting of Mrs. Meriwether and her lawyer.

After an hour or so, we adjourned to the dining room table. I heard rattles from the pantry as Mary—whose sight and hearing were fading fast—made her way back and forth.

My mother had solved the first course with jellied consommé. When we were through, I whisked the bowls into the pantry, shouting, "I've got it," to prevent a collision in the swinging doorway. For no reason, Mary would sometimes charge into the dining room, look around baffled, and then retreat into the pantry.

Every rattle and clatter brought a tense smile from my mother and nervous rearrangements of the silver. She did not relax until Mary staggered into the dining room carrying the platter of bluefish.

I asked her how the girl, Kate Latham, had been working out as her companion. You would have thought I'd dropped a bouquet of flowers on my mother's plate, for the surge of emotion the name gave her. "That girl!" she declared. "She's saved my life. I can't tell you, Alfred. We're like two peas in a pod."

She looked wary for a moment. Her eyes darted over the vast mahogany table, the Lowestoft, and sailing prints. "Of course, we know *nothing* about her family. We do know the father's a dentist—an oral surgeon, whatever that is—in Providence."

"So you like her," I said.

"I think she's just a bit too . . . too. What's the word?"

My mother searched through one of the most formidable arsenals of invective in the history of American social discourse. "Wholesome."

I was incredulous. *"Wholesome?"*

She looked relieved. Some weight of ambivalence or expectation of the unconscious had been satisfied. Perhaps somewhere in her mind she had expected the duck to come down and say the magic word—tart, or whatever.

With the yoke of hostility loosened, and the worst of her secret thoughts exposed, my mother became gay. She and Kate were off to Newport on the morrow. Kate must see the Casino, the Breakers, the Doll House. There would be trips to Meguntic, flower shows, Gilbert Stuart's birthplace, Watch Hill.

My mother wanted to make a last grand tour of the small state, touching all the bases, warming up the memories of ninety years. A foray into Providence possibly. Visits to a couple of old-timers. There would be velvet-glove clashes among the *grandes dames*. As the dutiful son I have witnessed these mongoose encounters conducted over rattling teacups—discreet eruptions over the most trivial things, like the temperature of that day in 1906.

"Do you think I'm senile?" she asked.

"No, I don't. Far from it."

"Fifty years ago I was middle-aged. *Seventy* years ago I was a mature young woman. Time has stabbed me in the back."

"You've always been extremely graphic," I said.

"I wonder what you'll think of Kate's paintings. Of course, they're very abstract and I prefer a more realistic mode. She drew a seascape the other day—a little drawing, delightful, of course—but isn't it interesting how you can sit next to someone for two hours, look at *exactly* the same ocean, and the other person will have a completely different idea of what is perfectly obvious. I find it annoying."

My mother sat back in her chair. She had not looked better in twenty years, at least since before my father went into his final glide. She told me that Winston could conceivably be President of the United States one day. "And that would make me, what?"

"First Mother-in-Law," I said.

"Winston doesn't know his real mother."

"First Mother?"

She gave the slightest inclination of her regal head. At this point I should have seen what was going on. But I didn't.

"I've lived through all the great events of this century. McKinley's assassination, the League of Nations, Prohibition. I even remember the *Maine*."

"Don't forget the Rough Riders," I said.

"I danced with Theodore Roosevelt at the Newport Cotillion in 1912. He was bursting out of his tuxedo vest, grinning like a monkey. Franklin, of course, had the most wonderful manners. Your grandfather met him in 1906—their law firms shared a building on Wall Street. Who could have known he was planning a Socialist revolution? It goes to show that you can't judge a book by its cover. Franklin had lovely manners and committed high treason. Winston has the manners of a mountain man. I've misjudged him all these years. What a startling success he's had."

She fiddled with the strand of pearls around her neck. She patted her beautiful white hair, hair like cotton. "What would you have done as a mother?" she asked the ceiling. "That summer I thought Dorothy would return from Europe with a prince in tow."

"Instead she came back with Thumper," I said.

"Thumper," she sighed. "A penniless basketball player cruising around Buffalo, looking for automobile accidents. Was that the kind of man I wanted to marry my precious? One just prayed that his real parents hadn't copulated in a mental institution. Of course, later on my fears proved groundless. My only grandchild turned out to be as blond and handsome as a young god, with a touch of the poet."

"He has his share of problems," I allowed.

She didn't want to hear about that. "Do you think Winston really has a chance to be President of the United States?"

"Did he say he did?"

"He asked me if I'd enjoy living in the White House. It scarcely seems possible that the giraffe who came bounding up the flagstones outside this house twenty years ago might be a President of the United States. I remember that yellow necktie he wore. I wondered if he'd thrown up on himself."

"It wasn't that bad." I felt odd, defending him.

"It was pretty bad," my mother insisted, with a dramatic shake of her head. "I loved him like a son from the very first, but I kept saying to myself, These are the crosses you bear, these are the crosses you bear. The next morning I took the car over to St. David's-By-The-Sea and flung myself into the last pew. Reverend Warren found me there, sobbing."

"I don't know how good his chances are," I said. "Who knows?"

My mother became instantly lucid. "What do you mean?"

"He might do something in Rhode Island politics. I guess his strong suit is defense policy."

"What could be more important than defense policy?" she asked, inspecting the dining room as if it was a missile silo.

"He tells me the President will make him Secretary of the Navy."

"Franklin Delano Roosevelt was only an *assistant* Secretary of the Navy, Winston said."

"I think you have to have the touch for politics. I don't know if he has the touch."

"He's always been the soul of graciousness to me. Always calling, doing me little favors, keeping me informed, taking an interest in the property."

There it was. "What exactly do you mean, taking an interest in the property?"

"He comes up with a new project every minute," my mother said. "Just yesterday he mentioned the possibility of having a marina on the Piscotaug River."

"Which side of the Piscotaug?" I asked, my voice rising. "What kind of boats?"

"Darling . . ." She gave a little wave of her hand, to ward off my questions. "All his charts gave me a splitting headache."

"It's a great idea." This is called giving an inch. "Of course, the problem is the pollution—if it's going to be a marina for power boats."

"Darling, that's *exactly* what I told him."

"And the garbage and gasoline, not to mention the increased river traffic."

"Exactly. . . ."

"What did he say when you told him?" I asked.

Her queenly brow furrowed. "He said the river was dying anyway. . . ."

"Yes, but the *reason* the river is dying is because of overuse by power boats. All that fuel these people dump ruins the mussel beds and lobster beds. The river's just too shallow to sustain that kind of traffic. We don't need more boats—we need no boats."

"All his plans for the New Wolcott. I must say I was impressed."

"The New Wolcott?" I groaned. "When did he tell you about the New Wolcott?"

"Yesterday Winston and I had the most delicious lunch in the Surf Club dining room." My mother's voice was low and rather seductive. "How long has it been since I've had champagne? You know, there's a kind of rough charm about Winston that I'd never noticed before."

"He told me about the New Wolcott yesterday."

She looked away from me. "He said the way you cross-examined him it was a tragedy. . . ." Her voice trailed off.

"What did you think of his plan?" I asked.

"I thought it was the best idea I'd ever heard in my life. An authentic re-creation of a New England whaling village, right down to the last detail. There'll be a long wharf right next to the seawall, with little shops, and at the end of the wharf a New England whaler, just like the one in Mystic. Maybe the townspeople will dress in period garb. You know, Alfred, he might have been describing my childhood. He certainly brought me out. I suppose Winston thought I was quite the pampered social butterfly in Newport, but I got around. Harpoons and whale blubber didn't frighten *me*."

My mother raised her hand and made a knife-thrust, evidently to demonstrate blubber-carving. It sent tremors through me. My face turned blubber-white.

"Look," I said palely. "He didn't mention anything about an authentic whaling community. He mentioned a lot of expensive condominiums and some building contractor in Meguntic nicknamed Charlie Tuna. He's got plans for gambling casinos along the seawall."

"Charlie Tuna?" My mother looked puzzled. "What a strange name."

"Jesus, a whaling village. Next thing you know Winston will be walking around with a parrot on his shoulder."

The image of the big fellow with a parrot on his shoulder made me giggle.

"Perhaps you're in favor of pornographic films involving small children."

"What are you talking about? I'm not in favor of pornographic films."

"I didn't say you were, darling. Winston certainly opened my eyes about Wolcott, Rhode Island. It's one of the leading centers for drug traffic in the state."

"That isn't true," I said. "It has almost no crime. Some broken windows, disorderly conduct, sleeping on the beach . . ."

"Of course, they're not *obvious* about it, but I got the lowdown on their operations."

"It's not true," I said. "It just isn't true. That's an untruth, and you know it."

"Winston says you'll defend Wolcott right down to the last bar and grill."

"Winston is a jerk."

My mother looked stern. She was on the verge of reproaching me, but then seemed to think better of it. Her hand fluttered around her necklace. Her eyes grew misty. "You're a bigger hero to us now than you ever were in World War II. If only Vice President Truman were alive, he'd pin another Distinguished Service Cross on your chest."

I was going to be killed with kindness and baby talk.

"Did Winston mention Sheriff Jim Sprague?" I asked.

"Just to say the poor man is terribly understaffed now that organized crime has moved in. It's all he can do to keep the hopheads off the beach in the evening."

"Do you think it may be necessary to destroy the town in order to save it?"

My mother gave a weighty nod. "Unless, as Winston says, the rustlers and outlaws decided pickings would be better on down the road a piece."

"What do you think would make the hopheads and porno film makers saddle up?"

"Winston thinks they're too entrenched, like a cancer that's seeped into the vitals of the town. New Wolcott will mean a new beginning."

"I'll talk to Winston," I said.

"Oh, do. It does my heart good to see you two together. You don't know how safe and secure it makes me feel—my two handsome lawyers. As a matter of fact, I've asked Winston to take a more active role in the management of the property."

"You've *what?*"

My mother smiled. "It's been on my mind for years. Don't you think three heads are better than one?"

"Christ, no."

"Now, darling—"

"Are you off your rocker?"

"Just on a trial basis . . ."

"He's a bounder," I said. "Don't you see that? For God's sake, Mom."

"Off my rocker?"

"That's a terrible idea. Winston would turn this place into a parking lot, if he thought there was money in it."

I leaned back in my chair, my hand at my throat. I felt harpooned. Just at a time when I had gotten a grip on my life, I suddenly lacked credibility.

"I don't like to see you so upset," she said soothingly. "You're beet-red."

The cut-up fruit for dessert looked like surgery—those ripe plums and slashed strawberries and banana brains.

"Charlie Tuna, gambling casinos, condominiums," my mother mused. She patted her mouth firmly with her napkin. "Off my rocker indeed."

Kate Latham, my mother's companion, was standing there looking at the vista when I wandered outside after lunch. She was dressed in cut-off blue jeans and a green T-shirt. Barefoot, she stood under one of the great split-leaf beech trees whose leaves shimmered in the light, as if they would drop all at once to the ground. In a scene—blond hair pulled back, tan arms, hazel eyes—in a scene—the sudden smile turning everything bronze and white. I felt old. I waved to her and lumbered toward my Caprice.

I was angry with my mother, but felt sorry for her, too. I wanted to tell her that she couldn't play in Winston's league—not with that kind of vanity.

Back at the house, while dressing for my golf game, I filled in Alice on my conversation with my mother. I picked out a sporty ensemble, running to powder blue.

Alice listened. She stood in the doorway, holding a bowl of snow peas.

"Are you going to marry that wharf rat?" my mother had asked my sister Dorothy that first night in 1962 at the big house. Well, Winston had come a long way since then.

Alice came over and sat down on the bed. With a certain formality she placed the bowl on the blanket beside her. "Maybe we should leave here," she said quietly. "I think you know how I feel."

I looked at her. "I think we ought to discuss it," I said quietly. "Tonight." A long talk, I decided, to explore the options. Perhaps our talk would help me toward a decisiveness that I didn't feel.

I grabbed my Footjoys from the closet.

At the entrance to our property, where the passage was blind, Winston and I nearly had a car accident. He came roaring out of nowhere in his silver Eldorado, with its front-wheel drive and blazing whip antennae, car telephone—in case of national emergency—and Citizen's Band radio and electric windows. It had every conceivable option that could be installed in a motor vehicle in the last fifth of the twentieth century.

For a fraction of a second, I was lost in the color-roar of silver, the bullwhips of his antennae. Only my fab reflexes saved the day. I swerved into some handy bushes. My Caprice's front end dipped like a bronco's amid the squeal of gripping radials, whirrs of sand. Winston hit his own braking system and we avoided the most terrible bumper-crunch—Caprice versus Eldorado, two classics dueling in the sun.

He came to a stop not ten feet away from me in dusty beams of sunlight. He promptly hit the switches on his electric windows —both of them—so even though he had stopped, everything was still in motion, going up and down. The antennae above him shivered like branches receiving the first warning of a tropical depression.

He immediately took the offensive,. "Why don't you watch where you're going, for Christ's sake?" he yelled, breaking the sudden forest stillness, including the lush vegetation containing my Caprice's blue snout.

There was the whiplash of his neck, the haloing Brillo of his hair. I saw the flintstones of his elbow. It had ripped into the ribs of a generation of uppity ballhawks. It had put his athletic conference on the map, digging and gouging under the boards. . . .

And something went Snap in my mind. It happened suddenly. My gorge rose and choked me and shook me until I was bouncing behind the steering wheel. Winston must have been doing thirty-five, purring at forty, when we narrowly escaped our head-on collision. But it wasn't just that; it was twenty years of accumulated rage—the way he treated his son; his thievery at the law firm; his plans for the New Wolcott; Charlie Tuna.

Instead of just blowing my top, the volcanic pressure of words opened fissures in my sentence structures. Sulphurous holes shot forth isolated rocks of abuse. My words hung in the air like balloons. They seemed to fulfill Winston's subtle prophecy to my mother that thirty years of alcoholism had burned out valuable cells in my cerebral cortex—razed judiciousness and leveled civility.

I couldn't shut myself up or shut up the small voice telling me to cool it. In my eagerness to get at the big fellow verbally, I banged my forehead against the window before I could roll it down. Verbiage tumbled over itself. I made chug-a-lug noises.

Winston stopped playing with his electric buttons and left both windows in the down position. He was the epitome of calmness and restraint and reasonability. He waited on my anger with the courtliness of an old family retainer, a resigned bow of his head to absorb every word.

I can't safely skip over all this—my bazaar of abuse. "Son of a bitch . . . Property . . . Shit . . . Mother . . . Lawyer . . . Handle . . . God . . . Damn . . . Fuck . . . Duck . . . Listen, Winston . . . Learn how to drive . . . Christ . . . Not any goddamn . . . Whaling . . . You can harpoon . . . Blubber . . . And shove it . . . Starkist . . . Up to here . . . Gills . . . Pack you in oil . . . You bastard . . . You got questions . . . Hey, you got questions . . . I'm her fucking lawyer . . . Shit . . ." I pounded the steering wheel for emphasis. "Any fast ones . . . End run around me . . ."

Half a century of repression danced in my face, tugging at my lips, fluttering my ruby cheeks, bunnying my chin.

Winston said, "Calm yourself, man."

This incensed me; the condescending "man." I might have just refused to face down a lion on the Serengeti. Winston, the great white hunter, had been forced to dispatch the beast himself. These tenderfeet—the way their eyes roll out here on the plains.

"You're sending your blood pressure off the charts. Perhaps I *was* going a bit fast. Still, that's no reason to shout at me. It's a free country. I can talk to your mother about any subject that I see fit. I am a member of this family, too, you know."

Winston's Eldorado fishtailed off in a burst of sand and dust. I thought the car's engine was turned off, but it had been idling silently. My forehead rested on the crescent of the steering wheel, against which it had bumped at the conclusion of my remarks.

11

It was Wednesday morning of that week. I sat in my beach chair at the Surf Club. The sun was never whiter, sheets of heat coated my oiled tummy. I sighed, opened *Daniel Deronda,* and read: "If this white-handed man with the perpendicular profile . . ."

It often happened with Eliot that I got fixated on a sentence or phrase. I mumbled the fragment aloud, "white-handed" and "perpendicular," and grunted with approval. "But self-confidence," she once wrote, "is apt to address itself to an imaginary dulness in others. . . ."

An enormous shadow chilled me. I felt a constriction in my ventricles and for a moment dared not look up. My feet shifted uneasily under the sand. It didn't help matters any that I had been muttering to myself. I had just added a "bop" to the "perp" in perpendicular—"bop-bop-perp-perp"—and must have sounded like an electric percolator. It was just another example of the kind of fun things I did.

Without any preamble except his shadow, Winston said, "I know I've been a jerk."

I looked up at him, or rather looked up into the sun, and said evenly, "You're too hard on yourself, Winston, by half."

"Forgive me?"

Goose pimples erupted in the muscle-pucker above my elbow. All I could feel at that precise moment was Winston's vigor and strength and thinly veiled hostility, matched against my own feeling of depletion and tiredness.

His presence on this day and during the remainder of the week was unexpected—he was supposed to have been off somewhere doing Navy things. And there I sat on the sand, preparing

with some trepidation for Gwendolyn's first meeting with Grand-
court. I awaited her fate with the most trembling anxiety—nine
hundred pages of it.

I strained against the harness of my own destiny. "No, I don't
think so, Winston," I should have said. "Let me itemize the
things that can't be forgiven."

"Can I plead overwork?" He sank to his knees. His face
landed five or six inches from my own. I marveled at the circum-
ference of his tanned pores. He wore khaki pants, a navy-blue
alligator shirt from which gray hair sprouted around the bottom
button, silver jogging shoes, and a pair of expensive mirrored
sunglasses.

"You can plead anything you want." I closed *Daniel Deronda*.
It made a literary *whump* sound. I suddenly felt as if I had all
day for Winston. George Eliot will do that to a man—make him
take the long view.

"I've got two nuke subs on my mind, shipyard problems in
Groton you wouldn't believe, a Secretary of the Navy who is permanently out to lunch. It's enough to make any man irascible."

"Oh, absolutely," I agreed.

"Shake."

"What?"

"Shake."

He had extended his hand across the metal armrest of my
beach chair. With extreme reluctance I offered him five digits.

"What say farther down the afternoon we bat the old ball
around?" He made flicking backhands resembling squash shots,
above me, then his left hand descended and covered our pledged
hands. Perhaps he had been in contact with his tennis pros in
Manhattan and the nation's capital on a conference call.

"I don't think so, Winston." I wriggled my hand from inside
his grip.

That afternoon at the Surf Club a reporter named Dace
Lesser, from the Providence *Herald*'s Sunday Style Section, came
to interview my mother.

She had to be coaxed for a millisecond into her ninety years of
memories. She took Dace upriver into Providence and out to the

mouth of Narragansett Bay. They endured hurricanes and rum-running, clambakes and shipwrecks; they talked about the geology of our white rocks, lobster pots, and the sex life of clams.

She divulged her secrets of longevity, which involved early-morning dips in the Piscotaug River and, like Satchel Paige, staying away from fried foods. She danced with Teddy Roosevelt at Newport again and this time felt the bully strength in his muscular arms. She told Dace how much my father had enjoyed the brisk air of the seashore. In fact, it had probably hastened his mildewed demise.

My mother explained to Dace how she still drove her own car. She beckoned over Kate Latham to take a bow. I was summoned reluctantly from the sand for a ringside introduction. My mother fumbled for my qualities before she got comfortable with my war record and tennis. This pretty much beached me in my late twenties.

A considerable portion of the interview concentrated on her remarkable spryness. She was amazing in this respect; instead of adding on years, she seemed to be jettisoning them. She glowed; her memory and eyes were as clear as blue bells.

My mother got a little competitive with Dace about career women and life in the business world. She described her own horse-killing schedule during the years before the invention of the electric washing machine. She caught Dace a little off guard about the importance of sound nutrition. This was a weak spot for a young reporter who probably lived on fast food. You would have thought the Meriwethers had invented fresh fruits and vegetables, that we'd never encountered a servant in our part of the state. My mother really gave a ride to the word "larder." She couldn't stay away from it; it was so well-stocked, the Meriwether larder. One might have expected a little mellowing after the age of eighty-five, but she perked right up about this career-woman business.

At the end of the interview, Dace closed her notebook, reached over, and flipped off the tape recorder. She leaned back in her wicker chair. She was a slim, dark-haired woman, so intense that I felt she might have been better off in the investigative division of her newspaper, instead of the style section. But now, with the interview in the can, so to speak, Dace seemed overcome with the emotions of the moment. She watched my mother take a last gander at the sun sashing her white rocks, turning gold now in their ageless lambency; she was enveloped like a satin cloak by the enriched sands of the past. Struggling to her feet, my mother bid adieu to Dace with a little your-whole-life-is-before-you-but-I-may-not-have-until-suppertime pat on her cheek.

Dace Lesser stood on the boardwalk across from me. She looked trim and elegant in her beige raw silk business suit. She held a snappy Gucci attaché case in one hand, a portable tape recorder in the other.

"She's a grand old lady, Mr. Meriwether," Dace said.

My mother descended into the parking lot, surrounded by cabana boys. She wobbled on the tarmac while Kate trotted over to bring up the Duesenberg.

"She's a real pain in the ass."

I thought I had muttered it under my breath, but evidently I hadn't. My mind traveled blithely on to other trivial thoughts. It took a while for the change in atmosphere to catch up with me. I gradually became aware of the descent of silence. I looked up in bewilderment, wondering where the party had gone, in time to see Dace's chin rise in disgust toward the tops of the far cabanas.

You can't run after a blurt and bring it back the way you can with tamer exclamations. Dace's high heels might have been tap-dancing on my skull for the pain her departure gave me. I hoped she wouldn't portray me in her article as a gross lush.

I did not see Winston for a couple of days. I knew he was around the property, but I didn't see him. Or my mother.

Then, on Friday afternoon, he strode up to my beach chair at the Surf Club. At first I thought he was just basking in the after-glow of the Dace Lesser interview. He looked as if he had run off a dozen unanswered points.

"You bring that reporter down here, Winston?" I asked, to confirm my suspicions.

"I confess everything," he said. "I can't wait to see her article. Look for it next Sunday."

He crossed his legs at the ankles in a balletic gesture and spread his arms.

"How'd you do it?"

"Oh, that." He shrugged, indicating it was routine. "That was nothing. I had lunch with Jack Fogarty the other week."

"Who's Jack Fogarty?" I asked.

"Publisher of the *Herald*. We share a lot of the same ideas about national defense. The big D. Jack gets a little *too* serious on the subject, whereas I see national defense more as a game between two tough opponents—winner take all."

Winston sat down on the boardwalk and stretched out his legs toward me. His head was in the shade; his legs were sunny.

"And you mentioned to Jack Fogarty that my mother might be a good subject for an article?"

"I don't say 'good' when I mean 'great.' He threw me a lunch the other week with his editors to pick my brain. After lunch I happened to mention my great mother-in-law. I told Jack that it seemed like a natural for his Sunday supplement. After all, Ma goes back to the clipper ships. He got all enthusiastic and said he'd carry the ball from there."

"Did you have a rough time convincing my mother to be interviewed?"

Winston laughed. "Are you kidding?"

He had my mother's number.

"I see," I said.

I longed to be rid of him. My toes gouged at the sand—all ten of them. I picked up *Daniel Deronda*—to bury myself in the plot, wrap myself inside the thickness, solidity, and closed social borders of the nineteenth century.

Winston leaned back into the shadows. His hands gripped a scarred knee. He began to rock himself back and forth—sometimes in the light, sometimes not. "Alfred, I think you made a tactical error," he said.

I reopened *Daniel Deronda*. This marked the first time in my life that I'd ever tried to banish someone from my presence. It was all very discouraging. "How's that?" I asked.

"Telling Ma she was off her rocker."

"What are you talking about?" I asked, startled.

"The other day. You told your mother she was off her rocker," he said. "It's just the kind of thing that's bound to upset her. A great woman, ninety years young."

"I don't think this is the time or place to rehash private conversations with my mother," I said calmly. "Do you, Winston?"

"No, of course not," he said.

He stood up then, stretched, and sighed. I could see the back of his head reflected in the oval mirror of the Meriwether cabana. Front and back, he seemed to loom over me.

I think it was then that I knew I was in for trouble. It had been my experience with Winston Bingham that every so often—when something important was at stake—he would dispense with his top-of-the-key bluster. Then would be revealed what I had always regarded as his most frightening single attribute—his first-class mind. Sometimes it was almost possible to look into his brain and watch his plans go clicking along implacably on their track.

"But I thought you'd like to know how it's going to be," he said quietly. "I'm sure your mother will be talking to you after she's calmed down. She and I have been having rather lengthy discussions these past few days."

"About what?" I asked.

"I believe your mother has decided it would be best for now if I advise her on her business affairs. For that purpose, she will transfer her power of attorney to me."

My face reddened. "Jesus," I said.

"Naturally, she hopes this will be a temporary arrangement. Until you get back on your feet."

I stared up at him. "What the hell do you mean—get back on my feet?"

Winston's voice was soft. "Alfred, I really don't know what she meant."

Daniel Deronda was spread across my stomach. My hands dove into the sand, carried sand to the surface on the tops of my fingers, then dove again. I could feel my gorge rising anew, the fissures of words bubbling up. The impulse to start yelling at Winston was almost overwhelming. My breath began to come in spurts. I fought to control myself. I knew that getting angry wouldn't do me any good. In fact, it would just encourage the notion that at some point I had suffered a severe frontal-lobe burnout.

A part of me was furious, but a part was also terribly saddened. I could see an intricate web spinning around my mother. It would be light and silky at first, but eventually its silken thread would lead to the best nursing home that money could buy. For a few moments, as I sat on the sand, she no longer seemed like the formidable matriarch of my Oedipal childhood and youth and middle age. A nightmare picture came into my mind of my mother's skin thinning out transparently across her skull. The blue glow of a television set flickered in front of her and she receded forever into the depths of her memories.

Winston spoke gently from above me about the Meriwether property. He used the civilized voice that I enjoyed hearing inside those nineteenth century clubs of my favorite novels, just as if we were old friends discussing a good grouse season. *Click-click*, that mind went down its track.

It was all crystal clear to him: villas for the elite; a new nine-hole golf course; power-broker clambakes; a landing strip for private planes; a pad for helicopters; a new marina on the Piscotaug; lobster pots off the rocks; a long private beach gouged out of our rough shoreline by Charlie Tuna's heavy equipment.

A man with dreams—a big man with big dreams—could do a lot with six hundred acres. All he needed was a little imagination.

Winston shrugged and put out his hands, palms up. His plans were crystal-clear and nothing more needed to be said. This was the way it was going to be.

Remain calm, I told myself. From somewhere I summoned a wan smile. "This is what I get," I said to him, "for beating you at tennis."

I guess he couldn't resist; it was in the blood. "Want to play?" he asked eagerly.

"No, Winston." I picked up *Daniel Deronda*. "I've already beaten you once."

One good thing did happen that week. I learned that my nephew, Winston Bingham, Jr., had developed—unbeknownst to anyone—a discreet and very private relationship with Kate Latham, my mother's companion.

It was Saturday evening around six-fifteen, and I had over-stayed my visit to the Surf Club. Cabana boys cleared the porches around me. The frying day was cooling off and a breeze came off the water. Over the course of the day my chair had sunk archeologically into the depths of the sand. This sinking sensation had been produced in large measure by hours of rest-less brooding.

My nephew arrived as usual for his evening swim. Had I not looked up after taking off my reading glasses, I would have missed Win as he slipped by. I hoped he wouldn't wind up doing what had produced a lot of shut-ins in the nineteenth cen-tury—that is, hang around to prop up his parents' marriage. I hoped he might get a chance to kick up his heels a bit before his days of apple-town youth ended. As it turned out, he really didn't need my advice.

I pulled out my beach chair from its wedged position in the sand, headed into the cabana, and got dressed in something sub-dued but nifty, mainly earth-tones. For some reason I wanted to try out a more laid-back sartorial style.

Barefoot, I left the cabana, waved to the cabana boys. I de-scended the staircase and tiptoed across the parking lot to my Caprice. The macadam was warm and smooth and undulated to-ward the turreted gate house at the entrance to the club. Bright yellow kiddie-bumps stretched from one side of the parking lot to the other.

The Duesenberg was almost beside me before the familiar sounds of its engine fully registered. I felt the heat from the long green hood, saw the sun sparkle off the mounted headlights. I looked up at Kate Latham's elbow.

"Hi, Mr. Meriwether," she said with a smile.

"Hello, Kate."

I thought to myself, This is a lovely sight and a sight for sore eyes—this supreme melding of youth and antiquity.

"How's the water?"

"Haven't been in since lunch. Warm then."

"Say, that's a great outfit," she enthused, referring to my earth-tones. "All you need is a pair of cowboy boots."

"Yup," I agreed.

I felt real good in the golden sunset. Just then. For a change.

Kate drummed her fingers on the steering wheel for a moment. "Well . . ." she said. "Catch you later."

"Sure," I said.

She put the car in gear and raised her chin, as if looking down the parking lot a far piece. Her blond hair caught the breeze and waved against the barn-wood backdrop of the cabana circle.

Under the softening streaks of sky, Kate Latham was blushing. Evidently she hadn't expected to encounter anyone that evening beside the deserted, trysting beach—except my nephew.

12

I went out on Sunday morning to pick up my New York *Times* at the Wolcott drug store. I encountered Sheriff Jim Sprague at the entrance to our property.

The lights on his patrol car throbbed. His beefy stomach was thrust against the door of a fisherman's pickup. He held a license and registration in his hand.

"Hey, Al," Rocco D'Erasmo, the fisherman, called as I pulled up beside his truck. Two gigantic millstones, upended, stood on either side of the road. Thick bushes bordered the open gates of white wood. It was there that Winston and I had had our Caprice-Eldorado confrontation a few days before.

"Hello, Rocco," I said, exiting my vehicle.

"*You* talk to the guy, will you, Al? I don't know what's going on." Rocco waved in disgust at Sprague.

"What's going on here?" I asked the sheriff. It surprised me a little to realize that I was several inches taller than Sprague; in fact, he was under six feet, so I was four or five inches taller than the good constable. Over the past few years—since I'd sworn off the sauce—I'd noticed that people had become their real size. Ever since childhood, evidently, I'd been overjudging people's height, adding on a few extra inches. This habit had continued into my late middle age.

Light filtered elegantly through the trees and made pools in the road. A thick shaft struck the sheriff directly across his face, whitening one side and turning the other an even more plumlike color than usual. The sheriff was not unacquainted—town legend knew—with massive doses of rectified substances.

Light and sun glinted off the huge millstones at the entrance—

the tonnage of our property, the sheer weight of it grinding toward the sea.

I was determined to remain cool and lawyerly, with a detachment befitting my new earth-toned persona. Gathering the facts,
assessing the situation. I'd left the door of my Caprice open by
mistake and briefly imagined it banged into by a silver Eldorado.
I saw the door sailing through the air in a burst of chrome-blue.
Winston and I would exchange insurance companies in the light-
filtered air. His insurance company would be named Bump &
Grind. He would know the name of a "chop shop" that could fix
me up with a new door in twenty minutes.

My hand went to my throat and scratched there idly.
"Mornin', Jim," I said to the sheriff.

"Hey, Mr. Meriwether," Jim said sheepishly.

"What's happenin'?" I asked in my new laconic style.

"I'm real sorry, Mr. Meriwether."

"What gives with my old friend Rocco?" I asked, surveying
the light-poured leaves above me, flittering, winking.

Jim's high-pitched voice was mismatched to his bulk. He
began to talk fast in the present tense, rubbing at the pavement
with a shiny black shoe. Evidently I represented an authority
figure to him. But I had no authority. "I get a call from Mr.
Meriwether yesterday—"

"You mean Mr. Bingham," I corrected.

"Yes, sir, that's who I mean—Mr. Bingham. And he tells me,
'Jimbo, doctor's orders—no more fishermen. Get the ones who are
on it off. Keep the ones who want to get in out. There're plenty
of other places in this state where they can fish.' Then he tells
me he wants me or a deputy up here to start spreading the
word."

I didn't want to put Jim in the middle—he was pitched too
high already—but there was the principle of the thing. The principle was that I had seen no papers turning over my mother's
power of attorney to Winston Bingham. I still ran the property
for her, or so I thought. Of course, she could call Jim Sprague
herself. But the principle was that Winston Bingham couldn't do
it, until I'd had a chance to talk with my mother and she had formally relieved me of command. I wasn't going to take Bingham's
word for anything.

"See here, Jim," I said, under the radiant summer light. I felt the power of the law just then. Sometimes my voice got small when I was under pressure, as if a child Alfred lurked in my larynx. But this time my voice was strong. And Jim might have thought, Is this the same hunk of human flotsam that I used to poke with my flashlight on the Wolcott beach? "I know you've got a job to do, and I appreciate you coming out here on a Sunday morning. But Mr. Bingham doesn't run this property—I do. I've been running it for going on fifteen years now."

"I know you have, Mr. Meriwether," Jim said truthfully. We were eye to eye now. He'd stopped examining the pavement.

"So what I'd like you to do is turn off those lights and go home. I don't care if our rocks are wall-to-wall fishermen."

"Yes, sir," Jim said.

"And if Mr. Bingham calls, have him call me. Tell him I think there's been some kind of misunderstanding. That should move him up."

I could tell Jim was worried as he hitched up his cartridge belt. He grimaced and said, "Yes, sir."

I nodded in the sun. "Thank you, Jim. You have a good day now. And don't forget to refer everything to me."

He adjusted his Smokey the Bear hat, walked to his patrol car. I was pleased to see that he turned off his flashing lights, which were blueing the millstones.

"Go on in, Rocco," I said to the fisherman, as I headed back to my Caprice.

Rocco tipped his Bosox cap. "Thanks, Al."

My new laconic style only got me so far, which was to a position sitting behind my steering wheel. Then I felt faint and dizzy. I clutched at the steering wheel, ran my fingers harshly along the ridges of the underside. Coronaries crossed my mind. "They" would find me slumped against my horn—hounded to death, massively insulted to the brain. Kate Latham would administer mouth-to-mouth resuscitation; my mother would attempt to jump into the grave with me, crying, "What have I done to him, my beautiful boy?" Winston would start speaking in tongues—heronfly, jumbofly. Dorothy would apologize for bringing Thumper home in the first place. Alice would murmur, "I stuck with him to the bitter end." And Jim Sprague would testify, "I hear the horn blowing, I look around, and his chin is just resting there on the steering wheel. He looked real peaceful."

I contemplated my funeral: a good "mix" of trusts and estates lawyers, grizzled fishermen, arthritic tennis players. Pancho Gonzales would fly in from Las Vegas: "Alfredo had all the equipment—great serve, great ground strokes. He covered a lot of court. But you know," he would fume, "maybe he didn't have it here." And Pancho would thump his "heart" area, the area where I didn't have it. My funeral would be held at St. David's-By-The-Sea. The congregation would give their lungs a workout with Martin Luther's overwhelming "A Mighty Fortress Is Our God." The organist would close with a mournful rendition of "My Way."

I punched in my Cruise Control and headed down to Wolcott. It was a lovely clear day. Rhode Island Sound sparkled on my left, gracefully fronted by the Wolcott seawall. I put on some "easy listening" music for the trip. The lush fruity strings seeped into my brain and calmed my synapses.

Coming home I saw Kate Latham, on a jog, just turning into the property. Holy Toledo, I thought, watching her long strides, the sheen of her arms, the flounce of her blond ponytail and admirable musculature. I wished that my Caprice whispered so that I could ride along unnoticed behind her for a while, as she ran through light and shadow along the dappled road. She wore blue jogging shorts, formidable blue-and-red Nikes, and a yellow T-shirt. I glimpsed a hiked expanse of buttock at mid-stride and knocked my temple against the side window. She turned then at the gasp of my eight-cylindered torque, gave me a smile, but did not break stride. The Nikes, the motion of her running, the black digital watch strapped mightily around her wrist, indicated that she was no-nonsense about her workouts. I waved as I went by, and sighed as she grew smaller in my rearview mirror—blond and bronze, yellow and red and blue in the mirror. She raised her watch to eye level.

I sailed past my mother's driveway. I hit my power brakes, stopped with a heavy buck, threw the car into reverse. I drove slowly up the hill toward the chimneys—both of them built to last for as long as it took, unyielding to the sky. Chimneys that warned of the weight of generations.

As I got out of my car and walked toward my mother's front door, I could see the young woman walking up the driveway. Beige furs of dust hung lightly in the air behind her shoes. She swung her arms, hiked and stretched back her shoulders, then stopped and did an erotic series of swooping hamstring exercises —elaborate palm-touches to the ground accomplished with a balletic professionalism. Oblivious, with her hands on her graceful hips—looking rather as if she were about to deal with an unruly child—she walked up toward the house, keeping her eyes on the ground and worrying a stone with the toe of her shoe. She looked as if she had a weight of thought on her yellow shoulders —streaked shirt, wet blond hair, pouring sweat as if she'd been caught in a summer shower.

In the morning light she reached the crest of the driveway, shimmering in the summer air. She still had her hands on her hips and head down—a field of yellow shades for just a moment, until her blue shorts came into view and then her divine legs. In the great distance of the enormous vista, an oil tanker ploughed along the horizon of the glassy sea. At the tip of our property, our twin files of rocks gleamed.

I pressed the buzzer of the front door. I had to find out what my mother and Winston Bingham had negotiated. I had to get the word from her lips.

After a longish wait Mary, the maid, opened the door a sliver and peered suspiciously at me. I could just make out her gnome-like head and feral eyes, the wild shocks of orange-red, almost Day-Glo hair wreathing her face. Although nutty as a fruitcake, she had somehow managed to attain old-family-retainer status in the Meriwether household.

Mary's eyes darted right and left. For all her suspicion, I might have been the vanguard of a regiment of English troops billeted in Wolcott. More sunlight slipped away. The rest of the day was going to be awfully long.

She pulled open the door—from a sliver to a slice of darkness. "Ralph," she snapped. "Your mother's in the attic."

She always called me Ralph. I didn't know why. She was an old woman, but I thought the least she could do when she reached old-family-retainer status was to get all the names right.

I gave Mary a grim smile. The door opened, she disappeared

behind it, and my eyes adjusted to night vision. There was a trickle of lamplight across the foyer rugs, like something spilled on the floor. A large oil painting of my mother's great-grand-father hung down at the opposite end of the foyer. I noticed his dandy's calves and powdered wig. His thin lips and sunken cheeks—pale as disease—gave no hint that he had made his first fortune out of the rum and Madeira trade; or that he had ever taken home a keg to get himself loose. His face spoke of the countinghouse and blotted ledger books, falconlike scrutiny of the cash flow.

Mary closed the door behind me, and shut out the last of the exterior world. She seemed to scurry between my legs like an or-ange cat—just a dart of orange in front of me. She raced toward the stairs and took them two at a time. Her left hand slapped at the shaky bannister for emphasis. Her gold-colored shoes struck the carpeted staircase like large sparks. Her footwear con-trasted with the black maid's uniform that she wore.

At the second floor landing, in sparks of gold, Mary shouted, "Ralph's here, ma'am. Come quickly."

I winced. My presence had precipitated a crisis. From Mary one always had the sense of which way the family wind blew— who was "in," who was "out," and especially who had lately fallen into disfavor. I had evidently entered a final phase.

I went into the living room and sat down by the fireplace. Andirons squatted amid the ashes in a space that was large enough to spit-roast an elk. The room itself had changed little over the years. Tall narrow windows opened onto the front lawn, but light and lawn were hidden by bushes. I saw only peeps of the outside, isolated reminders from the day.

My father sat in this chair in 1962, that first night with Win-ston. Thumper conducted Dad with his cigar hand and blew tiers of smoke. Over on that couch, Dorothy sat with her sherry and said, "A juice, Daddy. Winnie loves juices." My mother sat where I was sitting and offered her powdered neck to the gods. We all moved down the hall and into the dining room. Winston told a story about the *Titanic:* how he would have dressed up in women's clothing and jumped into the nearest lifeboat. After dinner we came back into the living room, and my father sat where I was sitting. A vein trickled down his temple. Something in his demeanor suggested he knew that not everyone had had the advantages he'd had. He was going to bend over backward for Winston—always a mistake with the big fellow.

Time passed slowly while I sat alone. My mother was not eager to see me. She chose to linger in her vast attic with her memories. I had accused her of being off her rocker—the first time I had ever spoken back to her. For this reason I was going to be given the silent treatment and then banished from my principality to live out my life in affluent isolation.

Ah, I thought, Alfred, the party's over. The party's over.

What stuck in my throat was the whole issue of my competence. Winston had offended me in a deeply lawyerly way. He regarded me as some kind of legal idiot, while regarding himself as the sole proprietor of a vast legal brain trust. He expected me to roll over and play dead. He thought he could just come bounding up to me on the beach and present his little triumphs to me. As if I was supposed to be a stupefied witness while he cut out my heart.

My mother stood in the doorway. She wobbled on the stairs leading down to the sunken cavernous living room. Her hand was at her forehead in a kind of wary salute, as though trying to make me out in the gloom. She descended a step and tottered, then took the last one and was into the room fully.

"I was up in the attic," she said. "Looking through your baby things."

Shaking my rattles, examining my snowsuits. Once upon a time she had tucked this quiet little boy into his snowsuit, and now he had grown up to be coarse and alcoholic and insulting.

I stood up and buttoned my invisible blazer. Had I been wearing it, I'm sure it would have made me feel more competent. My movements looked like what they were: a nervous hiking of the shoulders, a finger-fumble at the button of my *guayabera*, flowing and filigreed, tailored for the expansive gesture.

I went to my mother. It seemed that I knew just where to go and just what to do. For once I wasn't flustered or off balance, preparing for the worst. The "worst" had already happened and I was still on my feet.

"Mom," I said. "What in the world have you done?"

I so rarely called her Mom. She was my mother.

"I want Winston to be my lawyer now." It was as simple as that.

"There are things you don't know about him," I said. "There's something I must tell you."

She sighed and dropped her hand from her forehead. "Why, Alfred, I don't know what more there is to tell."

"Why don't we sit down on the couch."

"Very well," she agreed, sighing again and raising her chin.

"Just over here," I said—just a few steps. My hand went to the back of her white summer dress. I could feel the rickety cage of ribs.

We sat down on the couch, not more than a few inches from each other. From somewhere in the upper floors, Mary slammed a door and then bounced noisily down a flight of stairs.

My mother seemed to be preparing herself for news that could only be endured by a steely determination to get through the worst with her dignity intact. I thought, Her son is causing this reaction. Her golden boy is bringing unendurable news. Off-your-rocker insults, pleas to change her mind. Her folded hands fell to her lap abruptly. She was ready for anything.

I told her, "I think you're making a terrible mistake about the property."

"Yes, darling." Dust from the attic clung to the pleated hem of her dress—picked up from the trunks containing the treasures of my baby things. "But I've had to consider what's best."

"For the life of me, I can't understand why you would give Winston your power of attorney. It just doesn't make sense. I've handled the property for nearly twenty years—since Dad died. You've never complained. The property is as beautiful as the day you bought it."

"You've been spectacular," my mother declared.

"I don't know about that, but I've done the best I could. We've never had any disagreements."

"Never." She tossed her head, and her white hair seemed to glow by means of some interior phosphorescence of energy. The strong hands in her lap were fists to give thrust to her words. I felt that she possessed an awesome power of womanhood. When she spoke her voice was vibrant against the gathered darkness of old age. Her fists trembled for an instant above her lap, giving the impression that she was undergoing some fierce competition.

"But," she said, "there's *something* about him!" And this seemed to be a triumphant statement of Winston's best quality.

I leaned back in the couch. It was so uncomfortable that leaning back offered the same comfort as leaning forward, only with the added prospect that the springs might erupt at any moment and catapult me into the middle of the living room.

"*What* about him?" I asked. "What about him?" I repeated after a moment. My mother seemed to be off somewhere on an ego bliss-out.

"By God!" she exclaimed, throwing a short right that would have taken the wind out of anyone's sails. "By God, when Winston Bingham walks into a room, you know a *man* has walked into the room."

"Yeah, right," I muttered. I blew a little kiss to the fireplace and waved a twinkling good-bye to logic and chronology.

"He has energy, Alfred. I don't know how else to put it. He comes in and I feel a, a—" She searched for the word.

"A quickening," I said helpfully.

"Exactly!" she exclaimed. "A quickening. I've always said you were the sensitive one in the family. That's why you've had all these problems coping in life." There was a moment of silence. "Yes, a quickening," she mused, toying with the word. "Of course, you have to watch him like a hawk." She was watching me like a hawk. "He *is* a rough beast, isn't he?"

"Yes, he is," I said.

"I know you don't like him."

"No, I don't."

"With his breeding," she said, her voice trailing off.

I thought, Listen, breeding is *your* problem, Mom. I'm not on Winston's case because of his breeding.

"How can I explain it?" She looked around the living room, as if some visual aid might appear to provide a demonstration of Winston's qualities. "I feel rejuvenated. He has charts and maps and plans, and an idea a minute. He listens to me, too." She looked wary for a second, perhaps expecting that I would disagree with her. "He pretends that I have ten, twenty years to live."

"Well, maybe you do," I said.

She smiled and nodded heartily. "Well, by God, maybe I do at that. That's what I think. You're as young as you feel, and I *feel* a lot closer to fifty than to a hundred." She looked sly. "They expect me to rot in this house. Sit here and rot until they lower me into the ground. Being old is a dirty trick."

She pointed a bony finger at me indelicately. I wondered if she had picked up this gross habit from her son-in-law. Her hand was very trembly, but at that age it was to be expected. My hands had been trembly for many years from alcoholism. My fingers had jumped about like little gymnasts.

"Alfred, have I shown one—*one* trace of senility?"

"No," I said, recalling that at our lunch she had asked me the same question. "But you are showing poor judgment."

She surveyed the living room down her nose. "I think for the first time in my life, Alfred, that I'm exercising excellent judgment," she said, offended. "Sometimes in life you have to take a chance. That was the tragedy of your father. He was so careful and methodical, so lawyerly. You know, he wouldn't eat fish."

"Yes, I know."

"Here we were by the seashore with the most beautiful piece of property in the United States, and he was frightened of everything. The fog, the fish, the ocean, the wind. I think even those burly clambake makers scared him. All he wanted to do was sit in his library and draft wills, work on tax problems. Not that that isn't terribly important work. You and I know how wonderful he was."

"Yeah," I said. I missed Dad, frankly—wished I'd gotten to know him better.

"He was a saint," she sighed.

"Uh-huh."

"Have I told you about Winston's latest plan?"

"You mean the villas?" I asked.

She looked quizzical. "What villas?"

I couldn't bear to go into the villas, the landing strip, the nine-hole golf course, the beach gouged out of the shoreline. To go into such a lengthy description—and to be thought completely nuts in the process—would be too much.

I shrugged. "No, what's his latest plan?"

"He's determined that I should write my autobiography. I

happened to read him an except from my diary the other night, and he was quite taken with it. He expressed himself on the richness of detail. Well"—she patted her hair—"you know Winston"—Thumper's excesses of enthusiasm, his transports of romantic feeling—"when he gets it into his head about something, I don't care how often a person demurs, he can be very persuasive."

"It'll certainly keep you occupied," I said. You might not even notice the villas.

She looked at me reproachfully. "It's just possible, Alfred, that what little I have to say might be of permanent literary value."

I nodded. "You've seen a lot of things in ninety years."

"I daresay I won't be able to compete with literary titans, but perhaps a reader will find some interest in this obscure country life."

"Any title yet?" I asked.

"*A Woman Remembers*," she said promptly. "Winston seems to think . . ."

Winston. Winston. Winston. Couldn't get that name out of the conversation.

". . . that the big question is whether to go with an autobiography, or hire someone to give me the full treatment."

"The full treatment?" The phrase seemed freighted with sexuality.

"I told Winston that I wasn't sure I could sit still while someone *pored* over my life. He said it was fine with him—whatever I decided. He'd make all the arrangements. It's amazing the contacts he has in all walks of life. Like that Fogarty man, the publisher of the *Herald*. A little nobody who's been a member of the Winding Hollow Country Club for thirty years, and no one had ever met him, and suddenly he wants to know the story of my life. Winston did that. See, *that's* what I mean!" she exclaimed. For a moment I thought she was addressing another person in the room. I looked around. "It's the gumption, the pizzazz. He goes out and grabs life by the throat."

The reverse of my problem.

"I admire that in a man," she said fiercely. "It reminds me of the whaling days—strong men in little boats, facing Leviathan."

I hoped that I wouldn't be submitted to more blubber-carving—knifings in the air, strips of blubber cut away from my hulk.

Winston Bingham had managed to bury himself deep inside my mother's brain.

Carried away by the image of titans in frail crafts battling blubber-packed leviathans, my mother said haughtily, "And I believe, Alfred, that I'm the best judge of who should be entrusted with my holdings. *You* may think I've made a terrible mistake, but *I* think my biggest mistake was not taking a more active interest in my business affairs after your father died."

As she spoke her head became more thrown back. It looked sort of laid out and reposed on an angel-pillow of white hair. Her powdered neck presented an offering to burly Zeus in the clouds above our summer house. "I have already spent too much time in mourning," she said, letting her words gather power from the dark living room where no light flickered in the morning.

It was cool in the living room, its nicest feature at that moment. The chill of stones was calming. I cleared my throat. My mother's head was at peace, her nose in profile. Perhaps she wouldn't have minded too much if I just got up and left.

"Mom," I said.

I broke the spell and her eyes opened. She looked at me with a wonderful smile, as if remembering all the good things about her parenting. The gulf between us had opened even wider. "Yes, darling," she answered.

"There's something about Winston Bingham that I think you should know about."

I felt the first powerful throbs of anxiety.

She turned around a little on the couch to face me. She was still smiling, but something in her eyes had picked up on my tone. She looked wary. "About Winston?" she asked. "What is it?"

Her fingers curled in her lap, and I wondered if it wasn't to ward off the news. I sensed then that she had a suppressed glimmer about him—some intuition that something wasn't quite right with him. I think she knew the truth—it wasn't really her he was interested in—but to face that knowledge would mean more of the same desolation. Facing the truth meant she would continue to be a bit player, like the rest of us.

I wanted desperately to tell her that Winston was a thief. I would tell her and she would raise her fists and try to pound back the news, as if it was something palpable with which she could do battle. The last strength in her would be amazing.

Afterward I would be freed to the light. Home to Alice, golf in the afternoon, lawyerly brow-furrowings. "Well, it had to be done for her own good," I would insist. I didn't think anyone would gainsay me. Here was a man who wanted to turn six hundred virgin acres into a landing strip, bulldoze a whole town, and throw my mother into a nursing home when he was done with her. I saw a row of windows and each one had a blue glow in it.

I wanted to tell her that I planned to call Dickie Ramondino, formerly the head of the billing department at Waterman, Rhodes, Stevenson, and Meriwether. "There's a man I'd like you to talk to," I would have said to her. "I think you know him. His name is Dickie Ramondino."

"Why, Dickie," she would say. "I didn't know he was still alive."

"Retired from the firm about a year ago."

"He had the most wonderful manners," she would say.

I saw a high tea, a maximum of cordiality and comfort, perhaps right here in the living room. Two chairs drawn up beside a silver service—just Dickie and my mother. And finally, in the high afternoon, Dickie would get around to the matter of Winston's indelicacy, the little problem he had posed for the firm with that missing one hundred and twenty-five thousand dollars.

Dickie would explain it all to her in precisely the fashion she understood best. There would be no need to use the specific words: thief and crook and felony. Dickie would be horrified by such words; he would shrink back from them. But the words would be there after tea and after the powerful injection of manners had worn off.

And my mother's ferocity would be terrible. Winston, she would say, was worse than a wharf rat. It goes to show about breeding. He almost pulled the wool over my eyes. Using an old woman, using his own family that took him in from the gutter. He's no better than slime. Vermin you grind under your heels. A slug that crawled out from under a rock. We had a word for his type when I was a girl.

White nigger.

That's your Winston Bingham.

A white nigger.

Sometimes my mother would really fly off the handle, rhetoric-wise.

But as the words formed in my mind, the air seemed to leave the living room. My hand went to my throat and I worked to catch my breath. "I don't know quite how to say this"—I said slowly, testing the words. I could really feel the anxiety; it clenched at my chest and shut off air to my brain.

"Yes, darling," my mother said, poised with her little fists.

I realized suddenly that I didn't know how to say it, put it, get on with it, because I had no intention of saying anything. To think I had been up all night with the words.

"Lurks vengeance, footless, irresistible," wrote George Eliot.

There was a silence—awkward, painful. I shifted in the un-comfortable couch and my face reddened. Sentences formed and drifted away and there was no air and I felt that I was choking. My eyes roved around the living room—toward fireplace and windows—looking for any escape.

"I beat Winston at tennis," I blurted out at last.

Instantly, I wanted to run after the words and somehow bring them back.

My mother looked at me for a long moment. She stared at the global burnout beside her. Then she gave out with a long sigh. It was the soft sound of crosses borne, motherhood tested, genetic disasters, and bad seeds. She was absolving herself of me. Obvi-ously, once upon a time I had come from outer space, from some malign planet to test her resolve and Christian faith.

"My baby," she whispered.

How *could* I have said that? *That* wasn't what I meant.

I sighed, too, in the morning darkness.

My mother's long fingers came up toward me like delicate pincers—making shadow-crocodile openings and closings. They reached my red cheeks. Her fingers were cool, her palm soft and warm when she gently squeezed them into a trout expression. A little game we played when I was her best baby—something fishy.

I took her by the wrist in a grip that was not hard but not soft either—took her wrist in both my meaty hands. Her fingers were still in their delicate pincer mode. I held her wrist in the air for just a second. Then with a full forward motion, leaning out of the couch, I redeposited the appendage onto her lap and gave a couple of pats to keep it there.

Then I got up and left the house.

13

I went to my place out on the rocks. Three slabs—two vertical and one horizontal. As a child I pretended to rule a kingdom from that rough chair. Natural armrests bulged out of each vertical slab. They gave me a profound sense of kingly leisure.

The chair was the only place where I was content. From the upper-floor bedroom in my parents' house, I could hear the sound of the sea vividly, eternal plash after eternal plash. The narrow windows of the third floor acted like speaker systems to bring the sound right to me in stereo. I felt the water spread out along the beach, sizzle away into wild foam. Sometimes I went to my window in the deep night, and looked out to reassure myself that everything was in its normal rhythm. I took comfort from the raw silver of our rocks in the moonlight. They seemed like fortresses against some mysterious invading enemy.

Getting down to the chair was a bit precarious for an older man. I had to climb down backward—some twenty feet above the water—then hold on with both hands and turn myself in a space not wider than twelve inches. Facing the opposite file of rocks, which was some twenty yards across a narrow finger of ocean, I would ease myself down into a sitting position and get comfortable with the armrests and my feet dangling over the sheer face of rock.

When I was a child, I could scamper down and get comfortable in a matter of seconds. I had heedless confidence in my muscle-knowledge. Now, even though the chair was only a few feet below the crest of the file at its highest point, I found myself puffy and sweaty from the exertion.

I must have needed to get down there awfully badly. It helped me a bit to realize that a slip would have meant only a dunking.

The finger of water between files was quite deep, and the head of the rocks broke the surf and allowed for a gentle inlet. During hurricanes, though, it became a dangerous funnel of spuming water and the spray rode in quickly on a chute of power and smashed against the scrubland just below my house.

As soon as I sat down on the rock, got myself together, and caught my breath, I felt peace that week. It was an enclosed little world, hemmed in by the high spine of rocks directly opposite me, a wall behind me, the narrow finger of water below me, and scrubland rising to my right and obscuring my house.

I sat by the hour, trying to put it all together—where I had gone wrong, how it all should have been different. If I leaned out of the chair just a little, I could see an almost telescoped sliver of the Atlantic to my left—a patch of water the size of a postage stamp—now gunmetal, now green, now flashing with light, now glassy, now gray, stretching all the way to the horizon. Sometimes it was filled by an oil tanker, the flickering kinescopic sails from a regatta, the wavering bridge of a power boat. But mostly there was nothing, and there was silence.

The fishermen no longer came. Evidently the word had gone out or Sheriff Jim Sprague had set up his roadblock farther down the road. The rocks were bare. I could not remember a time, in all the years we had lived there, when they hadn't been populated by at least one fisherman. That was six decades. And now there was no one.

What was nice about the rock-chair was the total absence of vista. All of a sudden—after Winston, after my mother—I couldn't stand views and vistas and long stretches of anything: beaches, shoreline, seawall, town. From where I sat I couldn't see the property, and I didn't want to see it. But in my mind private planes came in for a landing over my rocks. Power boats chugged up the mighty Piscotaug, dripping diesel fuel. Villas turned pink at sunset. Flags waved over manicured putting greens.

When I went out to the chair in the morning, I refrained from looking to my left, because there was more Meriwether property down there. Rough shoreline—rocky and angry. The property annoyed me. Six hundred acres. There was far too much of it; it surrounded and engulfed you. The property taxes just killed you.

We should have given it to a nature conservancy twenty years ago.

I descended to the chair, inside the womblike division of rocks, and felt some sense of security coming back to me. Sometimes I hugged myself, as if against a storm. My feet dangled and epi-sodically my heels knocked together idly. I rubbed my hands against the glinting rock, which flashed in the sun from flecks of mica.

I made a point of staying away from the opposite file of rocks. It was perhaps fifty yards longer and ten yards higher than the file where I sat. From the high narrow spine, it offered a majestic view of the surrounding world—Wolcott in the distance; the bus-tling headwaters of the Piscotaug just below; the long Wolcott beach on the opposite shore; the gold cupola of the Surf Club. And, if one turned, there were the tiers of our property, rising to the stone chimneys of my parents' house. They were as majestic as some ancestral dwelling where one would think that all was peace and tranquility, and everyone slightly dotty in an engag-ing way.

The larger file of rocks had been popular with the fishermen. They liked to walk out to the farthest point, which ended in el-lipses of boulders—perhaps four hundred yards from shore—and set themselves up for the day. That file had once been a place I knew like the back of my hand. It was a children's world out there—with caves and tunnels and deep hiding places; secret gouges and slits in the rock, some large enough for a child to slip through; massive overhangs down near the water. There was a cave near the water where I once played pirates.

No one ever explored the rocks the way I had; no one had such need of secrecy. I liked to perch on an overhang and watch high tide fill the caves; or sit in a cave and let the tide lap around me until in the last minutes I would scamper away. Rock pools were choked with crabs and stranded starfish. Limbs of crabs bleached on the higher rocks, tossed up by some enor-mity of water in the night.

Most people didn't have time for the plateaus and outcrop-pings and caves and tunnels and snug overhangs that existed just below the spine of the great file thrusting whitely into the ocean. If most people looked at all, they looked around them at the magnificent view. They waved to bathers on the opposite side of the Piscotaug's headwaters—the Surf Club side. They moved on usually, and took their rest on one of the farthest boulders. But there was this other child's place just below them.

Now the spine was without human traffic. It was sharply silhouetted against the sky and below it ran the tangled rocky jumble. Great rocks had been thrown together like putty under the razor spine.

During that week I could see fear in Alice's eyes. She gave the impression of strength, but she wasn't so strong. I knew the questions behind her look: Are you going to start drinking again? Is it all going to begin again? The absences, the phone calls in the night, the varieties of incoherence, the sleeping on the beach. Are you going to give up everything you've worked so hard to achieve?

She watched my regression with a worried but clinical eye. Once I saw her at the tip of our lawn. She looked at me on the chair, with my topsiders clicking together and me hugging myself and rocking back and forth. She turned away on the lawn, and the sag of her shoulders indicated that she expected the worst.

"Can I help?" Alice asked. "Just let me help. *What's the problem?*"

"It's something I'll have to work out by myself."

"Would you like to talk to Mal Robinson?"

"No, I don't think so."

"It's just that I've never seen you this down before. I want to be able to *do* something."

"I'm all right. A lot of things hit me all at once. I need time to think."

"What things? Is it your mother? Winston?"

"Don't bother me," I said. "Please."

"You'll catch cold out there," Alice said.

My mother's voice gonged in my ears. She spoke to Winston from the back burners of my mind. ". . . at tennis. At tennis. I ask you. Ask you. I'm his mother. His mother. You raise a child, a child. You have such hopes, hopes. A mother's burden. I suppose it was the alcohol, the alcohol. I wish you could have seen him as a boy. How he seemed to flow across a tennis court. Now look at him. My husband's side of the family had many instances of insanity and instability. You raise a child, Winston, Winston, Winston. You let them out into the world, cruel world. You have to let them go sooner or later. You can't protect them forever, ever. Sometimes I believe that God is testing my faith, you know.

" 'I beat Winston at tennis.'

"Well, I just looked at him, at him, at him. I sighed and told him he'd always be my baby. You can only do so much. After all, he's over sixty years old. I think I kept him too long at my breast. For three years I suckled him.

"Frankly, I think at this point he is better off with that woman. That woman. That woman."

Winston and my mother spoke in the living room during those days of my upsetting emotional debilitation. I sat on the chair and covered my ears and rocked back and forth and clicked my heels. I felt self-pity; I felt murderous and forgiving; I plotted revenge. My mother came to me and begged to be taken back. I refused. Winston groveled before my throne and with a wiggle of my fingers guards seized him.

On the high chair I underwent massive yawings of emotion—from great anger to immense sadness; from self-love to a big hug for the world. Sometimes my fingers rested on my cheek the way Jack Benny's had in a trademark gesture of amazement and bewilderment.

At some point out on the chair, I asked myself, What *are* you doing out here? A mature man in the grand vintage of his years, sitting out on some rocks and acting like a baby. I stopped my heels from clicking, stopped hugging myself and rocking back and forth.

What *are* you doing out here?

The following Sunday morning I went into Wolcott and picked up the New York *Times* and the Providence *Herald*. It was a bright sunny day, and there was a surrounding hint of coolness in the air. It was still hot, but I felt an undercurrent of change, perhaps more psychic than meteorological.

In Wolcott I felt the heft and responsibility of the newspapers, publishing news of the real world. I got into my Caprice and

headed home. It was seven-thirty, eight o'clock in the morning—
sun-filled.

Alice was still asleep when I came back to the house. I removed the magazine section from the bulk of the *Herald*, folded
it and stuck the section lengthwise into my back pocket. I left
the remainder of the newspapers on my side of the bed.

I closed the front door softly behind me, made my way
through the scrub vegetation at the bottom of my property, then
climbed onto the first plateau of rocks. The sun was dazzling, the
glint off the stone terrific, and I had to squint as I walked. I
could feel the perspiration start, and I predicted the future of
the day, its gathering dense humidity. The left side of my body
absorbed the warmth. I longed for the coolness of the chair—so
deep and cool and shadowed in the morning, while the light
flashed off the two files of rocks, seeming to dart from one to the
other.

I descended to the chair carefully and sat down. I pulled the
magazine section from my pocket and stared at the picture of my
mother on the cover. She looked as happy as a clam. Her white
hair was fluffed benevolently. Some talent of the photographic
process had made her blue eyes seem twinkling and welcoming.
One could see her presiding at enormous family gatherings
where there was lots of good conversation, flowing wine, and
where the men went off in the afternoon to play their games.

In Dace Lesser's article, my mother retailed dancing with
Teddy Roosevelt, sharing a chuckle with FDR. She offered gar-
dening tips, reminisced about the "old" Rhode Island—whaling
in Wickham, tuna-fishing in Galilee, parties in Newport. A half
page of the article was devoted to her recipe for a clambake—
serves seventy. The only passage where she really let go with the
force of her personality occurred during a discourse on johnnycakes. She insisted that she, and she alone, held the one true
recipe. The white cornmeal had to be ground up with extreme
slowness. There had to be a proper mixture of this year's and last
year's cornmeal. But the real key to success, she declared, was in
not letting those millstones get too hot.

There were photographs of my mother standing in her lovely
garden, sitting in her classic Duesenberg, standing outside the
family manse with its stone chimneys rising in the background.

The Under Secretary of the Navy was even featured in one photograph, looming benevolently over the matriarch, contemplating—you heard it here first—a political career in the state he had come to love, so rich in tradition.

One particular thing in the article caught my eye. No mention was made anywhere that my mother had ever given birth to a male child. My sister Dorothy was mentioned a couple of times, mostly in her hostess capacity and strong-right-arm function as wife of the busy Under Secretary. My father was mentioned a few times—his strength and quiet dignity, his love of the seashore, his prominence as a lawyer. My nephew's budding career as a poet—tied into my mother's aspirations as an autobiographer—garnered a subordinate clause among the well-griddled johnnycakes.

But where was I? Alfred. Me. A careless reader, and even a careful one, would have been led to the conclusion that Alfred Meriwether did not exist—in the sense of "exist" as we know it from the metaphysicians. I found this omission disconcerting in the moments before I began to laugh. Discreet chuckles at first to test the water of my mirth, and then some heavy laughter.

If she left me out of her forthcoming autobiography, I would sue my mother in a court of law for involuntary orphan-making.

I am somebody, I said to myself. I am somebody. I am married, I am a lawyer, I am an uncle and a brother and a son. I served my country in the Second World War. I played tennis at Forest Hills in 1948. You could look it up.

At long last has it come down to this? I asked the sun. That my small mark in the world is to be obliterated entirely? You can't just take a man and pretend he doesn't exist.

It was funny, sad—and deeply offensive. For the first time in my life, I think, I experienced total distance from my mother. *This* was her summing-up, her satisfaction—newsprint and the cold eyes of strangers. If she ever got her bio published—through Winston's graces—she would probably go on the talk-show circuit, make the rounds with her book. She would appear on midday self-help shows and tell the host how to whip up some johnnycakes. She would be crusty but lovable, with a studioful of memories. But nowhere, in print or media, would she find time to mention that she had once given birth to a male child.

I gave the magazine a toss. It fluttered in the air, spread out upon air drafts, and hit the water with a little slap in the silence. The article drifted on the swells. My mother's photograph darkened and became heavy with waterlog and drifted out to sea between the files.

Kate Latham glistened with sweat. She took the opposite file of rocks at a run and moved quickly up to the topmost spine without breaking stride. She seemed saturated in light.

Already, in the few moments after I tossed my mother overboard, I was thinking about closing up my house. Little details of closing up were impinging on my consciousness. I had to call the gas company; I had to call the plumber to get the pipes drained, the water turned off. Alice and I would talk on this Sunday. I would climb back into bed with the newspapers as an extra layer of covering over my spindly legs, and we would talk.

Kate Latham was etched vividly just above the jumble of interfacing rocks and thrown-together formations, where I had once played as a child. Taking in the view at the end of her jog. I envied her balance. It was narrow up there on the backbone at the end of our property. She stopped just short of a point where she would have had to climb down toward the long string of boulders. She stood with her hands on her hips in blue jogging shorts and yellow T-shirt. Her hair was pulled back and tied in a ponytail. She stood on a massive butte of rock and caught her breath in the sunlight.

The view must have been majestic. It always had been. The tide on the Piscotaug would be coming in. The river would be furrowed with power below the butte upon which she stood. The gold cupola of the Surf Club would be gleaming. The waves on the Wolcott beach would be rolling heavily on this day, breaking with humid assurance. I could imagine what she saw on this morning. I felt a little cranky in my throne shadows—invisible and as damp as the air in my mother's living room.

Maybe I would go over and join her. I needed to be in touch for a minute or two with something healthy. We could discuss painting and clambakes, poetry and Duesenbergs. Maybe she would like to know what this place in Rhode Island had meant to me—how I had spent a lifetime here.

But it was all too tiring, and I slumped against the back of the

chair. I realized that it wasn't even necessary to announce myself. She was a good twenty yards away. The sun would be in
her eyes if she looked my way. There was no need for even a
hello across the finger of water.

All I could think was that at some point I had to call this
plumber in Meguntic. Then I had to call the gas company. I had
to seal up my fireplace, get a new lock for the front door. Move
the furniture in off the porch. Talk to some real estate people.

Talk to some real estate people. Talk to Alice first and then
we'll go over and talk to some real estate people. It felt as if winter was already upon me—with its demands of insulation, wood-
burning stoves, and pipe-drainings.

I didn't call hello to the lovely Kate Latham as she stood on
the butte across the water, taking in the view. But I did hope
jadedly that she might choose to swing into a warming-down ritual—something deliciously aerobic; some loosening of the ham-
strings; tautening of her abdomen, so important for the preven-
tion of lower-back strain; little archings and flexings, tanned
ripples. Already I was starting to perk up a bit.

I gave a little wave to Kate Latham, in response to a hello that
had never been given. She couldn't see me. I got up to go home.
I stood on my chair, embraced by the sides of the slab. I envied
my nephew—fortunate young man to have a summer with her.

He was there then.

Thumper.

The thousand lives of the rocks and the sea and the air continued. Gulls squealed, waves landed, a speedboat droned somewhere at the mouth of the Piscotaug. The beautiful girl didn't
see him. She had her back to him.

At a run he was larger and more formidable than he was on a
tennis court, or at a law firm, or at a cookout. I had the sense of
what he must have been like as a basketball player. Small College All-American. A kid the pros wanted. I had the sense of
how menacing he must have been under the boards. It must
have been Thumper's world—under the boards. He was big
across the chest and in the shoulders and forearms. In motion—
and he was in motion now, with a fixity of purpose that seemed
to define the word concentration—the power in his upper body
was galvanic.

I watched him from my chair. I leaned against the wall of stone, hemmed in by the vertical slabs—hidden. He was wearing white tennis shorts, silver jogging shoes, and a T-shirt with writing on it. I knew what the T-shirt said. He wore it for running. He had several of them. He had bought them in a novelty shop on Times Square. The shirt said HAVE A NICE DAY, but in smaller letters, just under HAVE A NICE DAY was printed ASSHOLE.

HAVE A NICE DAY
ASSHOLE

He got a kick out of it. He was a crude man.

The pourings of the sun lent his hair a frizzy luster. He took the gentle plateaus of rocks and then reached the high spine across and above where I stood. He seemed to take delight then in going into a couple of feinting moves atop the spine, little feats of balance as he moved, perhaps deep in the memory of youthful clearings-out. A coordination showed itself that had not been apparent on the tennis court. He suddenly threw a bolo punch that would have caught his imaginary opponent in the guzzle pipe.

Fifteen or twenty feet behind the oblivious Kate, he stopped abruptly. He walked toward her in an elaborate tiptoe; a silent-film planting with each step of his jogging shoes. He must have been several feet away from her when he said whatever it was he did say. From the angle of my vision it looked as if he whispered a sweet nothing directly into her exposed ear lobe; the blond hair pulled back to reveal the droplet.

At any rate—whatever he said and from wherever he said it—Kate Latham couldn't have been more surprised if she had been pecked by a gull. Her feet stayed in place but her upper body shuddered and she tucked in her arms as if at a sudden chill. Her thoughts had taken her on a long journey, far from the rocks.

Although her feet were planted, Winston stepped in and grabbed her arms to steady her against the dangers of the rocks, as if Kate Latham might lose her balance. Her body was facing out to sea, straight ahead, inside Winston's hold.

I was very concentrated on them: the distance and the closeness, the light between us, the sheen of her hair, the strength of his grip. She made a forlorn flapping gesture, still pinioned with her arm against her side. She was twisted upward toward Winston and I could see her face and the play of her fingers as they darted uncertainly around her heart area. Just for a moment. She was smiling up at him, but I thought perhaps there was just a tinge in the sun, a deepening in the color of her cheeks, that was very much like the illuminating blush I had seen at the Surf Club, when she had seen what I knew.

I watched Winston with unusual keenness. It was as though the action on the opposite rocks was being comprehended by my brain at a speed slightly faster than it was taking place. I was guarding Winston. We were under the boards together, and I could pretty much anticipate what he would do next.

He released the girl. No burns of lust seared her yellow T-shirt. I imagined a dialogue between them.

"Didn't mean to startle you," he must have said.

"Oh, that's all right, Mr. Bingham," she must have replied.

He stood then at the tip of the butte, on a pinnacle of rocks. He was the Under Secretary of the Navy. He put his hands gravely behind him, and they slapped together a couple of times. Shafts of sunlight sought him out. He may have been thinking nuclear thoughts. His great submarines were out there somewhere.

He saw missiles cutting through the undersea and lifting into the Rhode Island air. He knew the codes of destruction. He gave the sense, when he brushed by Kate Latham, that the very chartings of the sea were his. The rocks of the property seemed small. I huddled in the shadows with my interior monologues.

Kate shrugged and seemed about to leave him to his megathoughts—to take off and run home. But he beckoned her over. She looked prim beside him. He began to paint his dreams for her. Once or twice she stood on tiptoes—raised herself up off the heels of her shoes—as if she could peer over and look into the ocean itself to see how the world down there seethed with conflict, how close to shore the Russians patrolled, how their trawlers lingered nearby with sophisticated sonar equipment to watch every move we made on the Atlantic.

Perhaps Kate Latham didn't realize how close the enemy was.

They were listening to us even now beyond the horizon. She nodded and shielded her eyes, the better to see what he saw. I was imagining all this—all the things that Winston told her.

He swept the horizon one last time. Then his hand rested in the air in the direction of what would be the New Wolcott. There was a lot to point out in that direction. Winston seemed to pat New Wolcott into place with his hand. It was hard to tell whether he was giving Kate the whaling village-period garb–Mystic-johnnycakes version of the New Wolcott—which had captured my mother's heart—or the Charlie Tuna-barn-wood–condo–bluechip-Caesar's Palace version of the same place.

There seemed to be something about the vista of Winston's dreams that Kate Latham couldn't quite picture. Some alignment along the beach. Inside the new teacher-student rapport that had been established between them, Winston felt free to rest his arm lightly on her shoulder so that she would be able to follow the line of sight of his finger. There was so much to see. He explained the marina to her, and she nodded. He traced the course of the power boats through the channel between our rocks and the Wolcott beach. Perhaps he even made *putt-putt* noises.

No matter where he looked, there were possibilities. He turned full around and showed her the Meriwether property. With the spread of his hand, he seemed to indicate the enormity of the problem. The decay, the dense woods, the road through the property that would have to be widened to handle more traffic. The neglect was there for Kate Latham to see.

He touched her a couple of times to make his point. All innocence in his teaching mode. A couple of light touches to guide her vision, to help her understand the history of a place from his point of view. A little brush of the hand, a little pat on her forearm. He stepped back just a mini-step to let the property sink in —its tiers of neglect, the furry density of trees bespeaking woolly land management, woolly thinking that had been going on for more than half a century; woolly people; vain mothers, dipso sons, depressed fathers, hysterically aphonic daughters, a marathon-running son who had chosen a career in the high-paying poetry field. All that blockheadedness and denseness represented by those enormous chimneys. Behind those chimneys lurked darkness, footless, irresistible; eccentricity; neurosis; implosion; the whole vanity of human wishes.

Winston took a mini-step back from Kate Latham to let his angle on the property sink into her consciousness. Perhaps she felt they were sharing an imaginative leap. Frankly, I didn't know what she felt.

Winston feasted his eyes on her. He arched his troublesome neck to get a fuller glimpse from her velvet neck to her well-turned ankles. If looks alone could have penetrated into the marrow of her bones, she would have leapt away. She would have hit that rock face at a dead run and not stopped until she reached the chimneys of my parents' house. Because this guy—the one feasting himself on her buttocks, admiring the backs of her thighs, nibbling on her calves, licking contentedly at her ankles, practically burping with delight in the sun—this guy was trouble.

I didn't think that Kate Latham realized how perfectly the trap was sprung, how the cage had descended over her vulnerable contours. She was one-third naked already with gimme-a-T-gimme-an-H cheerleader eroticism that was bound to arouse him.

While gorging himself on Kate—as she looked at the property through his avid eyes—Winston Bingham seemed the soul of fatherly dignity. His hands were placed formally behind his back. He resembled an aging and arrow-thin curator instructing a rookie connoisseur.

I knew that Winston had been planning this escapade for weeks. He had been planning it ever since that afternoon at the Surf Club when he had been stricken by the vision of Kate Latham reclining in a bikini. He had planned it down to the last detail. Planning was his strong suit—he rarely made an unplanned move. My belief in his strategic outlook on life-events was based on years of experience with him. I felt I knew him like the back of my hand.

The key element in his strategic thinking—the thing that popped the cork on his lust—was his belief that Kate Latham was a nobody. He wouldn't pull a stunt like this on anyone whom he didn't regard as absolute shit. She was "trade"—a glorified babysitter, a mother's home companion, a carrier of picnic baskets. Her so-called artistic inclinations didn't hold any water with him. They just made her even more sluttish, connoting group-sex encounters and "modeling" orgies with hand-held cameras. Winston had worked his crude magic on secretaries, waitresses, and surfer girls during our long association. They occupied a special category for him, somewhere below that of prostitute. A prostitute at least demanded money for her favors.

Standing on my chair, watching this unfolding drama, I experienced shooting pains of sexual envy. I stamped my topsiders on the hard rock and the right side of my face twitched.

He had overhauled my law firm.

He had taken my property.

He had stolen my mother.

Now he was invading my fantasies.

Winston gestured solicitously and they moved across the butte of rocks. The sun was in their eyes and they couldn't see me. Winston pointed down to the jumbled world below—the plateaus, tiers, and overhangs that ran along the side of the rocks facing me. It was a place so unlike the high smooth spine along which most people traveled. Perhaps she had not been aware of this other world; few people were aware of it unless they chose to walk out along the shorter, less majestic file of rocks into which my chair was embedded.

Winston seemed to run his hand along the flank of rocks. Kate leaned over to look down and get a better view—and Winston peered into the gap of her T-shirt to get a better view of her breasts. He was talking all the while, explaining, and I believe he was telling her how incredible it was down there in the crazy-quilt darkness by the sea. Two hundred yards of total jumble that seemed to be clinging to a smoother, sturdier, healthier rock formation like some excrescent disease. He pointed vigorously down toward that other world. His gestures were quite theatrical. He could be terribly persuasive; he could be insistent; he could bully.

The air was still suddenly. There was a gauzy film of light across the water, and the couple—the older man and the woman young enough to be his granddaughter—shimmered and the older man's legs looked out of joint at the knees and ankles, and he seemed to be giving off shimmering heat from his silver jogging shoes.

"Don't go down there," I warned Kate Latham. I thought I had said it aloud, but in fact I hadn't even whispered it.

I had told Winston too much in the early days when it had seemed important to be polite to him. I took him into the interior of the property, gave him a guided tour of these amazing rock formations. I showed him where I had played as a child. He had said, "Uh-huh, uh-huh." What the hell are we doing here? he must have thought. Here in this netherworld. Let's get out of here. But somewhere in his photographic memory, the jumble of rocks had remained as clear to him as if he had taken a little stroll through it just the day before. Nothing had been discarded.

I continued to put words in their mouths:

Winston asked Kate Latham, "Want to take a look-see? This'll knock your eyes out. Come on," he said. He did not touch her. "There's a lot to see. Let me be your guide."

She looked at her watch. "Really, I'd like to, Mr. Bingham. But I have to be getting back."

"Nah," he said. "What's the hurry?"

Sunday morning. Up at the big house, the old battle-ax would still be snoozing away.

She shook her head. She didn't want to go down there.

"Five, ten minutes. Is that so very much to ask?"

Like a person poised at a pool's edge who was afraid of the water, Kate Latham stood on the rocks with her knees slightly bent. It was as if the momentum of her body would propel her into something that her mind didn't want to do.

Winston shrugged easily. I imagined that he said, "Suit yourself."

He hopped briskly down to the next plateau of rocks. Two hops took him to a position about five feet below where Kate Latham stood. He looked back up at about her crotch level, looking up at her slim legs, her jogging shorts, up at her breasts and blond hair, her knees bent invitingly.

She looked at her watch again. I imagined that she said, "I really have to go, Mr. Bingham. I'm really sorry. Maybe some other time."

She took a half step backward. Winston had his hands on his hips. I could see only his back. I imagined that he was smiling up at her, at the vista of his possibilities—the lengths of tanned thigh revealed to him, the outcroppings of breasts, the firm calves.

He spread out his arms in a "What can you do?" gesture that seemed almost a blessing on his possibilities, a sanctification of the moment lost. Easy come, easy go.

Obviously, my imagination had been working overtime. I had been constructing dialogues, interpreting gestures that I could barely see from across the space between the rocks. My imagination had been traveling along on its own track, using half-glimpsed pieces of information. What was happening seemed real enough to me, but perhaps it wasn't reality.

I felt guilty for allowing my dislike of Winston to run away with me. My brother-in-law had met my mother's young companion on the rocks. They had exchanged pleasantries for a few minutes. Now Winston was off to do his own thing, and she was off to the big house. Maybe she'd do some painting before my mother woke up.

Maybe I was getting paranoid. Pretty soon I would start thinking that Winston was aiming death rays at me, directing my thoughts with a remote-control device.

The last words I had uttered to my mother still rang in my ears: "I beat Winston at tennis." Those were not the words of a mature, healthy man in the prime of his life. Those were the words of a little boy.

I sighed, and my lips quivered troutishly.

Suddenly Kate Latham rose into the air. For just a second it seemed like a pure act of levitation. Her arms remained stiffly at her sides. She seemed to be diving upward. She rose and then I could see Winston's hands and a tanned expanse of the woman's midriff. She drifted off the butte like some fantastic Neptune temptress, suspended beside the whitish-yellow rocks. Her gorgeous legs kicked slowly back and forth, as though she were wearing diving flippers.

There was nothing fast about her levitation; it happened in liquid slow motion and she waved in the air. She was smiling as she descended, and her lips were moving, but I don't know if words were coming out or not.

Kate Latham disappeared. She vanished into the rocks, and in a fluid instant Winston Bingham vanished also. In the space of a few seconds, two people had vanished. The last thing I remembered was this blond swan in the air with her hands at her sides and her legs making scuba motions, and then she had vanished at the conclusion of her spectacular *pas de deux*, vanished with her magician right into the stage.

"Put me down," she could have said. "Unhand me, sir," she could have said.

"Take your hands off me, buster."

"Don't press the flesh, Mr. Bingham."

She could have screamed, she could have hollered, she could have given out with the slightest peep of alarm. She could have clutched at his hair and tugged at its frizziness. She could have gouged him in the face, ripped at the tendons of his vulnerable neck. She could have done a lot of things, but she didn't do anything. She smiled and was lifted off the rocks and down into the jumble.

It was possible that I had gotten her wrong. The air was rife with misunderstandings and I was filled with self-doubt. I felt emptiness in my summer. This was the final straw, getting it all wrong. Perhaps I had misinterpreted her blush. Maybe she was a sexpot. Maybe she was having an affair with *both* the son and the father; maybe there were Oedipal combinations that I hadn't even thought of yet. Maybe she wasn't even having an affair with the son. Maybe I just didn't know anything.

I looked over at the opposite file of rocks, where the couple had stood seconds before, acting out their bizarre *pas de deux*. I looked out at the naked rocks and an image came of my late father. He rose in the arms of Big Red. His arms were at his sides, his body was stiff. He had a smile on his face that wasn't a smile. His teeth ground against the insistent phlegm that stuck in his mouth—like gears that hadn't been well lubricated. I stood in the doorway of the porch. Dad's eyes pleaded with me as Big Red lifted him up to flip him over. His eyes gave him away.

Some people kick and scream; other people start closing their systems down after they've been frightened. They can't speak;

they can't move; their smiles freeze on their faces. One saw people like that in combat. You had to look once, twice, three times sometimes before you realized that they'd shut down.

Reality was all around me and reality said that such a thing—*rape*—could not be happening on a Sunday morning outdoors in the full blaze of sunlight on our property. I was speechless. Rape was a serious charge against the sun. Rape was real.

I took off—goosed by curiosity, jealousy, and alarm. I clambered up from my princely chair—where I had smiled upon my kingdom for so many years. I ran down the rocks, across a path through the scrub vegetation. I ran past my house, where my wife slept in our majestic double bed. I gashed my arm on an outcropping of bramble. I became more pigeon-toed as I ran, and moved in a kind of perpetual lunge. My interior monologues vanished.

A combination of out-of-shapedness and adrenaline rushes caused me an alarming shortness of breath. I made sounds as if I was laughing at some great comedy routine—soul-scraping *hahs* seared the air. I was not prepared for the force of the sun. The seepage of humidity mottled my *guayabera* and caused sweat-rivers against my love handles.

I was okay when I got to the first plateau of rocks, but experienced problems on the high narrow saddle that Winston and Kate Latham had jogged across with such ease. I started to feel dizzy. I stumbled on the spine—the sides seemed more sheer than I'd remembered. I saw the lickings of the Piscotaug directly below me, the roiling headwaters. The rocks seemed to gleam with unusual brightness and the reflection from mica-jewels hurt my eyes.

I planted my topsiders on either side of the spine and scurried across like a crab, gasping with every scuttle. My hands padded along the rocks. My feet moved as if I was pushing against a tackling dummy.

I knew it was going to end badly, but I couldn't stop myself. They were going to come upon me scurrying along crabwise. "Alfred," Winston would say, staring down at me when I ran into his knee.

"Mr. Meriwether," Kate Latham would say, with a saucy look of contempt. Winston might just reach out and topple me off the spine and walk on by me, ignoring my splash as I hit the Pisco-taug headfirst.

I would come upon them and they would be discussing Shake-speare in measured tones. I would stand above them—puffing, scratched and gasping, clutching my heart. My fevered eyes would give me away. This was the kind of story that would haunt me to my grave. They would be discussing painting, sub-marines, the White House, geology, history, basketball, whaling villages, johnnycakes.

She was facing me. Her yellow T-shirt seemed to shine in the demilight, seven or eight feet below where I stood. Winston had his back toward me and he was close against her.

"Please," she whispered. I think it was the longest word I've ever heard. The word just stretched out and reverberated in that small dark place.

Some raving of the eyes accidentally landed on me, but did not focus. She was filled with terror. Her whole face was hurt with it, from frozen mouth to see-a-ghost eyes. Her right arm was rigid at her side. It trembled inside an incredible tension of flex. The knuckles on her fist had turned entirely white, like the incipience of frostbite. Her fist was clenched so hard that she could have broken her fingers inside her own grip.

I stood on the butte.

"Hey," I said. "God *damn*, Winston."

His head instantly whipped around and upward. It was a per-fect imitation of one of his legendary neck spasms—the head whipping around like a cash register opening. "What the fuck do you want?" The thick curls of his hair seemed to give off sparks in the little light.

He had a second's trouble extricating his hand from up inside her T-shirt. It was lodged high up there with her breasts. A finger had perhaps caught on her jogger's bra in the upthrust of his need. His hand did not just come out of her T-shirt in an abrupt movement. It slid out and down across her stomach and pushed her more closely against the rocks, as if she were holding her breath.

Winston turned full around to confront me. The girl slipped from him and crawled up the rock face toward me. Her whole paralysis dissolved. She clawed at the rock as if it was someone's face. There was so much ferocity, so much terror released. She made deep grunting sounds. Tears sprayed from her eyes; she kept shaking her head and these droplets of tears flew. He had gone to work on her hair first. The ponytail had gone under his rough massage and her hair was streaming behind her. She ran by me in a crouch of fear, and fled across the butte of rocks in a fevered bundle of blue, yellow, and red.

Winston was enraged. He paced around in his bear pit below me. "What the fuck are you doing here? What is it with you? See this," he shouted, giving me the finger.

"You've done some things, Winston. My God."

He climbed up toward me, quicker than I'd expected. One moment he was padding around his pit, the next his head was beside my topsider and his hair was in the sunlight.

I lifted my topsider and brought it down the way you do when you're making a divot in the grass to set up a football for a placekick.

Winston yelled and his hand jerked upward. He lost his balance on the rough wall and fell backward onto the rocky floor. He lay on his back and his face twitched. He held on to his hand, using his good hand as a platter for his damaged fingers. I could see the divot-mark of my heel just above the knuckles. There was no blood, just a scar of purple. He made wincing expressions and I knew that I had done some damage to his hand.

He moaned and stretched out his body, as though to spread around the damage. His lower body was in darkness—I could see the pulsings of his chest under the HAVE-A-NICE-DAY-ASSHOLE T-shirt. The message was so glaring and incongruous that it seemed to ring out like neon.

"*Asshole, asshole, asshole!*" I shouted, and I think I wanted my epithets to act like dirt to cover his body. At that moment I hoped that I had broken his fingers, neck, back.

I left him there and he was still moaning. His fingers made telltale clawing motions, indicating that he had not been grievously injured.

I saw Kate Latham in the distance. She stood on the path just below my house. I could see my house, the chimneys of my parents' house, the Piscotaug River quilting below me. Kate Latham had both hands to her mouth. She stood stock-still and her hair looked wild. A poise in her legs threatened to cause her to jump away.

I tightroped my way across the spine of rocks. I was not comfortable; some fear of heights seized me there. My heart would not get back into control. It kept pounding against my chest. I spread out my arms to keep my balance. It seemed so precarious. I was determined not to get back into my tackling-dummy mode for that short walk. I wondered what had happened to the boy who had once run across these rocks with never a false move.

Kate Latham dropped her hands from her mouth, and I believe she shouted, "Please." In that moment, I wondered what she meant.

Winston hit me with a direct shot in the small of my back. I flew forward. When I hit the spine, my chest exploded with pain.

He was on top of me then, trying to turn me over in that narrow space. He picked at my body. I could feel his hands all over me, pawing me, looking for a grip on my shoulder. All I felt was this overwhelming pain. I heard the sound of my own gasps. Some distant voice shouted. Suddenly I was on my back and he was on top of me, and I could see the sky spinning, a glimpse of beach, Kate Latham's face, a fragment of window pane, and white sun.

I knew he was going to kill me. His hands closed around my neck and he had his knee in my crotch. I fought to keep his knee away from my damaged place. Whatever was damaged—ribs, lungs, stomach, or spleen—was damaged badly.

He was above me and I could taste his peppermint breath. I could hear shouting and there was a tremendous ringing in my ears. All I could think about was keeping his knee away, because that would cause more pain. He had his hands around my neck and he was choking me. I could feel a bursting in my head, but the pain and the prospect of more pain was killing me. Lettering stood out above me:

Nice . . . asshole . . . day . . .

I could feel his strength. His breath smelled benignly of peppermint. There was a waft of cologne, a lemon smell like the fierce Eau Sauvage. I tried to flex my neck, let the ripcords absorb the punishment.

Go for his neck. His neck. His neck.

My hands locked onto his neck with my thumbs and I shifted abruptly. I felt some slight movement to his body. Again, this shouting around me. I dug into him harder and could see his head shaking back and forth as if in fierce disagreement. I gouged at him with my thumbs. I pushed as hard as I could, feeling my shirt scrape harshly against the rock. I thought I was breaking through his flesh into some deep hollows between the tendons.

He shook again and again in saliva bursts. I dug into him. He reached behind him with his right hand to get at the things attacking his neck. I was buried under his weight. His hand went back and back to get at my nuisance thumbs. I got my hands to his chest and pushed with all my strength.

Winston leaned back heavily. His arms flapped in the air far above me in gigantic whooping movements. The whole thrust of his body now was backward. His black eyes looked down his nose and bulged like a malign schoolmaster's.

He had no purchase, no momentum anymore. I pushed again. He tipped and tipped some more. His enormous hands beat against the air, and then they clutched at the air as if willing the atmosphere to attain graspable substance, to offer him a handhold.

"Winston!" I gasped, as I felt him slipping. I reached out for him, but there was nothing in the air.

Winston tilted sideways and then simply fell off me. I saw the black waffle soles of his jogging shoes. I reached out. I felt that he had left before he was actually gone. His hands still clung to me, his knee still searched for the damaged place. His fingers kept trying to squeeze my neck until my head split open.

There was silence, very distinct, the absence of anything. It seemed to me that the silence was very long, and then I heard a hideous sound below me. It was a sound between a whump and a squish. It was such a heavy, final, wounded sound.

Something terrible had happened. I lay sprawled out on the spine of rocks. I could hear a pounding noise in the distance. Kate Latham was at the door of my house, ringing and pounding.

Something awful had happened, come quickly, come quickly.

The back of my head was bleeding. I could feel liquid mush

when I moved my head. I thought my ribs were broken. There was this intense weight of pain. I could not breathe properly. There was something wrong with my neck.

Something had happened. I could feel a kind of whiteness descending—it was palpable and white, a bleaching-out of all my scenes. I could watch it approach, gliding in palely. It was not unpleasant.

I raised my head. I had this weird fear that my brains were falling out of a hole in my head, right at the back where Winston had tried to pound me into the rock. It was important that I look down and see what had happened to him before all this whiteness claimed me, gliding in and clouding my vision.

"Winston?" I asked.

He was face down in the water. His head bumped against an outcropping of rock. The rock had turned into odd hallucinatory colors—pinks and reds. The last thing I saw before I went unconscious were these bathers strolling up the Wolcott beach toward our property. They carried umbrellas and picnic baskets. A child darted for the water and then playfully ran backward before the brush of the waves. I leaned back again onto the rock and passed out.

Where they found me.

14

Winston drifted downriver a ways. His body got caught in the current of the Piscotaug, which could be strong in spots. I visualized him spinning slowly as he drifted. Later on that Sunday, a few hours later, the Coast Guard in a motor launch picked him off a sandbar, where he had come to rest.

He either died of massive head injuries, or he drowned. This was a fine point at the inquest, held later in the week on a Friday morning at the Meguntic County courthouse.

The county medical examiner testified that he could not determine the exact cause of death. Then Kate Latham testified. She had driven down from Providence with her parents. She proved to be an effective witness after she settled down and found that she could use the phrase "sexual advances" as a euphemism for attempted rape. Sexual advances seemed to give her a little detachment from the trauma. And then she dropped the "sexual" and just said advances.

Either way, the story came out the same. Winston still hit me in the small of the back. I still fell and broke a rib. We still scuffled, she still watched, he still fell off the spine of rocks—the backbone, the saddle, the whatever—and rolled on his back and couldn't get himself righted and smashed his head. He died from that injury or he was still alive and died of drowning.

At the inquest I listened to complex medical terminology dealing with head trauma and lung-water and length-of-time-in-the-river. The actual human being got lost somewhere among the tissue samples. I didn't want to think about Thumper being autopsied, or about how the morgue people must have gathered around him and tagged his toe and weighed his brain. But I did think about it nonetheless.

I sat in the courtroom with bandaged ribs and thought, This must be reality.

Apart from the brief inquest proceeding itself, Winston's death caused a minor scandal. Old-line Wasp family. Death on the rocks. Under Secretary of the Navy. When the "sexual advances" angle came out, the case exploded for a day or two. It made the papers. Kate Latham was described as a "coed." Presumably, in the tabloid imagination, "coed" made her seem more sexy.

One New York tabloid bannered: SOCIALITES CLASH OVER COED BEAUTY—ONE DEAD.

Flashbulbs appeared at the courthouse steps, and television cameras. Microphones were thrust into my face. A brief celebrity attended my obscure country life for a day or two, but all I could think of was that my mother would have loved the attention. It was wasted on me.

I did not expect that my sister Dorothy would ever want to speak to me again. I expected that I would cease to exist for her, or that, if I ever came into her purview again, she would point a finger at me and hiss, "J'accuse."

But that isn't what happened. Dorothy said, "I'm sorry, Alfred," and leaned over and kissed me in my room at Providence Hospital. She just walked in, walked over to my bed, leaned down, and kissed me.

The hospital room was enveloped by Jean Patou. She turned around and exited abruptly. I think she just wanted to make clear, with punctuations of verve and perfume, that the episode was closed from that moment on. Life continued, she seemed to be saying—one bore up, she was sorry for everyone, it was no one's fault, but don't mention this incident to me again. I'm not as strong as I look, she seemed to be saying. My brother Alfred can tell you how once upon a time I was so scared that I frightened all the boys away on the shiniest night of my life and had to dance with my brother, dance after dance. I was so scared that I lost my voice for months. So scared. So scared.

I can't tell you how I felt about my sister Dorothy when she said, "I'm sorry, Alfred." But I felt something like brotherly love. This was my kid sister.

As for my mother, the politest word she had for Winston was

"oversexed." She really dragged out the heavy artillery and let him have it. We told her to stop, but she couldn't stop.

It was Alice, finally, who held everything together during those days. She stepped through the rubble of the Meriwether family's general stupefaction, and took over. She explained to us how it was going to be with the funeral, the burial, the guests—where we were going to go, where we were going to stand when we got there, when we were going to sit. She explained everything to us, and sometimes she explained it all again—patiently, politely—often using gestures. To Alice I think we Meriwethers must have resembled a group of foreign exchange students, each with an almost insurmountable language problem.

Winston's funeral was held at St. David's-By-The-Sea in Wolcott. Outside the church a mist hung in the air between spells of rain. I sat in the front pew, along with Alice, my mother, Dorothy, and young Win. The rest of the church was filled with brass. The Chief of Naval Operations was there. The Secretary of the Navy. The Secretary of Defense.

Reverend Warren read John Masefield's "Sea Fever" (the lonely sea and the sky). The St. David's organist played a stirring rendition of the Navy hymn. I thought about how far Winston had come from that afternoon in 1962 when he had arrived in Wolcott with Dorothy, an aging basketball player with a crick in his neck and no prospects.

After the funeral there was a lot of milling around in the rain. The Meriwether family waited for their limousines, as did the Navy people. Various assistants opened umbrellas over the heads of the brass, so no hairs would get wet during the long wait. The Secretary of Defense was the first to leave.

"Mr. Meriwether," a voice said. I turned around. "How's it going? I was a friend of Mr. Bingham's. Maybe he mentioned me."

"My God," I said. "You must be Charlie Tuna."

I had never encountered anyone who so closely lived up to his nickname. Charlie Tuna seemed to be vacuum-packed into his black suit. I estimated his weight at well over four hundred pounds. He stood not more than five and a half feet tall. He was flanked by two men, one of whom held an umbrella over him.

Tuna spoke in a breathless—or "beached"—voice. "Mr. Meriwether, my associates and me were deeply saddened about the late unpleasantness that happened to our good friend."

Tuna's every word rode on either a heavy intake or gasping exhalation of breath. These were combined with whistles through his nose and periodic winces as he fought for air. From a distance his winces might have been mistaken for continuous smiles.

"Thank you, Mr. Tuna." I couldn't remember his real name, but it didn't seem to make any difference.

"Listen," Tuna gasped. "Everyone calls me Charlie." A hike of his shoulders sent trembling waves of flesh against the fabric of his suit. "You meet my two associates now." It was not a request, but an order.

Charlie Tuna snapped his fingers in the rainy air—thick sausages striking each other in a rolling motion. Two hands shot out toward my stomach. "Vince, Tito, shake hands with Mr. Meriwether."

I shook hands with Vince and Tito. They might have been young associates at any prosperous Wall Street law firm—so pressed and buttoned-down and serious were they. I wondered if they carried guns.

A stretch-type limousine wheeled up in front of the church steps. "That's my car," Tuna panted. "Anything we can do, Mr. Meriwether, you call me. Anyway, I guess I'll be talking to you to wind up me and Mr. Bingham's business interests. We had a lot of interests, you know."

"Yes, Mr. Tuna," I said. "When the family settles the estate, I'm sure we'll be in touch."

He set off for the limousine, waddling along between his assistants. His hands made flipper movements, as though to provide inertial guidance. Tuna's amplitude and striking width gave the illusion of a great sea of mourners parting for him on the steps of the church—dowagers and defense secretaries, lawyers and lieutenants, widows and wives stepping back.

I thought the priority of limousines was interesting. First, the Secretary of Defense; then Charlie Tuna; then, presumably, the grieving family.

"Who was that obese individual?" my mother asked from her cantonment of black, under a heavy veil. She must have wondered what new humiliation Winston Bingham had in store for her from beyond the grave, as she entered her ninth decade.

I told her that the obese individual was none other than Charlie Tuna—he of the New Wolcott, the condominiums, and gambling casinos.

"There *is* a Charlie Tuna?" my mother asked. She looked utterly amazed. The fact of his nickname, combined with the astonishing obesity of his physical presence, packed quite a wallop for her.

"Yes," I said, adding that Mr. Tuna had invited himself to the funeral.

My mother stared down at the mourners, who huddled in the rain under umbrellas at the church steps. She leaned on two formidable canes. "You invest your hopes in someone," she said, "but breeding always tells." She waved one of her canes then, as if it was still possible to do battle with Winston. "He has brought disgrace upon this family."

After Winston's burial in the family plot outside Wolcott, the Meriwethers gathered at the big house. We spoke in low tones in the living room. Dorothy was composed—she asked me how the funeral had gone. I said it seemed to have gone pretty well. I mentioned that the flowers were lovely. She asked me if I thought "Sea Fever" was a bit much. I said no, I thought it was a nice touch.

I sat for a while with my nephew. All things considered—and there was a lot to be considered—he seemed to be holding up pretty well. I asked him about Kate Latham.

"Katie's still shaken up about the whole thing," he allowed, but didn't want to volunteer any more information.

I hesitated for a moment and then plunged in. I wondered aloud if—long pause for the sixty-four-dollar question—if—that is —not wanting to invade his privacy—if he was going to be seeing her again.

My nephew looked surprised. "Sure," he said with a shrug. "I mean, why not?"

Why not, indeed. I patted his arm and got up.

After a while, I went over and sat with my mother. "Well, I still have my beautiful boy, don't I?" she asked, her eyes brimming. "My Prince Charming."

For a fleeting moment it *still* seemed possible to share in the royalty of childhood. Just for a moment and then the moment was gone.

I wandered out to the verandah, where my father once sat amid wicker furniture in his declining years. Fog had closed in around the house in the late afternoon, obscuring the wonderful vista. It made no difference. I was overcome with private images —the sparkle of the lawn; the white rocks; an antique Duesenberg; my father tip-tapping on the glass to make sure that the sea was at a safe distance. I could have told him. And I thought of an outsized coffin being wheeled on its carriage up the aisle of a seaside church.

Winston Bingham.

Thumper.

I turned away. There was nothing to see anyway. I went inside to find Alice.

15

It was a sunny afternoon in Manhattan, a few weeks later. After seeing a client uptown, I stopped in at the Games Club on Madison Avenue to call Alice and let her know I'd be home early.

I left the phone booth on the bottom floor, just off the lobby. I stood next to the front desk, talking with Tony, the club's doorman. I watched the members as they entered from Madison Avenue and headed up the stairs. They stopped by the desk for keys and messages; an older group, my generation and older, in the middle of the afternoon. Something powerful in me longed to join the gang upstairs at the great bar and then snooze it off in one of the reading room's chairs. That was one reason why I rarely visited the Games Club anymore.

"You look real good, Mr. Meriwether," Tony said. Perhaps he didn't know about my summer, or was too polite to mention it. He hitched up the pants of his gray uniform and shot his explosive cuffs. His voice did not rise above a hoarse whisper. I always had the impression that Tony had just returned from a city confrontation where he had shouted himself silly—some taxicab unseemliness or a Knicks victory.

From the side of his mouth, as if we were conspirators, he told me about a coronary event in the steam room yesterday; big bucks dropped at the backgammon tables; real estate developers who wanted to buy the club's air space and put up a hotel. "You know, you look real *good*, Mr. Meriwether. Real good. Mr. Carroll has a walker now. They say it's progressive. Same disease killed the Ironman, Lou Gehrig. Say, do you know what Mr. Mulloy Junior calls his son, Mr. Mulloy the Third?"

"The Turd," I said.

Tony nodded. "He says it right in front of me, too. 'Where's The Turd?' How do you answer a question like that? I said, 'He just went upstairs, Mr. Mulloy.'"

Upstairs. I looked at the carpeted staircase across the lobby, whose walls were lined with portraits in oil. The grand parade of club presidents receded into mustachios and muttonchops—two flights of tradition, carrying the members backward in time as they climbed. My father, an old-fashioned man, looked the picture of lean modernity at the foot of the stairs. My grandfather, who believed this nation was built on trusts—the bigger the better—ran to suet on the second floor. A watch chain stretched like a gold fence across his vest. My great-grandfather had carried the club through the hard years of the Civil War—the thirsty years. Just outside the entrance to the bar.

I touched Tony's arm. "Tony, you remember the night I fell down the stairs?"

What does he want to ask me that for? Tony's eyes asked. He glanced nervously at the door. He hiked up his pants. "Yeah, I saw the whole thing. This is going back some years." He kept his eyes on the door. "Thought you'd killed yourself. You just kept rolling and rolling. I remember I really got on them about the carpeting. Suppose it had been one of our older members who took a header?"

"I'm glad they fixed the carpeting."

Tony warmed to the subject. "Yeah, hell. You went down one whole *flight*—boom, boom, boom. It was like in slow motion. Want to know the weird thing?"

"What's that?" I asked.

"You landed on your feet. I couldn't believe it. I'm standing there, watching. Boom, boom, boom—you bounce down to the bottom of the stairs and I'm thinking, Call an ambulance. Mr. Meriwether, he's gone. The next thing I know you've got your briefcase tucked under your arm and you're walking toward me like it was spring in Central Park. You're walking like Maurice Chevalier. You're always a friendly guy anyway, so I'm thinking, It's a miracle. Phone up the priests. So what happens? You take maybe twenty steps and it was like Joe Louis walked through that door and landed a short right on your button." Tony bobbed and weaved and threw a short right in the direction of Madison

Avenue. "You crumpled to the floor." He pointed dramatically at the marble spot in the lobby. "Right over there."

"I don't remember," I said.

Tony shrugged. "It could have been a lot worse, Mr. Meriwether. It could have been a broken neck. It could have been the Big Casino."

I gave a last look at the stairs and took Tony by the arm. "Tony, let's see if we can rustle up a Checker. I might as well head home."

"You got it, Mr. Meriwether." I think he was relieved to be summoned into action. "Say, you know you look real good. Rhode Island must be agreeing with you."

Socialites clash over coed beauty—one dead.

"Maybe it's the salt air," I said.

"Yeah, you can't beat that salt air," Tony agreed. He made it sound in his hoarse whisper as if he knew a guy who could corner the market on the stuff.

Tony and I walked outside to Madison Avenue. He hailed a cab, opened the door, and bid me inside with a courtly bow. I tipped him, said thanks and good-bye. He said, "Be seeing you, Mr. Meriwether."

Tony closed the door, and the cab pulled away. The notion came to me in a rush that certain places—the Games Club, the property in Rhode Island—were gone forever. I felt like crying on that sunny afternoon, as the cab carried me home to Eighty-seventh Street. I thought that growing up had been pretty rough —especially at my age.